F. Kafka

Translated from the German by WILLA and EDWIN MUIR

Revised, and with additional material translated by E. M. BUTLER

With excerpts from Kafka's *Diaries*

Drawings by FRANZ KAFKA

FRANZ

KAFKA

THE
TRIAL

DEFINITIVE EDITION

SCHOCKEN BOOKS NEW YORK

All rights under International and Pan-American Copyright
Conventions. Published in the United States by
Schocken Books, Inc., New York.
Distributed by Pantheon Books, a division of Random House, Inc.,
New York. This work is a translation of the German *Der Prozess*,
edited by Max Brod. Copyright 1925 by Verlag die Schmiede.
Copyright renewed 1952 by Schocken Books Inc. Copyright 1935
by Schocken Verlag. Copyright renewed 1963 by Schocken Books
Inc. Copyright 1946 by Schocken Books Inc. Copyright renewed
1974 by Schocken Books Inc.

Library of Congress Cataloging-in-Publication Data

Kafka, Franz, 1883–1924.
The trial.

(Schocken Kafka library)
Translation of: Der prozess.
I. Title.   II. Series.
PT2621.A26P713   1988   833'.912   87-32345
ISBN 0-8052-0848-8

Manufactured in the United States of America
2468B9753

Display typography by Jessica Shatan

First Schocken paperback edition published in 1968

CONTENTS

NOTE: Asterisks (*) in the text show where Franz Kafka deleted passages; these passages will be found in Appendix II, pages 257-263, with identifying text page numbers.

CHAPTER ONE

The Arrest · Conversation with Frau Grubach · Then Fräulein Bürstner

SOMEONE must have been telling lies about Joseph K., for without having done anything wrong he was arrested one fine morning. His landlady's cook, who always brought him his breakfast at eight o'clock, failed to appear on this occasion. That had never happened before. K. waited for a little while longer, watching from his pillow the old lady opposite, who seemed to be peering at him with a curiosity unusual even for her, but then, feeling both put out and hungry, he rang the bell. At once there was a knock at the door and a man entered whom he had never seen before in the house. He was slim and yet well knit, he wore a closely fitting black suit furnished with all sorts of pleats, pockets, buckles, and buttons, as well as a belt, like a tourist's outfit, and in consequence looked eminently practical, though one could not quite tell what actual purpose it served. "Who are you?" asked K., half raising himself in bed. But the man ignored the question, as though his appearance needed no explanation, and merely said: "Did you ring?"

1

"Anna is to bring me my breakfast," said K., and then studied the fellow, silently and carefully, trying to make out who he could be. The man did not submit to this scrutiny for very long, but turned to the door and opened it slightly so as to report to someone who was evidently standing just behind it: "He says Anna is to bring him his breakfast." A short guffaw from the next room came in answer; and it rather sounded as if several people had joined in. Although the strange man could not have learned anything from it that he did not know already, he now said to K., as if passing on a statement: "It can't be done." "This is news indeed," cried K., springing out of bed and quickly pulling on his trousers. "I must see what people these are next door, and how Frau Grubach can account to me for such behavior." Yet it occurred to him at once that he should not have said this aloud and that by doing so he had in a way admitted the stranger's right to superintend his actions; still, that did not seem important to him at the moment. The stranger, however, took his words in some such sense, for he asked: "Hadn't you better stay here?" "I shall neither stay here nor let you address me until you have introduced yourself." "I meant well enough," said the stranger, and then of his own accord threw the door open. In the next room, which K. entered more slowly than he had intended, everything looked at first glance almost as it had the evening before. It was Frau Grubach's living room; perhaps among all the furniture, rugs, china, and photographs with which it was crammed there was a little more free space than usual, yet one did not perceive that at first, especially as the main change consisted in the presence of a man who was sitting at the open window reading a book, from which he now glanced up. "You should have stayed in your room! Didn't Franz tell you that?" "Yes, but what are you doing here?" asked K., looking from his new acquaintance to the man called Franz, who was still standing by the door, and then back again. Through the open window he had another glimpse of the old woman, who with truly senile inquisitiveness had moved along to the window exactly opposite, in order to go on seeing all that could be seen. "I'd better get Frau Grubach—" said K., as if wrenching himself away from the two men (though they were standing at quite a distance from him) and making as if to go out. "No," said the man at the window, flinging the book down on the table and getting up. "You can't go out, you are arrested." "So it seems," said K. "But what for?" he added. "We are not authorized to tell you that. Go to your room and wait there. Proceedings have been instituted against you, and you will be informed of everything in due course. I am exceeding my instructions in speaking freely to you like this. But I hope nobody hears me except Franz, and he himself has been too free with you, against his express instructions. If you continue to have as good luck as you have had in the choice of your warders, then you can be confident of the final result." K. felt he must sit down, but now he saw that there was no seat in the whole room except the chair beside the window. "You'll soon discover that we're telling you the truth," said Franz, advancing toward him simultaneously with the other man. The latter overtopped K. enormously and kept clapping him on the shoulder. They both examined his nightshirt and said that he would have to wear a less fancy shirt now, but that they would take charge of this one and the rest of his underwear and, if his case turned out well, restore them to him later. "Much better give these things to us than hand them over to the depot," they said, "for in the depot there's lots of thieving, and besides they sell everything there after a certain length of time, no matter whether your case is settled or not. And you never know how long these cases will last, especially these days. Of course you would get the money out of the depot in the long run, but in the first place the prices they pay you are always wretched, for they sell your things to the best briber, not the best bidder, and anyhow it's well known that money dwindles a lot if it passes from hand to hand from one year to another." K. paid hardly any attention to this advice. Any right to dispose of his own things which he might possess he did not prize very highly; far more important to him was the necessity to understand his situation clearly; but with these people beside him he could not even think. The belly of the second warder—for they could only be warders—kept butting against him in an almost friendly way, yet if he looked up he caught sight of a face which did not in the least suit that fat body, a dry, bony face with a great nose, twisted to one side, which seemed to be consulting over his head with the other warder. Who could these men be? What were they talking about? What authority could they represent? K. lived in a country with a legal constitution, there was universal peace, all the laws were in force; who dared seize him in his own dwelling? He had always been inclined to take things easily, to believe in the worst only when the worst happened, to take no care for the morrow even when the outlook was threatening. But that struck him as not being the right policy here, one could certainly regard the whole thing as a joke, a rude joke which his colleagues in the Bank had concocted for some unknown reason, perhaps because this was his thirtieth birthday, that was of course possible, perhaps he had only to laugh knowingly in these men's faces and they would laugh with him, perhaps they were merely porters from the street corner—they looked very like it— nevertheless his very first glance at the man Franz had decided him for the time being not to give away any advantage that he might possess over these people. There was a slight risk that later on his friends might possibly say he could not take a joke, but he had in mind—though it was not usual with him to learn from experience—several occasions, of no importance in themselves, when against all his friends' advice he had behaved with deliberate reckless- ness and without the slightest regard for possible conse- quences, and had had in the end to pay dearly for it. That must not happen again, at least not this time; if this was a comedy he would insist on playing it to the end.

But he was still free. "Allow me," he said, passing quickly between the warders to his room. "He seems to have some sense," he heard one of them saying behind him. When he reached his room he at once pulled out the drawer of his desk. Everything lay there in perfect order, but in his agita- tion he could not find at first the identification papers for which he was looking. At last he found his bicycle license and was about to start off with it to the warders, but then it seemed too trivial a thing, and he searched again until he found his birth certificate. As he was re-entering the next room the opposite door opened and Frau Grubach showed herself. He saw her only for an instant, for no sooner did she recognize him than she was obviously over- come by embarrassment, apologized for intruding, van- ished, and shut the door again with the utmost care. "Come in, do," he would just have had time to say. But he merely stood holding his papers in the middle of the room, looking at the door, which did not open again, and was only re- called to attention by a shout from the warders, who were sitting at a table by the open window and, as he now saw, devouring his breakfast. "Why didn't she come in?" he asked. "She isn't allowed to," said the tall warder, "since you're under arrest." "But how can I be under arrest? And particularly in such a ridiculous fashion?" "So now you're beginning it all over again?" said the warder, dipping a slice of bread and butter into the honey-pot. "We don't answer such questions." "You'll have to answer them," said K. "Here are my papers, now show me yours, and first of all your warrant for arresting me." "Oh, good Lord," said

the warder. "If you would only realize your position, and
if you wouldn't insist on uselessly annoying us two, who
probably mean better by you and stand closer to you than
any other people in the world." "That's so, you can believe
that," said Franz, not raising to his lips the coffee cup he
held in his hand, but instead giving K. a long, apparently
significant, yet incomprehensible look. Without wishing it
K. found himself decoyed into an exchange of speaking
looks with Franz, none the less he tapped his papers and
repeated: "Here are my identification papers." "What are
your papers to us?" cried the tall warder. "You're behaving
worse than a child. What are you after? Do you think you'll
bring this fine case of yours to a speedier end by wrangling
with us, your warders, over papers and warrants? We are
humble subordinates who can scarcely find our way
through a legal document and have nothing to do with
your case except to stand guard over you for ten hours a
day and draw our pay for it. That's all we are, but we're
quite capable of grasping the fact that the high authorities
we serve, before they would order such an arrest as this,
must be quite well informed about the reasons for the
arrest and the person of the prisoner. There can be no mistake about that. Our officials, so far as I know them, and I
know only the lowest grades among them, never go hunting
for crime in the populace, but, as the Law decrees, are
drawn toward the guilty and must then send out us
warders. That is the Law. How could there be a mistake
in that?" "I don't know this Law," said K. "All the worse
for you," replied the warder. "And it probably exists nowhere but in your own head," said K.; he wanted in some
way to enter into the thoughts of the warders and twist
them to his own advantage or else try to acclimatize himself to them. But the warder merely said in a discouraging
voice: "You'll come up against it yet." Franz interrupted;
"See, Willem, he admits that he doesn't know the Law and

yet he claims he's innocent." "You're quite right, but you'll never make a man like that see reason," replied the other. K. gave no further answer; Must I, he thought, let myself be confused still worse by the gabble of those wretched hirelings?—they admit themselves that's all they are. They're talking of things, in any case, which they don't understand. Plain stupidity is the only thing that can give them such assurance. A few words with a man on my own level of intelligence would make everything far clearer than hours of talk with these two. He walked up and down a few times in the free part of the room; at the other side of the street he could still see the old woman, who had now dragged to the window an even older man, whom she was holding round the waist. K. felt he must put an end to this farce. "Take me to your superior officer," he said. "When he orders me, not before," retorted the warder called Willem. "And now I advise you," he went on, "to go to your room, stay quietly there, and wait for what may be decided about you. Our advice to you is not to let yourself be distracted by vain thoughts, but to collect yourself, for great demands will be made upon you. You haven't treated us as our kind advances to you deserved, you have forgotten that we, no matter who we may be, are at least free men compared to you; that is no small advantage. All the same, we are prepared, if you have any money, to bring you a little breakfast from the coffeehouse across the street."

Without replying to this offer K. remained standing where he was for a moment. If he were to open the door of the next room or even the door leading to the hall, perhaps the two of them would not dare to hinder him, perhaps that would be the simplest solution of the whole business, to bring it to a head. But perhaps they might seize him after all, and if he were once down, all the superiority would be lost which in a certain sense he still retained. Accordingly, instead of a quick solution he chose that certainty which the natural course of things would be bound to bring, and went back to his room without another word having been said by him or by the warders.

He flung himself on his bed and took from the washstand a fine apple which he had laid out the night before for his breakfast. Now it was all the breakfast he would have, but in any case, as the first few bites assured him, much better than the breakfast from the filthy night café would have been, which the grace of his warders might have secured him. He felt fit and confident, he would miss his work in the Bank that morning, it was true, but that would be easily overlooked, considering the comparatively high post he held there. Should he give the real reason for his absence? He considered doing so. If they did not believe him, which in the circumstances would be understandable, he could produce Frau Grubach as a witness, or even the two odd creatures over the way, who were now probably meandering back again to the window opposite his room. K. was surprised, at least he was surprised considering the warders' point of view, that they had sent him to his room and left him alone there, where he had abundant opportunities to take his life. Though at the same time he also asked himself, looking at it from his own point of view, what possible ground he could have to do so. Because two warders were sitting next door and had intercepted his breakfast? To take his life would be such a senseless act that, even if he wished, he could not bring himself to do it because of its very senselessness. If the intellectual poverty of the warders were not so manifest, he might almost assume that they too saw no danger in leaving him alone, for the very same reason. They were quite at liberty to watch him now while he went to a wall-cupboard where he kept a bottle of good brandy, while he filled a glass and drank it down to make up for his breakfast, and then drank a second to give him courage, the last one only as a precaution, for the improbable contingency that it might be needed.

Then a shout came from the next room which made him start so violently that his teeth rattled against the glass. "The Inspector wants you," was its tenor. It was merely the tone of it that startled him, a curt, military bark with which we would never have credited the warder Franz. The command itself was actually welcome to him. "At last," he shouted back, closing the cupboard and hurrying at once into the next room. There the two warders were standing, and, as if that were a matter of course, immediately drove him back into his room again. "What are you thinking of?" they cried. "Do you imagine you can appear before the Inspector in your shirt? He'll have you well thrashed, and us too." "Let me alone, damn you," cried K., who by now had been forced back to his wardrobe. "If you grab me out of bed, you can't expect to find me all dressed up in my best suit." "That can't be helped," said the warders, who as soon as K. raised his voice always grew quite calm, indeed almost melancholy, and thus contrived either to confuse him or to some extent bring him to his senses. "Silly formalities!" he growled, but immediately lifted a coat from a chair and held it up for a little while in both hands, as if displaying it to the warders for their approval. They shook their heads. "It must be a black coat," they said. Thereupon K. flung the coat on the floor and said—he did not himself know in what sense he meant the words—"But this isn't the capital charge yet." The warders smiled, but stuck to their: "It must be a black coat." "If it's to dispatch my case any quicker, I don't mind," replied K., opening the wardrobe, where he searched for a long time among his many suits, chose his best black one, a lounge suit which had caused almost a sensation among his acquaintances because of its elegance, then selected another shirt and began to dress with great care. In his secret heart he thought he had managed after all to speed up the proceedings, for the warders had forgotten to make him take a bath. He kept an eye on them to see if they would remember the ducking, but of course it never occurred to them, yet on the other hand Willem did not forget to send Franz to the Inspector with the information that K. was dressing.

When he was fully dressed he had to walk, with Willem treading on his heels, through the next room, which was now empty, into the adjoining one, whose double doors were flung open. This room, as K. knew quite well, had recently been taken by a Fräulein Bürstner, a typist, who went very early to work, came home late, and with whom he had exchanged little more than a few words in passing. Now the night table beside her bed had been pushed into the middle of the floor to serve as a desk, and the Inspector was sitting behind it. He had crossed his legs, and one arm was resting on the back of the chair.*

In a corner of the room three young men were standing looking at Fräulein Bürstner's photographs, which were stuck into a mat hanging on the wall. A white blouse dangled from the latch of the open window. In the window over the way the two old creatures were again stationed, but they had enlarged their party, for behind them, towering head and shoulders above them, stood a man with a shirt open at the neck and a reddish, pointed beard, which he kept pinching and twisting with his fingers. "Joseph K.?" asked the Inspector, perhaps merely to draw K.'s roving glance upon himself. K. nodded. "You are presumably very much surprised at the events of this morning?" asked the Inspector, with both hands rearranging the few things that lay on the night table, a candle and a matchbox, a book and a pincushion, as if they were objects which he required for his interrogation. "Certainly," said K., and he was filled with pleasure at having encountered a sensible man at last, with whom he could discuss the matter. "Certainly, I am

surprised, but I am by no means very much surprised."
"Not very much surprised?" asked the Inspector, setting the
candle in the middle of the table and then grouping the
other things round it. "Perhaps you misunderstand me," K.
hastened to add. "I mean"—here K. stopped and looked
round him for a chair. "I suppose I may sit down?" he
asked. "It's not usual," answered the Inspector. "I mean,"
said K. without further parley, "that I am very much surprised, of course, but when one has lived for thirty years in
this world and had to fight one's way through it, as I have
had to do, one becomes hardened to surprises and doesn't
take them too seriously. Particularly the one this morning." * "Why particularly the one this morning?" "I won't
say that I regard the whole thing as a joke, for the preparations that have been made seem too elaborate for that.
The whole staff of the boarding-house would have to be
involved, as well as all you people, and that would be past
a joke. So I don't say that it's a joke." "Quite right," said
the Inspector, looking to see how many matches there were
in the matchbox. "But on the other hand," K. went on,
turning to everybody there—he wanted to bring in the
three young men standing beside the photographs as well
—"on the other hand, it can't be an affair of any great importance either. I argue this from the fact that though I
am accused of something, I cannot recall the slightest
offense that might be charged against me. But that even is
of minor importance, the real question is, who accuses me?
What authority is conducting these proceedings? Are you
officers of the law? None of you has a uniform, unless your
suit"—here he turned to Franz—"is to be considered a
uniform, but it's more like a tourist's outfit. I demand a
clear answer to these questions, and I feel sure that after
an explanation we shall be able to part from each other on
the best of terms." The Inspector flung the matchbox down
on the table. "You are laboring under a great delusion," he

said. "These gentlemen here and myself have no standing whatever in this affair of yours, indeed we know hardly anything about it. We might wear the most official uniforms and your case would not be a penny the worse. I can't even confirm that you are charged with an offense, or rather I don't know whether you are. You are under arrest, certainly, more than that I do not know. Perhaps the warders have given you a different impression, but they are only irresponsible gossips.* However, if I can't answer your questions, I can at least give you a piece of advice; think less about us and of what is going to happen to you, think more about yourself instead. And don't make such an outcry about your feeling innocent, it spoils the not unfavorable impression you make in other respects. Also you should be far more reticent, nearly everything you have just said could have been implied in your behavior with the help of a word here and there, and in any case does not redound particularly to your credit."

K. stared at the Inspector. Was he to be taught lessons in manners by a man probably younger than himself? To be punished for his frankness by a rebuke? And about the cause of his arrest and about its instigator was he to learn nothing?

He was thrown into a certain agitation, and began to walk up and down—nobody hindered him—pushed back his cuffs, fingered his shirt-front, ruffled his hair, and as he passed the three young men said: "This is sheer nonsense!" Whereupon they turned toward him and regarded him sympathetically but gravely; at last he came to a stand before the Inspector's table. "Hasterer, the lawyer, is a personal friend of mine," he said. "May I telephone to him?" "Certainly," replied the Inspector, "but I don't see what sense there would be in that, unless you have some private business of your own to consult him about." "What sense would there be in that?" cried K., more in amazement than

exasperation. "What kind of man are you, then? You ask
me to be sensible and you carry on in the most senseless
way imaginable yourself! It's enough to sicken the dogs.
People first fall upon me in my own house and then lounge
about the room and put me through my paces for your
benefit. What sense would there be in telephoning to a
lawyer when I'm supposed to be under arrest? All right, I
won't telephone." "But do telephone if you wànt to," replied the Inspector, waving an arm toward the entrance
hall, where the telephone was, "please do telephone." "No,
I don't want to now," said K., going over to the window.
Across the street the party of three was still on the watch,
and their enjoyment of the spectacle received its first slight
check when K. appeared at the window. The two old people moved as if to get up, but the man at the back pacified
them. "Here's a fine crowd of spectators!" cried K. in a loud
voice to the Inspector, pointing at them with his finger. "Go
away," he shouted across. The three of them immediately
retreated a few steps, the two ancients actually took cover
behind the younger man, who shielded them with his massive body and to judge from the movements of his lips was
saying something which, owing to the distance, could not
be distinguished. Yet they did not remove themselves altogether, but seemed to be waiting for the chance to return
to the window again unobserved. "Officious, inconsiderate
wretches!" said K. as he turned back to the room again.
The Inspector was possibly of the same mind, K. fancied,
as far as he could tell from a hasty side-glance. But it was
equally possible that the Inspector had not even been listening, for he had pressed one hand firmly on the table and
seemed to be comparing the length of his fingers. The two
warders sat on a chest draped with an embroidered cloth,
rubbing their knees. The three young men were looking
aimlessly round them with their hands on their hips. It was
as quiet as in some deserted office. "Come, gentlemen,"

cried K.—it seemed to him for the moment as if he were responsible for all of them—"from the look of you this affair of mine seems to be settled. In my opinion the best thing now would be to bother no more about the justice or injustice of your behavior and settle the matter amicably by shaking hands on it. If you are of the same opinion, why, then—" and he stepped over to the Inspector's table and held out his hand. The Inspector raised his eyes, bit his lips, and looked at K.'s hand stretched out to him; K. still believed he was going to close with the offer. But instead he got up, seized a hard round hat lying on Fräulein Bürstner's bed, and with both hands put it carefully on his head, as if he were trying it on for the first time. "How simple it all seems to you!" he said to K. as he did so. "You think we should settle the matter amicably, do you? No, no, that really can't be done. On the other hand I don't mean to suggest that you should give up hope. Why should you? You are only under arrest, nothing more. I was requested to inform you of this. I have done so, and I have also observed your reactions. That's enough for today, and we can say good-by, though only for the time being, naturally. You'll be going to the Bank now, I suppose?" "To the Bank?" asked K. "I thought I was under arrest?" K. asked the question with a certain defiance, for though his offer to shake hands had been ignored, he felt more and more independent of all these people, especially now that the Inspector had risen to his feet. He was playing with them. He considered the idea of running after them to the front door as they left and challenging them to take him prisoner. So he said again: "How can I go to the Bank, if I am under arrest?" "Ah, I see," said the Inspector, who had already reached the door. "You have misunderstood me. You are under arrest, certainly, but that need not hinder you from going about your business. Nor will you be prevented from leading your ordinary life." "Then being

arrested isn't so very bad," said K., going up to the Inspector. "I never suggested that it was," said the Inspector.
"But in that case it would seem there was no particular
necessity to tell me about it," said K., moving still closer.
The others had drawn near too. They were all gathered
now in a little space beside the door. "It was my duty," said
the Inspector. "A stupid duty," said K. inflexibly. "That may
be," replied the Inspector, "but we needn't waste our time
with such arguments. I was assuming that you would want
to go to the Bank. As you are such a quibbler over words,
let me add that I am not forcing you to go to the Bank, I
was merely assuming that you would want to go. And to
facilitate that, and render your arrival at the Bank as un-
obtrusive as possible, I have detained these three gentlemen here, who are colleagues of yours, to be at your disposal." "What?" cried K., gaping at the three of them.
These insignificant anemic young men, whom he had observed only as a group standing beside the photographs,
were actually clerks in the Bank, not colleagues of his—that
was putting it too strongly and indicated a gap in the
omniscience of the Inspector—but they were subordinate
employees of the Bank all the same. How could he have
failed to notice that? He must have been very much taken
up with the Inspector and the warders not to recognize
these three young men. The stiff Rabensteiner swinging his
arms, the fair Kullich with the deep-set eyes, and Kaminer
with his insupportable smile, caused by a chronic muscular
twitch. "Good morning!" said K. after a pause, holding out
his hand to the three politely bowing figures. "I didn't
recognize you. Well, shall we go to our work now, eh?"
The young men nodded, smilingly and eagerly, as if they
had been waiting all the time merely for this, but when
K. turned to get his hat, which he had left in his room, they
all fled one after the other to fetch it, which seemed to
indicate a certain embarrassment. K. stood still and

watched them through the two open doors; the languid Rabensteiner, naturally, brought up the rear, for he merely minced along at an elegant trot. Kaminer handed over the hat and K. had to tell himself expressly, as indeed he had often to do in the Bank, that Kaminer's smile was not intentional, that the man could not smile intentionally if he tried. Then Frau Grubach, who did not appear to be particularly conscious of any guilt, opened the front door to let the whole company out, and K. glanced down, as so often before, at her apron string, which made such an unreasonably deep cut in her massive body. Down below he decided, his watch in his hand, to take a taxi so as to save any further delay in reaching the Bank, for he was already half an hour late. Kaminer ran to the corner to get a taxi, the other two were obviously doing their best to distract K., when suddenly Kullich pointed to the opposite house door, where the tall man with the reddish, pointed beard was emerging into sight, and immediately, a little embarrassed at showing himself in his full height, retreated against the wall and leaned there. The old couple must be still coming down the stairs. K. was annoyed at Kullich for drawing his attention to the man, whom he had already identified, indeed whom he had actually expected to see. "Don't look across," he said hurriedly, without noticing how strange it must seem to speak in that fashion to grown-up men. But no explanation proved necessary, for at that moment the taxi arrived, they took their seats and drove off. Then K. remembered that he had not noticed the Inspector and the warders leaving, the Inspector had usurped his attention so that he did not recognize the three clerks, and the clerks in turn had made him oblivious of the Inspector. That did not show much presence of mind, and K. resolved to be more careful in this respect. Yet in spite of himself he turned round and craned from the back of the car to see if he could perhaps catch sight of the Inspector and the warders. But he immediately turned away again and leaned back comfortably in the corner without even having attempted to distinguish one of them. Unlikely as it might seem, this was just the moment when he would have welcomed a few words from his companions, but the others seemed to be suddenly tired: Rabensteiner gazed out to the right, Kullich to the left, and only Kaminer faced him with his nervous grin, which, unfortunately, on grounds of humanity could not be made a subject of conversation.

That spring K. had been accustomed to pass his evenings in this way: after work whenever possible—he was usually in his office until nine—he would take a short walk, alone or with some of his colleagues, and then go to a beer hall, where until eleven he sat at a table patronized mostly by elderly men. But there were exceptions to this routine, when, for instance, the Manager of the Bank, who highly valued his diligence and reliability, invited him for a drive or for dinner at his villa. And once a week K. visited a girl called Elsa, who was on duty all night till early morning as a waitress in a cabaret and during the day received her visitors in bed.

But on this evening—the day had passed quickly, filled with pressing work and many flattering and friendly birthday wishes—K. resolved to go straight home. During every brief pause in the day's work he had kept this resolve in mind; without his quite knowing why, it seemed to him that the whole household of Frau Grubach had been thrown into great disorder by the events of the morning and that it was his task alone to put it right again. Once order was restored, every trace of these events would be obliterated and things would resume their old course. From the three clerks themselves nothing was to be feared, they had been absorbed once more in the great hierarchy of the Bank, no change was to be remarked in them. K. had

several times called them singly and collectively to his
room, with no other purpose than to observe them: each
time he had dismissed them again with a quiet mind.*

When at half past nine he arrived at the house where he
lived he found a young lad in the street doorway, standing
with his legs wide apart and smoking a pipe. "Who are
you?" K. asked at once, bringing his face close to the lad's
—one could not see very well in the darkness of the entrance. "I'm the house-porter's son, sir," said the lad, taking
the pipe from his mouth and stepping aside. "The house-
porter's son?" asked K., tapping his stick impatiently on the
ground. "Do you want anything, sir? Shall I fetch my
father?" "No, no," said K., and his voice had a reassuring
note, as if the lad had done something wrong but was to
be forgiven. "It's all right," he said and went on, yet before
he climbed the stair he turned round for another look.

He had intended to go straight to his room, but as he
wanted to speak to Frau Grubach he stopped instead to
knock at her door. She was sitting darning at a table, on
which lay a heap of old stockings. K. excused himself awk-
wardly for knocking so late, but Frau Grubach was most
cordial and would hear of no apology, she was always glad
to have a talk with him, he knew very well that he was her
best and most valued boarder. K. looked round the room; it
had reverted completely to its old state, the breakfast dishes
which had stood that morning on the table by the window
had apparently been cleared away. Women's hands are
quietly effective, he thought. He himself might have
smashed the dishes on the spot, but he certainly could
never have quietly carried them away. He gazed at Frau
Grubach with a certain gratitude. "Why are you still working at this late hour?" he asked. They were both sitting at
the table now, and from time to time K. buried one hand
in the pile of stockings. "There's a lot to do," she said;
"during the day my time belongs to my boarders; for keep-

ing my own things in order I have only the evenings." "I'm afraid I've been responsible for giving you extra work today." "How is that?" she asked, becoming more intent, the work resting in her lap. "I mean the men who were here this morning." "Oh, that," she said, resuming her composure, "that didn't give me much to do." K. looked on in silence while she took up her darning again. (She seems surprised that I mentioned it, he thought, she seems to think it not quite right that I should mention it. All the more need for me to do so. I couldn't mention it to anyone but this old woman.) "It must certainly have made more work," he said at last, "but it won't happen again." "No, that can't happen again," she said reassuringly, with an almost sorrowful smile. "Do you really mean it?" asked K. "Yes," she said softly, "and above all you mustn't take it too much to heart. Lots of things happen in this world! As you've spoken so frankly to me, Herr K., I may as well admit to you that I listened for a little behind the door and that the two warders told me a few things too. It's a matter of your happiness, and I really have that at heart, more perhaps than I should, for I am only your landlady. Well, then, I heard a few things, but I can't say that they were particularly bad. No. You are under arrest, certainly, but not as a thief is under arrest. If one's arrested as a thief, that's a bad business, but as for this arrest—. It gives me the feeling of something very learned, forgive me if what I say is stupid, it gives me the feeling of something learned which I don't understand, but which there is no need to understand."

"What you've just said is by no means stupid, Frau Grubach, at least I'm partly of the same opinion, except that I judge the whole thing still more severely. There's nothing learned about it. It's completely null and void. I was taken by surprise, that was all. If immediately on wakening I had got up without troubling my head about

Anna's absence and had come to you without regarding anyone who tried to bar my way, I could have breakfasted in the kitchen for a change and could have got you to bring me my clothes from my room; in short, if I had behaved sensibly, nothing further would have happened, all this would have been nipped in the bud. But one is so unprepared. In the Bank, for instance, I am always prepared, nothing of that kind could possibly happen to me there, I have my own attendant, the general telephone and the office telephone stand before me on my desk, people keep coming in to see me, clients and clerks, and above all, my mind is always on my work and so kept on the alert, it would be an actual pleasure to me if a situation like that cropped up in the Bank. Well, it's past history now and I didn't really intend to speak about it again, only I wanted to hear your judgment, the judgment of a sensible woman, and I am very glad we are in agreement. But now you must give me your hand on it, an agreement such as this must be confirmed with a handshake."

Will she take my hand? The Inspector wouldn't do it, he thought, gazing at the woman with a different, a critical eye. She stood up because he had stood up, she was a little embarrassed, for she had not understood all that he had said. And because of her embarrassment she said something which she had not intended to say and which was, moreover, rather out of place. "Don't take it so much to heart, Herr K.," she said with tears in her voice, forgetting, naturally, to shake his hand. "I had no idea that I was taking it to heart," said K., suddenly tired and seeing how little it mattered whether she agreed with him or not.

At the door he asked: "Is Fräulein Bürstner in?" "No," replied Frau Grubach, and in giving this dry piece of information she smiled with honest if belated sympathy. "She's at the theater. Do you want to ask her something? Shall I give her a message?" "Oh, I just wanted a word or two with her." "I'm afraid I don't know when she will be back; when she goes to the theater she's usually late." "It's of no consequence," said K., turning to the door, his head sunk on his breast. "I only wanted to apologize to her for having borrowed her room today." "That's quite unnecessary, Herr K., you are too scrupulous, Fräulein Bürstner knows nothing about it, she hasn't been back since early this morning, everything has been put back in its place again too, see for yourself." And she opened the door of Fräulein Bürstner's room. "Thanks, I believe you," said K., but went in through the open door all the same. The moon shone softly into the dark chamber. As far as one could see everything was really in its proper place, and the blouse was no longer dangling from the latch of the window. The pillows on the bed looked strangely high, they were lying partly in the moonlight. "She often comes home late," said K., looking at Frau Grubach as if she were to blame for it. "Young people are like that," said Frau Grubach apologetically. "Certainly, certainly," said K., "but it can go too far." "That it can," said Frau Grubach, "how right you are, Herr K.! In this case especially, perhaps. I have no wish to speak ill of Fräulein Bürstner, she is a dear, good girl, kind, decent, punctual, industrious, I admire all these qualities in her, but one thing is undeniable, she should have more pride, should keep herself more to herself. This very month I have met her twice already on outlying streets, and each time with a different gentleman. It worries me, and as sure as I stand here, Herr K., I haven't told anybody but you, but I'm afraid there's no help for it, I shall have to talk to Fräulein Bürstner herself about it. Besides, it isn't the only thing that has made me suspicious of her." "You're quite on the wrong track," said K., with a sudden fury which he was scarcely able to hide, "and you have obviously misunderstood my remark about Fräulein Bürstner, it wasn't meant in that way. In fact I frankly warn you against saying anything to her; you're quite mistaken, I know Fräulein Bürstner very well, there isn't a word of truth in what you say. But perhaps I'm going too far myself. I don't want to interfere, you can say what you like to her. Good night." "Good night, Herr K.," said Frau Grubach imploringly, hurrying after him to his door, which he had already opened, "I don't really mean to say anything to her yet, of course I'll wait to see what happens before I do anything, you're the only one I've spoken to, in confidence. After all, it must be to the interest of all my boarders that I try to keep my house respectable, and that is all I'm anxious about in this case." "Respectable!" cried K., through the chink of the door; "if you want to keep your house respectable you'll have to begin by giving me notice." Then he shut the door and paid no attention to the faint knocking that ensued.

On the other hand, as he felt no desire to sleep, he resolved to stay awake and take the opportunity of noting at what hour Fräulein Bürstner returned. Perhaps when she did so it might still be possible, unsuitable though the hour was, to have a few words with her. As he lounged by the window and shut his tired eyes, he actually considered for a moment paying Frau Grubach back by persuading Fräulein Bürstner to give notice along with him. Yet he saw at once that this was an excessive reaction, and he began to suspect himself of wishing to change his lodgings because of that morning's events. Nothing could be more senseless, not to say pointless and contemptible.*

When he became weary of gazing out into the empty street he lay down on the sofa, after having slightly opened the door to the entrance hall, so that from where he was lying he might see at once anyone who came in. Until about eleven he lay quietly on the sofa smoking a cigar. But then he could not endure lying there any longer and took a step or two into the entrance hall, as if that would make Fräulein Bürstner come all the sooner. He felt no special desire to see her, he could not even remember exactly how she looked, but he wanted to talk to her now, and he was exasperated that her being so late should further disturb and derange the end of such a day. She was to blame, too, for the fact that he had not eaten any supper and that he had put off the visit to Elsa he had proposed making that evening. He could remedy both omissions still, it was true, by going straight to the wine restaurant where Elsa worked. He would do that later, he decided, after his talk with Fräulein Bürstner.

It was a little after half past eleven when he heard somebody on the stairs. Absorbed in his thoughts, he had been marching up and down the entrance hall for some time as if it were his own room, and now he fled behind his bedroom door. It was Fräulein Bürstner coming in. As she locked the front door she shivered and drew her silk shawl round her slim shoulders. In a minute she would be going into her room, where K. certainly could not intrude at such an hour; he would therefore have to speak to her now, but unfortunately he had forgotten to switch on the light in his room, so that if he were to emerge from the darkness it would look as if he were waylaying her and at least must be somewhat alarming. No time was to be lost, so in his confusion he whispered through the chink of the door: "Fräulein Bürstner." It sounded like a prayer, not like a summons. "Is anyone there?" asked Fräulein Bürstner, looking round with wide-open eyes. "It's I," said K., stepping forward. "Oh, Herr K.!" said Fräulein Bürstner, smiling. "Good evening," and she held out her hand to him. "I should like to have a word or two with you, will you allow me to do so now?" "Now?" asked Fräulein Bürstner. "Must it be now? A little unusual, isn't it?" "I've been waiting for you ever since nine." "Well, I was at the theater, you know, I had no idea you were waiting." "What I want

to talk to you about didn't happen till today." "Oh, well,
I have no serious objection, except that I am so tired I
can scarcely stand on my feet. So come for a few minutes
to my room. We can't possibly talk here, we should waken
everybody, and I should dislike that for our own sakes even
more than for theirs. Wait here till I have turned on the
light in my room, and then you can switch off the light
here." K. did so, but waited until Fräulein Bürstner from
her room again invited him, in a whisper, to come in.
"Take a seat," she said, pointing to the sofa; she herself
stood leaning against the foot of the bed in spite of her
confessed weariness; she did not even take off her small but
lavishly flower-bedecked hat. "Well, what is it? I am really
curious." She crossed her ankles. "Perhaps you will say,"
began K., "that there was no urgent need to speak about
it now, but—" "I never listen to preambles," said Fräulein
Bürstner. "That makes it easier for me," said K. "This morning your room was thrown into some slight confusion and
the fault was mine in a certain sense, it was done by
strange people against my will, and yet as I have said the
fault was mine; I want to beg your pardon for this." "My
room?" asked Fräulein Bürstner, and she cast a critical eye
round the room instead of looking at him. "That is so," said
K., and now they gazed into each other's eyes for the first
time. "The actual manner in which it happened isn't worth
mentioning." "But surely that is the really interesting part,"
said Fräulein Bürstner. "No," said K. "Well," said Fräulein
Bürstner, "I don't want to pry into secrets; if you insist that
it is uninteresting, I shall not argue the point. You have
begged my pardon and I herewith freely grant it, particularly as I can find no trace of disturbance." With her open
palms pressed to her hips, she made a tour of the room.
Beside the mat where the photographs were stuck she
stopped. "Look here," she cried, "my photographs are all
mixed up! That is really odious. So someone has actually

been in my room who had no right to come in." K. nodded and silently cursed the clerk Kaminer, who could never control his stupid, meaningless fidgeting. "It is curious," said Fräulein Bürstner, "that I should be compelled now to forbid you to do something which you ought to forbid yourself to do, that is to enter my room in my absence." "But I have explained to you, Fräulein," said K., going over to the photographs, "that it was not I who interfered with these photographs; still, as you won't believe me, I have to confess that the Court of Inquiry brought three Bank clerks here, one of whom, and I shall have him dismissed at the first opportunity, must have meddled with your photographs." In answer to the Fräulein's inquiring look he added: "Yes, there was a Court of Inquiry here today." "On your account?" asked the Fräulein. "Yes," replied K. "No!" cried the girl, laughing. "Yes, it was," said K. "Why, do you think I must be innocent?" "Well, innocent," said Fräulein Bürstner, "I don't want to commit myself, at a moment's notice, to a verdict with so many possible implications, besides, I don't really know you; all the same, it must be a serious crime that would bring a Court of Inquiry down on a man. Yet as you are still at large—at least I gather from the look of you that you haven't just escaped from prison—you couldn't really have committed a serious crime." "Yes," said K., "but the Court of Inquiry might have discovered, not that I was innocent, but that I was not so guilty as they had assumed." "Certainly, that is possible," said Fräulein Bürstner, very much on the alert. "You see," said K., "you haven't much experience in legal matters." "No, I haven't," said Fräulein Bürstner, "and I have often regretted it, for I would like to know everything there is to know, and law courts interest me particularly. A court of law has a curious attraction, hasn't it? But I'll soon remedy my ignorance in that respect, for next month I am joining the clerical staff of a lawyer's office." "That's excel-

lent," said K. "Then you'll be able to help me a little with
my case." "That may well be," said Fräulein Bürstner, "why
not? I like to make good use of my knowledge." "But I
mean it seriously," said K., "or at least half-seriously, as
you yourself mean it. The case is too trifling to need a
lawyer, but I could do very well with an adviser." "Yes,
but if I am to be an adviser I must know what it's all
about," said Fräulein Bürstner. "That's just the trouble,"
said K. "I don't know that myself." "Then you've simply
been making fun of me," said Fräulein Bürstner, extrava-
gantly disappointed, "it was surely unnecessary to choose
this late hour for doing so." And she walked away from
the photographs, where they had been standing together
for a long time. "But, Fräulein," said K., "I'm not making
fun of you. Why won't you believe me? I have already told
you all I know. In fact more than I know, for it was not a
real Court of Inquiry. I called it that because I didn't know
what else to call it. There was no interrogation at all, I
was merely arrested, but it was done by a Commission."
Fräulein Bürstner sat down on the sofa and laughed again.*
"What was it like, then?" she asked. "Horrible," said K., but
he was no longer thinking of what he was saying, for he
was completely taken up in staring at Fräulein Bürstner,
who was leaning her head on one hand—her elbow was
resting on the sofa cushions—while with the other she
slowly caressed her hip. "That's too general," she said.
"What's too general?" asked K. Then he came to himself
and asked: "Shall I let you see how it happened?" He
wanted to move about and yet he did not want to leave.
"I'm tired," said Fräulein Bürstner. "You came home so
late," said K. "So you've gone the length of reproaching me,
and I deserve it, too, for I should never have let you in.
And there was no need for it, either, that's evident." "There
was a need for it. I'll make you see that in a minute," said
K. "May I shift this night table from beside your bed?"

"What an idea!" cried Fräulein Bürstner. "Of course not!" "Then I can't show you how it happened," said K. in agitation, as if some immeasurable wrong had been inflicted upon him. "Oh, if you need it for your performance, shift the table by all means," said Fräulein Bürstner, and after a pause added in a smaller voice: "I'm so tired that I'm letting you take too many liberties." K. stationed the table in the middle of the room and sat down behind it. "You must picture to yourself exactly where the various people are, it's very interesting. I am the Inspector, over there on the chest two warders are sitting, beside the photographs three young men are standing. At the latch of the window—just to mention it in passing—a white blouse is dangling. And now we can begin. Oh, I've forgotten about myself, the most important person; well, I'm standing here in front of the table. The Inspector is lounging at his ease with his legs crossed, his arm hanging over the back of the chair like this, an absolute boor. And now we can really begin. The Inspector shouts as if he had to waken me out of my sleep, he actually bawls; I'm afraid, if I am to make you understand, I'll have to bawl too, but he only bawls my name." Fräulein Bürstner, who was listening with amusement, put her finger to her lips to keep K. from shouting, but it was too late, K. was too absorbed in his role, he gave a long-drawn shout: "Joseph K.," less loud indeed than he had threatened, but with such explosive force that it hung in the air a moment before gradually spreading through the room.

Then there was a knocking at the door of the adjoining room, a loud, sharp, regular tattoo. Fräulein Bürstner turned pale and put her hand to her heart. K. was violently startled, it took him a moment or so to withdraw his thoughts from the events of the morning and the girl before whom he was acting them. No sooner had he come to himself than he rushed over to Fräulein Bürstner and seized

her hand. "Don't be afraid," he whispered, "I'll put everything right. But who can it be? There's only the living
room next door, nobody sleeps there." "No," Fräulein
Bürstner whispered in his ear, "since yesterday a nephew
of Frau Grubach has been sleeping there, a Captain. There
was no other room he could have. I forgot all about it.
Why did you have to shout like that? I'm all upset." "There's
no need for that," said K., and as she sank back on the
cushions he kissed her on the brow. "Away with you, away
with you," she said, hastily sitting up again, "do go away,
do go now, what are you thinking about, he's listening at
the door, he hears everything. How you torment me!" "I
won't go," said K., "until you are a little calmer. Come to
the far corner of the room, he can't hear us there." She let
herself be led there. "You forget," he said, "that though
this may mean unpleasantness for you, it is not at all serious. You know how Frau Grubach, who has the decisive
voice in this matter, particularly as the Captain is her
nephew, you know how she almost venerates me and believes absolutely everything I say. She is also dependent
on me, I may say, for she has borrowed a fair sum of
money from me. I shall confirm any explanation of our
being together here that you like to invent, if it is in the
least practicable, and I pledge myself to make Frau Grubach not only publicly accept it but also really and hon-
estly believe it. You needn't consider me at all. If you
want to have it announced that I assaulted you, then Frau
Grubach will be informed accordingly and she will believe
it without losing her confidence in me, she's so devoted to
me." Fräulein Bürstner, silent and somewhat limp, stared
at the floor. "Why shouldn't Frau Grubach believe that I
assaulted you?" K. added. He was gazing at her hair: it
was reddish hair, parted in the middle and fastened with
a bun at the back, and very neatly dressed. He expected

her to look up at him, but she said without changing her posture: "Forgive me, I was terrified at the sudden knocking rather than at any consequence of the Captain's being there. It was so still after you shouted and then there came these knocks, that was why I was so terrified, I was sitting quite near the door, too, the knocking seemed to be just beside me. I thank you for your offer, but I'm not going to accept it. I can bear the responsibility for anything that happens in my room, no matter who questions it. I'm surprised you don't see the insult to me that is implied in your suggestion, together with your good intentions, of course, which I do appreciate. But now go, leave me to myself, I need more than ever to be left in peace. The few minutes you begged for have stretched to half an hour and more." K. clasped her hand and then her wrist. "But you aren't angry with me?" he asked. She shook his hand off and answered: "No, no, I'm never angry with anybody." He felt for her wrist again, she let him take it this time and so led him to the door. He was firmly resolved to leave. But at the door he stopped as if he had not expected to find a door there; Fräulein Bürstner seized this moment to free herself, open the door, and slip into the entrance hall, where she whispered: "Now, please do come! Look"—she pointed to the Captain's door, underneath which showed a strip of light—"he has turned on his light and is amusing himself at our expense." "I'm just coming," K. said, rushed out, seized her, and kissed her first on the lips, then all over the face, like some thirsty animal lapping greedily at a spring of long-sought fresh water. Finally he kissed her on the neck, right on the throat, and kept his lips there for a long time. A slight noise from the Captain's room made him look up. "I'm going now," he said; he wanted to call Fräulein Bürstner by her first name, but he did not know what it was. She nodded wearily, resigned her hand for

him to kiss, half turning away as if she were unaware of
what she did, and went into her room with down-bent
head. Shortly afterwards K. was in his bed. He fell asleep
almost at once, but before doing so he thought for a little
about his behavior, he was pleased with it, yet surprised
that he was not still more pleased; he was seriously concerned for Fräulein Bürstner because of the Captain.

CHAPTER TWO

First Interrogation

K. was informed by telephone that next Sunday a short inquiry into his case would take place. His attention was drawn to the fact that these inquiries would now follow each other regularly, perhaps not every week, but at more frequent intervals as time went on. It was in the general interest, on the one hand, that the case should be quickly concluded, but on the other hand the interrogations must be thorough in every respect, although, because of the strain involved, they must never last too long. For this reason the expedient of these rapidly succeeding but short interrogations had been chosen. Sunday had been selected as the day of inquiry so that K. might not be disturbed in his professional work. It was assumed that he would agree to this arrangement, but if he preferred some other day they would meet his wishes to the best of their ability. For instance, it would be possible to hold the inquiries during the night, although then K. would probably not be fresh enough. At any rate they would expect him on Sunday, if

K. had no objection. It was, of course, understood that he must appear without fail, he did not need to be reminded of that. He was given the number of the house where he had to go, it was a house in an outlying suburban street where he had never been before.

On receiving this message K. replaced the receiver without answering; his mind was made up to keep the appointment on Sunday, it was absolutely essential, the case was getting under way and he must fight it; this first interrogation must also be the last. He was still standing thoughtfully beside the telephone when he heard behind him the voice of the Assistant Manager, who wanted to telephone and found K. barring his way. "Bad news?" asked the Assistant Manager casually, not really wanting to know but merely eager to get K. away from the telephone. "No, no," said K., stepping aside but without going away. The Assistant Manager lifted the receiver and said, speaking round it while he waited to be connected: "Oh, a word with you, Herr K. Would you do me the favor of joining a party on my yacht on Sunday morning? There will be quite a large party, doubtless some of your friends will be among them. Herr Hasterer, the lawyer, among others. Will you come? Do come!" K. made an effort to attend to what the Assistant Manager was saying. It was of no slight importance to him, for this invitation from a man with whom he had never got on very well was a sort of friendly overture and showed how important K. had become to the Bank and how valuable his friendship or at least his neutrality had become to its second highest official. The Assistant Manager had definitely humbled himself in giving this invitation, even though he had merely dropped it casually while waiting at the telephone to get a connection. Yet K. had to humble the man a second time, for he said: "Thanks very much. But I'm sorry I have no time on Sunday, I have a previous engagement." "A pity," said the Assistant Man-

ager, turning to speak into the telephone, which had just
been connected. It was not a short conversation, but in his
confusion K. remained standing the whole time beside the
instrument. Not till the Assistant Manager had rung off did
he start out of his reverie in some alarm and say, to excuse
his aimless loitering: "I have just been rung up and asked
to go somewhere, but they forgot to tell me at what time."
"Well, you can ring up and ask," said the Assistant Manager. "It isn't so important as all that," said K., though in
saying so he crippled still further his first lame excuse. The
Assistant Manager, turning to go, went on making remarks
about other topics. K. forced himself to answer, but what
he was really thinking was that it would be best to go to
the address at nine o'clock on Sunday morning, since that
was the hour at which all the law courts started their business on weekdays.

Sunday was dull. K. was tired, for he had stayed late
at his restaurant the night before because of a celebration;
he had nearly overslept. In a great hurry, without taking
time to think or co-ordinate the plans which he had drawn
up during the week, he dressed and rushed off, without his
breakfast, to the suburb which had been mentioned to him.
Strangely enough, though he had little time to study
passers-by, he caught sight of the three clerks already involved in his case: Rabensteiner, Kullich, and Kaminer. The
first two were journeying in a streetcar which crossed in
front of him, but Kaminer was sitting on the terrace of a
café and bent inquisitively over the railing just as K.
passed. All three were probably staring after him and wondering where their chief was rushing off to; a sort of defiance had kept K. from taking a vehicle to his destination,
he loathed the thought of chartering anyone, even the most
casual stranger, to help him along in this case of his, also
he did not want to be beholden to anyone or to initiate
anyone even remotely in his affairs, and last of all he had

no desire to belittle himself before the Court of Inquiry by a too scrupulous punctuality. Nevertheless he was hurrying so as to arrive by nine o'clock if possible, although he had not even been required to appear at any specified time.

He had thought that the house would be recognizable even at a distance by some sign which his imagination left unspecified, or by some unusual commotion before the door. But Juliusstrasse, where the house was said to be and at whose end he stopped for a moment, displayed on both sides houses almost exactly alike, high gray tenements inhabited by poor people. This being Sunday morning, most of the windows were occupied, men in shirt-sleeves were leaning there smoking or holding small children cautiously and tenderly on the window ledges. Other windows were piled high with bedding, above which the disheveled head of a woman would appear for a moment. People were shouting to one another across the street; one shout just above K.'s head caused great laughter. Down the whole length of the street at regular intervals, below the level of the pavement, there were little general grocery shops, to which short flights of steps led down. Women were thronging into and out of these shops or gossiping on the steps outside. A fruit hawker who was crying his wares to the people in the windows above, progressing almost as inattentively as K. himself, almost knocked K. down with his pushcart. A phonograph which had seen long service in a better quarter of the town began stridently to murder a tune.

K. penetrated deeper into the street, slowly, as if he had now abundant time, or as if the Examining Magistrate might be leaning from one of the windows with every opportunity of observing that he was on the way. It was a little after nine o'clock. The house was quite far along the street, it was of unusual extent, the main entrance was particularly high and wide. It was clearly a service entrance

for trucks, the locked doors of various warehouses surrounded the courtyard and displayed the names of firms
some of which were known to K. from the Bank ledgers.
Against his usual habit, he studied these external appearances with close attention and remained standing for a little
while in the entrance to the courtyard. Near him a barefooted man was sitting on a crate reading a newspaper.
Two lads were seesawing on a hand-barrow. A sickly young
girl was standing at a pump in her dressing-jacket and
gazing at K. while the water poured into her bucket. In
one corner of the courtyard a line was stretched between
two windows, where washing was already being hung up
to dry. A man stood below superintending the work with
an occasional shout.

K. turned toward the stairs to make his way up to the
Court of Inquiry, but then came to a standstill again, for
in addition to this staircase he could see in the courtyard
three other separate flights of stairs and besides these a
little passage at the other end which seemed to lead into
a second courtyard. He was annoyed that he had not been
given more definite information about the room, these people showed a strange negligence or indifference in their
treatment of him, he intended to tell them so very positively and clearly. Finally, however, he climbed the first
stairs and his mind played in retrospect with the saying of
the warder Willem that an attraction existed between the
Law and guilt, from which it should really follow that the
Court of Inquiry must abut on the particular flight of stairs
which K. happened to choose.

On his way up he disturbed many children who were
playing on the stairs and looked at him angrily as he strode
through their ranks. "If I ever come here again," he told
himself, "I must either bring sweets to cajole them with or
else a stick to beat them." Just before he reached the first
floor he had actually to wait for a moment until a marble

came to rest, two children with the lined, pinched faces of adult rogues holding him meanwhile by his trousers; if he had shaken them off he must have hurt them, and he feared their outcries.

His real search began on the first floor. As he could not inquire for the Court of Inquiry he invented a joiner called Lanz—the name came into his mind because Frau Grubach's nephew, the Captain, was called Lanz—and so he began to inquire at all the doors if a joiner called Lanz lived there, so as to get a chance to look into the rooms. It turned out, however, that that was quite possible without further ado, for almost all the doors stood open, with children running out and in. Most of the flats, too, consisted of one small single-windowed room in which cooking was going on. Many of the women were holding babies in one arm and working over the stove with the arm that was left free. Half-grown girls who seemed to be dressed in nothing but an apron kept busily rushing about. In all the rooms the beds were still occupied, sick people were lying in them, or men who had not wakened yet, or others who were resting there in their clothes. At the doors which were shut K. knocked and asked if a joiner called Lanz lived there. Generally a woman opened, listened to his question, and then turned to someone in the room, who thereupon rose from the bed. "The gentleman's asking if a joiner called Lanz lives here." "A joiner called Lanz?" asked the man from the bed. "Yes," said K., though it was beyond question that the Court of Inquiry did not sit here and his inquiry was therefore superfluous. Many seemed convinced that it was highly important for K. to find the joiner Lanz, they took a long time to think it over, suggested some joiner who, however, was not called Lanz, or a name which had some quite distant resemblance to Lanz, or inquired of their neighbors, or escorted K. to a door some considerable distance away, where they fancied such a man

might be living as a lodger, or where there was someone
who could give better information than they could. In the
end K. scarcely needed to ask at all, for in this way he was
conducted over the whole floor. He now regretted his plan,
which at first had seemed so practical. As he was approaching the fifth floor he decided to give up the search, said
good-by to a friendly young workman who wanted to conduct him farther, and descended again. But then the use-
lessness of the whole expedition filled him with exasperation, he went up the stairs once more and knocked at the
first door he came to on the fifth story. The first thing he
saw in the little room was a great pendulum clock which
already pointed to ten. "Does a joiner called Lanz live
here?" he asked. "Please go through," said a young woman
with sparkling black eyes, who was washing children's
clothes in a tub, and she pointed with her damp hand to
the open door of the next room.

K. felt as though he were entering a meeting-hall. A
crowd of the most variegated people—nobody troubled
about the newcomer—filled a medium-sized two-windowed
room, which just below the roof was surrounded by a gallery, also quite packed, where the people were able to
stand only in a bent posture with their heads and backs
knocking against the ceiling. K., feeling the air too thick
for him, stepped out again and said to the young woman,
who seemed to have misunderstood him: "I asked for a
joiner, a man called Lanz." "I know," said the woman,
"just go right in." K. might not have obeyed if she had
not come up to him, grasped the handle of the door, and
said: "I must shut this door after you, nobody else must
come in." "Very sensible," said K., "but the room is surely
too full already." However, he went in again.

Between two men who were talking together just inside
the door—the one was making with both outstretched
hands a gesture as if paying out money while the other

was looking him sharply in the eye—a hand reached out
and seized K. It belonged to a little red-cheeked lad.
"Come along, come along," he said. K. let himself be led
off, it seemed that in the confused, swarming crowd a
slender path was kept free after all, possibly separating
two different factions; in favor of this supposition was the
fact that immediately to right and left of him K. saw
scarcely one face looking his way, but only the backs of
people who were addressing their words and gestures to
the members of their own party. Most of them were
dressed in black, in old, long, and loosely hanging Sunday
coats. These clothes were the only thing that baffled K.,
otherwise he would have taken the gathering for a local
political meeting.*

At the other end of the hall, toward which K. was being
led, there stood on a low and somewhat crowded platform
a little table, set at a slant, and behind it, near the very edge
of the platform, sat a fat little wheezing man who was
talking with much merriment to a man sprawling just behind him with his elbow on the back of the chair and his
legs crossed. The fat little man now and then flung his
arms into the air, as if he were caricaturing someone. The
lad who was escorting K. found it difficult to announce his
presence. Twice he stood on tiptoe and tried to say something, without being noticed by the man up above. Not till
one of the people on the platform pointed out the lad did
the man turn to him and bend down to hear his faltering
words. Then he drew out his watch and with a quick
glance at K., "You should have been here an hour and five
minutes ago," he said. K. was about to answer, but had no
time to do so, for scarcely had the man spoken when a
general growl of disapproval followed in the right half of
the hall. "You should have been here an hour and five
minutes ago," repeated the man in a raised voice, casting
another quick glance into the body of the hall. Immediately

the muttering grew stronger and took some time to subside, even though the man said nothing more. Then it became much quieter in the hall than at K.'s entrance. Only the people in the gallery still kept up their comments. As far as one could make out in the dimness, dust, and reek, they seemed to be worse dressed than the people below. Some had brought cushions with them, which they put between their heads and the ceiling, to keep their heads from getting bruised.

K. made up his mind to observe rather than speak, consequently he offered no defense of his alleged lateness in arriving and merely said: "Whether I am late or not, I am here now." A burst of applause followed, once more from the right side of the hall. "These people are easy to win over," thought K., disturbed only by the silence in the left half of the room, which lay just behind him and from which only one or two isolated handclaps had come. He considered what he should say to win over the whole of the audience once and for all, or if that were not possible, at least to win over most of them for the time being.

"Yes," said the man, "but I am no longer obliged to hear you now"—once more the muttering arose, this time unmistakable in its import, for, silencing the audience with a wave of the hand, the man went on: "yet I shall make an exception for once on this occasion. But such a delay must not occur again. And now step forward." Someone jumped down from the platform to make room for K., who climbed on to it. He stood crushed against the table, the crowd behind him was so great that he had to brace himself to keep from knocking the Examining Magistrate's table and perhaps the Examining Magistrate himself off the platform.

But the Examining Magistrate did not seem to worry, he sat quite comfortably in his chair and after a few final words to the man behind him took up a small notebook, the only object lying on the table. It was like an ancient school exercise book, grown dog-eared from much thumbing. "Well, then," said the Examining Magistrate, turning over the leaves and addressing K. with an air of authority, "you are a house painter?" "No," said K., "I'm the chief clerk of a large Bank." This answer evoked such a hearty outburst of laughter from the right party that K. had to laugh too. People doubled up with their hands on their knees and shook as if in spasms of coughing. There were even a few guffaws from the gallery. The Examining Magistrate, now indignant, and having apparently no authority to control the people in the body of the hall, proceeded to vent his displeasure on those in the gallery, springing up and scowling at them till his eyebrows, hitherto inconspicuous, contracted in great black bushes above his eyes.

The left half of the hall, however, was still as quiet as ever, the people there stood in rows facing the platform and listened unmoved to what was going on up there as well as to the noise in the rest of the hall, indeed they actually suffered some of their members to initiate conversations with the other faction. These people of the left party, who were not so numerous as the others, might in reality be just as unimportant, but the composure of their bearing made them appear of more consequence. As K. began his speech he was convinced that he was actually representing their point of view.

"This question of yours, Sir, about my being a house painter—or rather, not a question, you simply made a statement—is typical of the whole character of this trial that is being foisted on me. You may object that it is not a trial at all; you are quite right, for it is only a trial if I recognize it as such. But for the moment I do recognize it, on grounds of compassion, as it were. One can't regard it except with compassion, if one is to regard it at all. I do not say that your procedure is contemptible, but I should like to present that epithet to you for your private consumption." K. stopped and looked down into the hall. He had spoken sharply, more sharply than he had intended, but with every justification. His words should have merited applause of some kind, yet all was still, the audience were clearly waiting intently for what was to follow; perhaps in that silence an outbreak was preparing which would put an end to the whole thing. K. was annoyed when the door at the end of the hall opened at that moment, admitting the young washerwoman, who seemed to have finished her work; she distracted some of the audience in spite of all the caution with which she entered. But the Examining Magistrate himself rejoiced K.'s heart, for he seemed to be quite dismayed by the speech. Until now he had been on his feet, for he had been surprised by K.'s speech as he got up to rebuke the gallery. In this pause he resumed his seat, very slowly, as if he wished his action to escape remark. Presumably to calm his spirit, he turned over the notebook again.

"That won't help you much," K. continued, "your very notebook, Sir, confirms what I say." Emboldened by the mere sound of his own cool words in that strange assembly, K. simply snatched the notebook from the Examining Magistrate and held it up with the tips of his fingers, as if it might soil his hands, by one of the middle pages, so that the closely written, blotted, yellow-edged leaves hung down on either side. "These are the Examining Magistrate's records," he said, letting it fall on the table again. "You can continue reading it at your ease, Herr Examining Magistrate, I really don't fear this ledger of yours though it is a closed book to me, for I would not touch it except with my finger tips and cannot even take it in my hand." It could only be a sign of deep humiliation, or must at least be interpreted as such, that the Examining Magistrate now took up the notebook where it had fallen on the table, tried to put it to rights again, and once more began to read it.

The eyes of the people in the first row were so tensely fixed upon K. that for a while he stood silently looking down at them. They were without exception elderly men, some of them with white beards. Could they possibly be the influential men, the men who would carry the whole assembly with them, and did they refuse to be shocked out of the impassivity into which they had sunk ever since he began his speech, even though he had publicly humiliated the Examining Magistrate?

"What has happened to me," K. went on, rather more quietly than before, trying at the same time to read the faces in the first row, which gave his speech a somewhat disconnected effect, "what has happened to me is only a single instance and as such of no great importance, especially as I do not take it very seriously, but it is representative of a misguided policy which is being directed against many other people as well. It is for these that I take up my stand here, not for myself."

He had involuntarily raised his voice. Someone in the audience clapped his hands high in the air and shouted: "Bravo! Why not? Bravo! And bravo again!" A few men in the first row pulled at their beards, but none turned round at this interruption. K., too, did not attach any importance to it, yet felt cheered nevertheless; he no longer considered it necessary to get applause from everyone, he would be quite pleased if he could make the audience start thinking about the question and win a man here and there through conviction.

"I have no wish to shine as an orator," said K., having come to this conclusion, "nor could I if I wished. The Examining Magistrate, no doubt, is much the better speaker, it is part of his vocation. All I desire is the public ventilation of a public grievance. Listen to me. Some ten days ago I was arrested, in a manner that seems ridiculous even to myself, though that is immaterial at the moment. I was seized in bed before I could get up, perhaps—it is not unlikely, considering the Examining Magistrate's statement —perhaps they had orders to arrest some house painter who is just as innocent as I am, only they hit on me. The room next to mine was requisitioned by two coarse warders. If I had been a dangerous bandit they could not have taken more careful precautions. These warders, moreover, were degenerate ruffians, they deafened my ears with their gabble, they tried to induce me to bribe them, they attempted to get my clothes and underclothes from me under dishonest pretexts, they asked me to give them money ostensibly to bring me some breakfast after they had brazenly eaten my own breakfast under my eyes. But that was not all. I was led into a third room to confront the Inspector. It was the room of a lady whom I deeply respect, and I had to look on while this room was polluted, yes, polluted, on my account but not by any fault of mine, through the presence of these warders and this Inspector. It was not easy for me to remain calm. I succeeded, however, and I asked the Inspector with the utmost calm—if he were here, he would have to substantiate that—why I had been arrested. And what was the answer of this Inspector, whom I can see before me now as he lounged in a chair belonging to the lady I have mentioned, like an embodiment of crass arrogance? Gentlemen, he answered in effect nothing at all, perhaps he really knew nothing; he had arrested me and that was enough. But that is not all, he had brought three minor employees of my Bank into the lady's room, who amused themselves by fingering and disarranging certain photographs, the property of the lady. The presence of these employees had another object as well, of course, they were expected, like my landlady and her maid, to spread the news of my arrest, damage my public reputation, and in particular shake my position in the Bank. Well, this expectation has entirely failed of its success, even my landlady, a quite simple person—I pronounce her name in all honor, she is called Frau Grubach —even Frau Grubach has been intelligent enough to recognize that an arrest such as this is no more worth taking seriously than some wild prank committed by stray urchins at the street corners. I repeat, the whole matter has caused me nothing but some unpleasantness and passing annoyance, but might it not have had worse consequences?"

When K. stopped at this point and glanced at the silent Examining Magistrate, he thought he could see him catching someone's eye in the audience, as if giving a sign. K. smiled and said: "The Examining Magistrate sitting here beside me has just given one of you a secret sign. So there are some among you who take your instructions from up here. I do not know whether the sign was meant to evoke applause or hissing, and now that I have divulged the matter prematurely I deliberately give up all hope of ever learning its real significance. It is a matter of complete indifference to me, and I publicly empower the Examining Magistrate to address his hired agents in so many words, instead of making secret signs to them, to say at the proper moment: Hiss now, or alternatively: Clap now."

The Examining Magistrate kept fidgeting on his chair with embarrassment or impatience. The man behind him to whom he had been talking bent over him again, either to encourage him or to give him some particular counsel. Down below, the people in the audience were talking in low voices but with animation. The two factions, who had seemed previously to be irreconcilable, were now drifting together, some individuals were pointing their fingers at K., others at the Examining Magistrate. The fuggy atmosphere in the room was unbearable, it actually prevented one from seeing the people at the other end. It must have been particularly inconvenient for the spectators in the gallery, who were forced to question the members of the audience in a low voice, with fearful side-glances at the Examining Magistrate, to find out what was happening. The answers were given as furtively, the informant generally putting his hand to his mouth to muffle his words.

"I have nearly finished," said K., striking the table with his fist, since there was no bell. At the shock of the impact the heads of the Examining Magistrate and his adviser started away from each other for a moment. "I am quite detached from this affair, I can therefore judge it calmly, and you, that is to say if you take this alleged court of justice at all seriously, will find it to your great advantage to listen to me. But I beg you to postpone until later any comments you may wish to exchange on what I have to say, for I am pressed for time and must leave very soon."

At once there was silence, so completely did K. already dominate the meeting. The audience no longer shouted confusedly as at the beginning, they did not even applaud, they seemed already convinced or on the verge of being convinced.

"There can be no doubt—" said K., quite softly, for he was elated by the breathless attention of the meeting; in that stillness a subdued hum was audible which was more exciting than the wildest applause—"there can be no doubt that behind all the actions of this court of justice, that is to say in my case, behind my arrest and today's interrogation, there is a great organization at work. An organization which not only employs corrupt warders, oafish Inspectors, and Examining Magistrates of whom the best that can be said is that they recognize their own limitations, but also has at its disposal a judicial hierarchy of high, indeed of the highest rank, with an indispensable and numerous retinue of servants, clerks, police, and other assistants, perhaps even

hangmen, I do not shrink from that word. And the significance of this great organization, gentlemen? It consists in
this, that innocent persons are accused of guilt, and senseless proceedings are put in motion against them, mostly
without effect, it is true, as in my own case. But considering the senselessness of the whole, how is it possible for
the higher ranks to prevent gross corruption in their agents?
It is impossible. Even the highest Judge in this organization cannot resist it. So the warders try to steal the clothes
off the bodies of the people they arrest, the Inspectors
break into strange houses, and innocent men, instead of being fairly examined, are humiliated in the presence of
public assemblies. The warders mentioned certain depots
where the property of prisoners is kept; I should like to
see these depots where the hard-earned property of arrested men is left to rot, or at least what remains of it after
thieving officials have helped themselves."

Here K. was interrupted by a shriek from the end of the
hall; he peered from beneath his hand to see what was
happening, for the reek of the room and the dim light together made a whitish dazzle of fog. It was the washerwoman, whom K. had recognized as a potential cause of
disturbance from the moment of her entrance. Whether she
was at fault now or not, one could not tell. All K. could see
was that a man had drawn her into a corner by the door
and was clasping her in his arms.* Yet it was not she who
had uttered the shriek but the man; his mouth was wide
open and he was gazing up at the ceiling. A little circle
had formed round them, the gallery spectators near by
seemed to be delighted that the seriousness which K. had
introduced into the proceedings should be dispelled in this
manner. K.'s first impulse was to rush across the room, he
naturally imagined that everybody would be anxious to
have order restored and the offending couple at least
ejected from the meeting, but the first rows of the audience

remained quite impassive, no one stirred and no one would let him through. On the contrary they actually obstructed him, someone's hand—he had no time to turn round— seized him from behind by the collar, old men stretched out their arms to bar his way, and by this time K. was no longer thinking about the couple, it seemed to him as if his freedom were being threatened, as if he were being arrested in earnest, and he sprang recklessly down from the platform. Now he stood eye to eye with the crowd. Had he been mistaken in these people? Had he overestimated the effectiveness of his speech? Had they been disguising their real opinions while he spoke, and now that he had come to the conclusion of his speech were they weary at last of pretense? What faces these were around him! Their little black eyes darted furtively from side to side, their beards were stiff and brittle, and to take hold of them would be like clutching bunches of claws rather than beards. But under the beards—and this was K.'s real discovery— badges of various sizes and colors gleamed on their coat-collars. They all wore these badges, so far as he could see. They were all colleagues, these ostensible parties of the right and the left, and as he turned round suddenly he saw the same badges on the coat-collar of the Examining Magistrate, who was sitting quietly watching the scene with his hands on his knees. "So!" cried K., flinging his arms in the air, his sudden enlightenment had to break out, "every man jack of you is an official, I see, you are yourselves the corrupt agents of whom I have been speaking, you've all come rushing here to listen and nose out what you can about me, making a pretense of party divisions, and half of you applauded merely to lead me on, you wanted some practice in fooling an innocent man. Well, much good I hope it's done you, for either you have merely gathered some amusement from the fact that I expected you to defend the innocent, or else—keep off or I'll strike you," cried

K. to a trembling old man who had pushed quite close to him—"or else you have really learned a thing or two. And I wish you joy of your trade." He hastily seized his hat, which lay near the edge of the table, and amid universal silence, the silence of complete stupefaction, if nothing else, pushed his way to the door. But the Examining Magistrate seemed to have been still quicker than K., for he was waiting at the door. "A moment," he said. K. paused but kept his eyes on the door, not on the Examining Magistrate; his hand was already on the latch. "I merely wanted to point out," said the Examining Magistrate, "that today—you may not yet have become aware of the fact—today you have flung away with your own hand all the advantages which an interrogation invariably confers on an accused man." K. laughed, still looking at the door. "You scoundrels, I'll spare you future interrogations," he shouted, opened the door, and hurried down the stairs. Behind him rose the buzz of animated discussion, the audience had apparently come to life again and were analyzing the situation like expert students.

CHAPTER THREE

In the Empty Courtroom · The Student · The Offices

DURING THE next week K. waited day after day for a new summons, he would not believe that his refusal to be interrogated had been taken literally, and when no appointment was made by Saturday evening, he assumed that he was tacitly expected to report himself again at the same address and at the same time. So he betook himself there on Sunday morning, and this time went straight up through the passages and stairways; a few people who remembered him greeted him from their doors, but he no longer needed to inquire of anybody and soon came to the right door. It opened at once to his knock, and without even turning his head to look at the woman, who remained standing beside the door, he made straight for the adjoining room. "There's no sitting today," said the woman. "Why is there no sitting?" he asked; he could not believe it. But the woman convinced him by herself opening the door of the next room. It was really empty and in its emptiness looked even more sordid than on the previous Sunday. On the table, which still stood on the platform as before, several books were lying. "May I glance at the books?" asked K., not out of any particular curiosity, but merely that his visit here might not be quite pointless. "No," said the woman, shutting the door again, "that isn't allowed. The books belong to the Examining Magistrate." "I see," said K., nodding, "these books are probably law books, and it is an essential part of the justice dispensed here that you should be condemned not only in innocence but also in ignorance." "That must be it," said the woman, who had not quite understood him. "Well, in that case I had better go again," said K. "Shall I give the Examining Magistrate a message?" asked the woman. "Do you know him?" asked K. "Of course," replied the woman, "my husband is an usher, you see." Only then did K. notice that the anteroom, which had contained nothing but a washtub last Sunday, now formed a fully furnished living room. The woman remarked his surprise and said: "Yes, we have free houseroom here, but we must clear the room on the days when the Court is sitting. My husband's post has many disadvantages." "I'm not so much surprised at the room," said K., looking at her severely, "as at the fact that you're married." "Perhaps you're hinting at what happened during the last sitting, when I caused a disturbance while you were speaking," said the woman. "Of course I am," said K. "It's an old story by this time, and almost forgotten, but at the moment it made me quite furious. And now you say yourself that you're a married woman." "It didn't do you any harm to have your speech interrupted; what you said made a bad enough impression, to judge from the discussion afterwards." "That may be," said K., evading that issue, "but it does not excuse you." "I stand excused in the eyes of everyone who knows me," said the woman. "The man you saw embracing me has been persecuting me for a long time. I may not be a temptation to most men, but I am to him. There's no way of keeping him off, even my husband has grown reconciled to it now; if he isn't to lose his job he must put up with it, for that man you saw is one of the students and will probably rise to great power yet. He's always after me, he was here today, just before you came." "It is all on a par," said K., "it doesn't surprise me." "You are anxious to improve things here, I think," said the woman slowly and watchfully, as if she were saying something which was risky both to her and to K., "I guessed that from your speech, which personally I liked very much. Though, of course, I only heard part of it, I missed the beginning and I was down on the floor with the student while you were finishing. It's so horrible here," she said after a pause, taking K.'s hand. "Do you think you'll manage to improve things?" K. smiled and caressed her soft hands. "Actually," he said, "it isn't my place to improve things here, as you put it, and if you were to tell the Examining Magistrate so, let us say, he would either laugh at you or have you punished. As a matter of fact, I should never have dreamed of interfering of my own free will, and shouldn't have lost an hour's sleep over the need for reforming the machinery of justice here. But the fact that I am supposed to be under arrest forces me to intervene—I am under arrest, you know—to protect my own interests. But if I can help you in any way at the same time, I shall be very glad, of course. And not out of pure altruism, either, for you in turn might be able to help me." "How could I do that?" asked the woman. "By letting me look at the books on the table there, for instance." "But of course!" cried the woman, dragging him hastily after her. They were old dog-eared volumes, the cover of one was almost completely split down the middle, the two halves were held together by mere threads. "How dirty everything is here!" said K., shaking his head, and the woman had to wipe away the worst of the dust with her apron before K. would put out his hand to touch the books. He opened the first of them and found an indecent picture. A man and a woman were sitting naked on a sofa, the obscene intention of the draftsman was evident enough, yet his skill was so small that nothing emerged from the picture save the all-too-solid figures of a man and a woman sitting rigidly upright, and because of the bad perspective, apparently finding the utmost difficulty even in turning toward each other. K. did not look at any of the other pages, but merely glanced at the title page of the second book, it was a novel entitled: *How Grete Was Plagued by Her Husband Hans.* "These are the law books that are studied here," said K. "These are the men who are supposed to sit in judgment on me." "I'll help you," said the woman. "Would you like me to?" "Could you really do that without getting yourself into trouble? You told me a moment ago that your husband is quite at the mercy of the higher officials." "I want to help you, all the same," said the woman. "Come, let us talk it over. Don't bother about the danger to me. I only fear danger when I want to fear it. Come." She settled herself on the edge of the platform and made room for him beside her. "You have lovely dark eyes," she said, after they had sat down, looking up into K.'s face, "I've been told that I have lovely eyes too, but yours are far lovelier. I was greatly struck by you as soon as I saw you, the first time you came here. And it was because of you that I slipped later into the courtroom, a thing I never do otherwise and which, in a manner of speaking, I am actually forbidden to do." So this is all it amounts to, thought K., she's offering herself to me, she's corrupt like the rest of them, she's tired of the officials here, which is understandable enough, and accosts any stranger who takes her fancy with compliments about his eyes. And K. rose to his feet as if he had uttered his thoughts aloud and sufficiently explained his position. "I don't think that could help me," he said; "to help me effectively one would need connections with the

higher officials. But I'm sure you know only the petty subordinates that swarm round here. You must know them
quite well and could get them to do a lot, I don't doubt,
but the utmost that they could do would have no effect
whatever on the final result of the case. And you would
simply have alienated some of your friends. I don't want
that. Keep your friendship with these people, for it seems
to me that you need it. I say this with regret, since to make
some return for your compliment, I must confess that I like
you too, especially when you gaze at me with such sorrowful eyes, as you are doing now, though I assure you there's
no reason whatever for it. Your place is among the people
I have to fight, but you're quite at home there, you love
this student, no doubt, or if you don't love him at least you
prefer him to your husband. It's easy to tell that from what
you say." "No," she cried without getting up but merely
catching hold of K.'s hand, which he did not withdraw
quickly enough. "You mustn't go away yet, you mustn't go
with mistaken ideas about me. Could you really bring yourself to go away like that? Am I really of so little account
in your eyes that you won't even do me the kindness of
staying for a little longer?" "You misunderstand me," said
K., sitting down, "if you really want me to stay I'll stay
with pleasure, I have time enough; I came here expecting
to find the Court in session. All that I meant was merely to
beg you not to do anything for me in this case of mine. But
that needn't offend you when you consider that I don't
care at all what the outcome of the case is, and that I
would only laugh at it if I were sentenced. Assuming, that
is, that the case will ever come to a proper conclusion,
which I very much doubt. Indeed, I fancy that it has
probably been dropped already or will soon be dropped,
through the laziness or the forgetfulness or it may be even
through the fears of those who are responsible for it. Of
course it's possible that they will make a show of carrying

it on, in the hope of getting money out of me, but they needn't bother, I can tell you now, for I shall never bribe anyone. That's something you could really do for me, however; you could inform the Examining Magistrate, or anyone who could be depended on to spread the news, that nothing will induce me to bribe these officials, not even any of the artifices in which they are doubtless so ingenious. The attempt would be quite hopeless, you can tell them that frankly. But perhaps they have come to that conclusion already, and even if they haven't, I don't much mind whether they get the information or not. It would merely save them some trouble and me, of course, some unpleasantness, but I should gladly endure any unpleasantness that meant a setback for them. And I shall take good care to see that it does. By the way, do you really know the Examining Magistrate?" "Of course," said the woman. "He was the first one I thought of when I offered you my help. I didn't know that he was only a petty official, but as you say so it must naturally be true. All the same, I fancy that the reports he sends up to the higher officials have some influence. And he writes out so many reports. You say that the officials are lazy, but that certainly doesn't apply to all of them, particularly to the Examining Magistrate, he's always writing. Last Sunday, for instance, the session lasted till late in the evening. All the others left, but the Examining Magistrate stayed on in the courtroom, I had to bring a lamp for him, I only had a small kitchen lamp, but that was all he needed and he began to write straight away. In the meantime my husband came home, he was off duty on that particular Sunday, we carried back our furniture, set our room to rights again, then some neighbors arrived, we talked on by candlelight, to tell the truth we simply forgot the Examining Magistrate and went to bed. Suddenly, in the middle of the night, it must have been far into the night by then, I woke up, the Examining Magistrate was

standing beside our bed shielding the lamp with his hand
to keep the light from falling on my husband, a needless
precaution, for my husband sleeps so soundly that not even
the light would have wakened him. I was so startled that
I almost cried out, but the Examining Magistrate was very
kind, warned me to be careful, whispered to me that he had
been writing till then, that he had come to return the lamp,
and that he would never forget the picture I had made lying asleep in bed. I only tell you this to show that the
Examining Magistrate is kept really busy writing reports,
especially about you, for your interrogation was certainly
one of the main items in the two days' session. Such long
reports as that surely can't be quite unimportant. But besides that you can guess from what happened that the
Examining Magistrate is beginning to take an interest in
me, and that at this early stage—for he must have noticed
me then for the first time—I could have great influence
with him. And by this time I have other proofs that he is
anxious to win my favor. Yesterday he sent me a pair of
silk stockings through the student, who works with him
and whom he is very friendly with, making out that it was
a reward for cleaning the courtroom, but that was only an
excuse, for to do that is only my duty and my husband is
supposed to be paid for it. They're beautiful stockings,
look"—she stretched out her legs, pulled her skirts above
her knees, and herself contemplated the stockings—"they're
beautiful stockings, but too fine, all the same, and not suitable for a woman like me."

Suddenly she broke off, laid her hand on K.'s hand as if
to reassure him, and said: "Hush, Bertold is watching us."
K. slowly raised his eyes. In the door of the courtroom a
young man was standing; he was small, his legs were
slightly bowed, and he strove to add dignity to his appearance by wearing a short, straggling, reddish beard, which
he was always fingering. K. stared at him with interest, this

was the first student of the mysterious jurisprudence whom
he had encountered, as it were, on human terms, a man,
too, who would presumably attain to one of the higher
official positions some day. The student, however, seemed
to take not the slightest notice of K., he merely made a
sign to the woman with one finger, which he withdrew for
a moment from his beard, and went over to the window.
The woman bent over K. and whispered: "Don't be angry
with me, please don't think badly of me, I must go to him
now, and he's a dreadful-looking creature, just see what
bandy legs he has. But I'll come back in a minute and then
I'll go with you if you'll take me with you, I'll go with you
wherever you like, you can do with me what you please,
I'll be glad if I can only get out of here for a long time,
and I wish it could be forever." She gave K.'s hand a last
caress, jumped up, and ran to the window. Despite himself
K.'s hand reached out after hers in the empty air. The
woman really attracted him, and after mature reflection he
could find no valid reason why he should not yield to that
attraction. He dismissed without difficulty the fleeting suspicion that she might be trying to lay a trap for him on the
instructions of the Court. In what way could she entrap
him? Wasn't he still free enough to flout the authority of
this Court once and for all, at least as far as it concerned
him? Could he not trust himself to this trifling extent? And
her offer of help had sounded sincere and was probably
not worthless. And probably there could be no more fitting
revenge on the Examining Magistrate and his henchmen
than to wrest this woman from them and take her himself.
Then some night the Examining Magistrate, after long and
arduous labor on his lying reports about K., might come to
the woman's bed and find it empty. Empty because she
had gone off with K., because the woman now standing in
the window, that supple, voluptuous warm body under the
coarse, heavy, dark dress, belonged to K. and to K. alone.

After arguing himself in this way out of his suspicions, he began to feel that the whispered conversation in the window was going on too long, and started knocking on the table with his knuckles and then with his fist. The student glanced briefly at K. across the woman's shoulder, but did not let himself be put out, indeed moved closer to her and put his arms around her. She drooped her head as if attentively listening to him, and as she did so he kissed her loudly on the throat without at all interrupting his remarks. In this action K. saw confirmed the tyranny which the student exercised over the woman, as she had complained, and he sprang to his feet and began to pace up and down the room. With occasional side-glances at the student he meditated how to get rid of him as quickly as possible, and so it was not unwelcome to him when the fellow, obviously annoyed by his walking up and down, which had turned by now into an angry tramping, said: "If you're so impatient, you can go away. There was nothing to hinder your going long ago, nobody would have missed you. In fact, it was your duty to go away, and as soon as I came in too, and as fast as your legs could carry you." There was intense rage in these words, but there was also the insolence of a future official of the Court addressing a displeasing prisoner. K. stepped up quite close to the student and said with a smile: "I am impatient, that is true, but the easiest way to relieve my impatience would be for you to leave us. Yet if by any chance you have come here to study—I hear that you're a student—I'll gladly vacate the room and go away with this woman. I fancy you've a long way to go yet in your studies before you can become a Judge. I admit I'm not very well versed in the niceties of your legal training, but I assume that it doesn't consist exclusively in learning to make rude remarks, at which you seem to have attained a shameless proficiency." "He shouldn't have been allowed to run around at large," said the student, as if seeking to explain K.'s insulting words to the woman. "It was a mistake, I told the Examining Magistrate that. He should at least have been confined to his room between the interrogations. There are times when I simply don't understand the Examining Magistrate." * "What's the use of talking?" said K., stretching out his hand to the woman. "Come along." "Ah, that's it," said the student, "no, no, you don't get her," and with a strength which one would not have believed him capable of he lifted her in one arm and, gazing up at her tenderly, ran, stooping a little beneath his burden, to the door. A certain fear of K. was unmistakable in this action, and yet he risked infuriating K. further by caressing and clasping the woman's arm with his free hand. K. ran a few steps after him, ready to seize and if necessary to throttle him, when the woman said: "It's no use, the Examining Magistrate has sent for me, I daren't go with you; this little monster," she patted the student's face, "this little monster won't let me go." "And you don't want to be set free," cried K., laying his hand on the shoulder of the student, who snapped at it with his teeth. "No," cried the woman, pushing K. away with both hands. "No, no, you mustn't do that, what are you thinking of? It would be the ruin of me. Let him alone, oh, please let him alone! He's only obeying the orders of the Examining Magistrate and carrying me to him." "Then let him go, and as for you, I never want to see you again," said K., furious with disappointment, and he gave the student a punch in the back that made him stumble for a moment, only to spring off more nimbly than ever out of relief that he had not fallen. K. slowly walked after them, he recognized that this was the first unequivocal defeat that he had received from these people. There was no reason, of course, for him to worry about that, he had received the defeat only because he had insisted on giving battle. While he stayed quietly at home and went about

his ordinary vocations he remained superior to all these
people and could kick any of them out of his path. And he
pictured to himself the highly comic situation which would
arise if, for instance, this wretched student, this puffed-up
whippersnapper, this bandy-legged beaver, had to kneel by
Elsa's bed some day wringing his hands and begging for
favors. This picture pleased K. so much that he decided, if
ever the opportunity came, to take the student along to visit
Elsa.

Out of curiosity K. hurried to the door, he wanted to see
where the woman was being carried off to, for the student
could scarcely bear her in his arms across the street. But
the journey was much shorter than that. Immediately opposite the door a flight of narrow wooden stairs led, as it
seemed, to a garret, it had a turning so that one could not
see the other end. The student was now carrying the
woman up this stairway, very slowly, puffing and groaning,
for he was beginning to be exhausted. The woman waved
her hand to K. as he stood below, and shrugged her
shoulders to suggest that she was not to blame for this
abduction, but very little regret could be read into that
dumb show. K. looked at her expressionlessly, as if she
were a stranger, he was resolved not to betray to her either
that he was disappointed or even that he could easily get
over any disappointment he felt.

The two had already vanished, yet K. still stood in the
doorway. He was forced to the conclusion that the woman
not only had betrayed him, but also had lied in saying that
she was being carried to the Examining Magistrate. The
Examining Magistrate surely could not be sitting waiting in
a garret. The little wooden stairway did not reveal anything, no matter how long one regarded it. But K. noticed
a small card pinned up beside it, and crossing over he read
in childish, unpracticed handwriting: "Law Court Offices
upstairs." So the Law Court offices were up in the attics

of this tenement? That was not an arrangement likely to inspire much respect, and for an accused man it was re- assuring to reckon how little money this Court could have at its disposal when it housed its offices in a part of the building where the tenants, who themselves belonged to the poorest of the poor, flung their useless lumber. Though, of course, the possibility was not to be ignored that the money was abundant enough, but that the officials pocketed it be- fore it could be used for the purposes of justice. To judge from K.'s experience hitherto, that was indeed extremely probable, yet if it were so, such disreputable practices, while certainly humiliating to an accused man, suggested more hope for him than a merely pauperized condition of the Law Courts. Now K. could understand too why in the be- ginning they had been ashamed to summon him into their attics and had chosen instead to molest him in his lodgings. And how well-off K. was compared with the Magistrate, who had to sit in a garret, while K. had a large room in the Bank with a waiting room attached to it and could watch the busy life of the city through his enormous plate-glass window. True, he drew no secondary income from bribes or peculation and could not order his attendant to pick up a woman and carry her to his room. But K. was per- fectly willing to renounce these advantages, at least in this life.

K. was still standing beside the card when a man came up from below, looked into the room through the open door, from which he could also see the courtroom, and then asked K. if he had seen a woman about anywhere. "You are the usher, aren't you?" asked K. "Yes," said the man. "Oh, you're the defendant K., now I recognize you, you're welcome." And he held out his hand to K., who had not expected that. "But no sitting was announced for to- day," the usher went on, as K. remained silent. "I know," said K., gazing at the man's civilian clothes, which displayed on the jacket, as the sole emblem of his office, two gilt buttons in addition to the ordinary ones, gilt buttons that looked as if they had been stripped from an old army coat. "I was speaking to your wife a moment ago. She's not here now. The student has carried her up to the Examining Magistrate." "There you are," said the usher, "they're always carrying her away from me. Today is Sunday too, I'm not supposed to do any work, but simply to get me away from the place they sent me out on a useless errand. And they took care not to send me too far away, so that I had some hopes of being able to get back in time if I hurried. And there was I running as fast as I could, shouting the message through the half-open door of the office I was sent to, nearly breathless so that they could hardly make me out, and back again at top speed, and yet the student was here before me, he hadn't so far to come, of course, he had only to cut down that short wooden staircase from the attics. If my job were not at stake, I would have squashed that student flat against the wall here long ago. Just beside this card. It's a daily dream of mine. I see him squashed flat here, just a little above the floor, his arms wide, his fingers spread, his bandy legs writhing in a circle, and splashes of blood all round. But so far it's only been a dream." "Is there no other remedy?" asked K., smiling. "Not that I know of," said the usher. "And now it's getting worse than ever, up till now he has been carrying her off for his own pleasure, but now, as I've been expecting for a long time, I may say, he's carrying her to the Examining Magistrate as well." "But isn't your wife to blame too?" asked K.; he had to keep a grip on himself while asking this, he still felt so jealous. "But of course," said the usher, "she's actually most to blame of all. She simply flung herself at him. As for him, he runs after every woman he sees. In this building alone he's already been thrown out of five flats he managed to insinuate himself into. And my wife is the best-looking woman in the whole tenement, and I'm in a position where I can't defend myself." "If that's how things stand, then there's no help, it seems," said K. "And why not?" asked the usher. "If he only got a good thrashing some time when he was after my wife—he's a coward, anyway—he would never dare to do it again. But I can't thrash him, and nobody else will oblige me by doing it, for they're all afraid of him, he's too influential. Only a man like you could do it." "But why a man like me?" asked K., in astonishment. "You're under arrest, aren't you?" said the usher. "Yes," said K., "and that means I have all the more reason to fear him, for though he may not be able to influence the outcome of the case, he can probably influence the preliminary interrogations." "Yes, that's so," said the usher, as if K.'s view of the matter were as self-evident as his own. "Yet as a rule all our cases are foregone conclusions." "I am not of that opinion," said K., "but that needn't prevent me from taking the student in hand." "I should be very grateful to you," said the usher rather formally; he did not appear really to believe that his heart's desire could be fulfilled. "It may be," K. went on, "that some more of your officials, probably all of them, deserve the same treatment." "Oh, yes," said the usher, as if he were assenting to a commonplace. Then he gave K. a confidential look, such as he had not yet ventured in spite of all his friendliness, and added: "Everyone is always rebellious." But the conversation seemed to have made him uneasy, all the same, for he broke it off by saying: "I must report upstairs now. Would you like to come too?" "I have no business there," said K. "You can have a look at the offices. Nobody will pay any attention to you." "Why, are they worth seeing?" asked K. hesitatingly, but suddenly feeling a great desire to go. "Well," said the usher, "I thought it might interest you." "Good," said K. at last, "I'll come with you." And he ran up the stairs even more quickly than the usher.

On entering he almost stumbled, for behind the door there was an extra step. "They don't show much consideration for the public," he said. "They show no consideration of any kind," replied the usher. "Just look at this waiting-room." It was a long passage, a lobby communicating by ill-fitting doors with the different offices on the floor. Although there was no window to admit light, it was not entirely dark, for some of the offices were not properly boarded off from the passage but had an open frontage of wooden rails, reaching, however, to the roof, through which a little light penetrated and through which one could see a few officials as well, some writing at their desks, and some standing close to the rails peering through the interstices at the people in the lobby. There were only a few people in the lobby, probably because it was Sunday. They made a very modest showing. At almost regular intervals they were sitting singly along a row of wooden benches fixed to either side of the passage. All of them were carelessly dressed, though to judge from the expression on their faces, their bearing, the cut of their beards, and many almost imperceptible little details, they obviously belonged to the upper classes. As there was no hat-rack in the passage, they had placed their hats under the benches, in this probably following each other's example. When those who were sitting nearest the door caught sight of K. and the usher, they rose politely, followed in turn by their neighbors, who also seemed to think it necessary to rise, so that everyone stood as the two men passed. They did not stand quite erect, their backs remained bowed, their knees bent, they stood like the street beggars. K. waited for the usher, who kept slightly behind him, and said: "How humbled they must be!" "Yes," said the usher, "these are the accused men, all of them are defendants." "Indeed!" said K. "Then they're colleagues of mine." And he turned to the nearest, a tall, slender, almost gray-haired man. "What are you waiting here for?" asked K. courteously. But this unexpected question confused the man, which was the more deeply embarrassing as he was obviously a man of the world who would have known how to comport himself anywhere else and would not lightly have renounced his natural superiority. Yet in this place he did not know even how to reply to a simple question and gazed at the others as if it were their duty to help him, as if no one could expect him to answer should help not be forthcoming. Then the usher stepped up and said, to reassure the man and encourage him: "This gentleman merely asked what you are waiting for. Come, give him an answer." The familiar voice of the usher had its effect: "I'm waiting—" the man started to say, but could get out no more. He had obviously begun by intending to make an exact reply to the question, but did not know how to go on. Some of the other clients had drifted up and now clustered round, and the usher said to them: "Off with you, keep the passage clear." They drew back a little, but not to their former places. Meanwhile the man had collected himself and actually replied with a faint smile: "A month ago I handed in several affidavits concerning my case and I am waiting for the result." "You seem to put yourself to a great deal of trouble," said K. "Yes," said the man, "for it is my case." "Everyone doesn't think as you do," said K. "For example, I am under arrest too, but as sure as I stand here I have neither put in any affidavit nor attempted anything whatever of the kind. Do you consider such things necessary, then?" "I can't exactly say," replied the man, once more deprived of all assurance; he evidently thought that K. was making fun of him, and appeared to be on the point of repeating his first answer all over again for fear of making a new mistake, but under K.'s impatient eye he merely said: "Anyhow, I have handed in my affidavits." "Perhaps you don't believe that I am under arrest?" asked K. "Oh, yes, certainly," said the man, stepping somewhat aside, but there was no belief in his answer, merely apprehension. "So you don't really believe me?" asked K. and, provoked without knowing it by the man's humility, he seized him by the arm as if to compel him to believe. He had no wish to hurt him, and besides had grasped him quite loosely, yet the man cried out as if K. had gripped him with glowing pincers instead of with two fingers. That ridiculous outcry was too much for K.; if the man would not believe that he was under arrest, so much the better; perhaps he actually took him for a Judge. As a parting gesture he gripped the man with real force, flung him back on the bench, and went on his way. "Most of these accused men are so sensitive," said the usher. Behind them almost all the clients were now gathered round the man, whose cries had already ceased, and they seemed to be eagerly asking him about the incident. A guard came up to K., he was mainly recognizable by his sword, whose sheath, at least to judge from its color, was of aluminum. K. gaped at it and actually put out his hand to feel it. The guard, who had come to inquire into the commotion, asked what had happened. The usher tried to put him off with a few words, but the guard declared that he must look into this matter himself, saluted, and strutted on with hasty but very short steps, probably resulting from gout.

K. did not trouble his head for long over him and the people in the lobby, particularly as, when he had walked halfway down the lobby, he saw a turning leading to the right through an opening which had no door. He inquired of the usher if this was the right way, the usher nodded, and K. then turned into it. It troubled him that he had always to walk one or two paces ahead of the usher, in a place like this it might look as if he were a prisoner under escort. Accordingly he paused several times to wait for the usher, but the man always dropped behind again. At last K. said, to put an end to his discomfort: "I've seen the

place now, and I think I'll go." "You haven't seen everything yet," said the usher innocently. "I don't want to see
everything," said K., who by now felt really tired. "I want
to get away, how does one reach the outside door?" "You
surely haven't lost your way already?" asked the usher in
surprise. "You just go along here to the corner and then
turn to the right along the lobby straight to the door."
"You come too," said K. "Show me the way, there are so
many lobbies here, I'll never find the way." "There's only
the one way," said the usher reproachfully. "I can't go back
with you, I must deliver my message and I've lost a great
deal of time through you already." "Come with me," said
K. still more sharply, as if he had at last caught the usher
in a falsehood. "Don't shout like that," whispered the usher,
"there are offices everywhere hereabouts. If you don't want
to go back by yourself, then come a little farther with me,
or wait here until I've delivered my message, then I'll be
glad to take you back." "No, no," said K., "I won't wait and
you must come with me now." K. had not yet even glanced
round the place where he was, and only when one of the
many wooden doors opened did he turn his head. A girl
whose attention must have been caught by K.'s raised voice
appeared and asked: "What does the gentleman want?" A
good way behind her he could also see a male figure approaching in the half-light. K. looked at the usher. The man
had said that nobody would pay any attention to him, and
now two people were already after him, it wouldn't take
much to bring all the officials down on him, demanding an
explanation of his presence. The only comprehensible and
acceptable one was that he was an accused man and
wished to know the date of his next interrogation, but that
explanation he did not wish to give, especially as it was
not even in accordance with the truth, for he had come
only out of curiosity or, what was still more impossible as
an explanation of his presence, out of a desire to assure

himself that the inside of this legal system was just as loathsome as its external aspect. And it seemed, indeed, that he had been right in that assumption, he did not want to make any further investigation, he was dejected enough by what he had already seen, he was not at that moment in a fit state to confront any higher official such as might appear from behind one of these doors, he wanted to quit the place with the usher, or, if need be, alone.

But his dumb immobility must make him conspicuous, and the girl and the usher were actually gazing at him as if they expected some great transformation to happen to him the next moment, a transformation which they did not want to miss. And at the end of the passage now stood the man whom K. had noticed before in the distance; he was holding on to the lintel of the low doorway and rocking lightly on his toes, like an eager spectator. But the girl was the first to see that K.'s behavior was really caused by a slight feeling of faintness; she produced a chair and asked: "Won't you sit down?" K. sat down at once and leaned his elbows on the arms of the chair so as to support himself still more securely. "You feel a little dizzy, don't you?" she asked. Her face was close to him now, it had that severe look which the faces of many women have in the first flower of their youth. "Don't worry," she said. "That's nothing out of the common here, almost everybody has an attack of that kind the first time they come here. This is your first visit? Well, then, it's nothing to be surprised at. The sun beats on the roof here and the hot roof-beams make the air stuffy and heavy. That makes this place not particularly suitable for offices, in spite of the other great advantages it has. But the air, well, on days when there's a great number of clients to be attended to, and that's almost every day, it's hardly breathable. When you consider, too, that washing of all sorts is hung up here to dry—you can't wholly prohibit the tenants from washing their dirty linen—you won't find it surprising that you should feel a little faint. But in the end one gets quite used to it. By the time you've come back once or twice you'll hardly notice how oppressive it is here. Do you really feel better now?" K. did not answer, he realized too painfully the shame of being delivered into the hands of these people by his sudden weakness; besides, even now that he knew the cause of the faintness, it did not get any better but grew somewhat worse instead. The girl noticed this at once, and to help K. seized a bar with a hook at the end that leaned against the wall and opened with it a little skylight just above K. to let in the fresh air. Yet so much soot fell in that she had to close the skylight again at once and wipe K.'s hands clean with her handkerchief, since K. was too far gone to attend to himself. He would have preferred to sit quietly there until he recovered enough strength to walk away, yet the less he was bothered by these people the sooner he would recover. But now the girl said: "You can't stay here, we're causing an obstruction here"—K. glanced round inquiringly to see what he could be obstructing—"if you like, I'll take you to the sick-room. Please give me a hand," she said to the man standing in the door, who at once came over. But K. had no wish to go to the sick-room, he particularly wanted to avoid being taken any farther, the farther he went the worse it must be for him. "I'm quite able to go away now," he said and got up from his comfortable seat, which had relaxed him so that he trembled as he stood. But he could not hold himself upright. "I can't manage it after all," he said, shaking his head, and with a sigh sat down again. He thought of the usher, who could easily get him out of the place in spite of his weakness, but he seemed to have vanished long ago. K. peered between the girl and the man standing before him, but could see no sign of the usher.

"I fancy," said the man, who was stylishly dressed and

was wearing a conspicuously smart gray waistcoat ending in two long sharp points, "that the gentleman's faintness is due to the atmosphere here, and the best thing to do—and what he would like best—is not to take him to the sickroom at all, but out of these offices altogether." "That's it!" cried K., so delighted that he almost broke into the man's words, "I should feel better at once, I'm sure of it, I'm not so terribly weak either, I only need a little support under my arms, I won't give you much trouble, it isn't very far after all, just take me to the door, then I'll sit for a little on the stairs and recover in no time, for I don't usually suffer from these attacks, I was surprised myself by this one. I am an official too and accustomed to office air, but this is really more than one can bear, you said so yourselves. Will you have the goodness, then, to let me lean upon you a little, for I feel dizzy and my head goes round when I try to stand up by myself." And he lifted his shoulders to make it easier for the two of them to take him under the arms.

Yet the man did not respond to his request but kept his hands quietly in his pockets and laughed. "You see," he said to the girl. "I hit the nail on the head. It's only here that this gentleman feels upset, not in other places." The girl smiled too, but tapped the man lightly on the arm with her finger tips, as if he had gone too far in jesting like that with K. "But dear me," said the man, still laughing, "I'll show the gentleman to the door, of course I will!" "Then that's all right," said the girl, inclining her elegant head for a moment. "Don't take his laughter too much to heart," she said to K., who had sunk again into vacant melancholy and apparently expected no explanation. "This gentleman— may I introduce you?" (the gentleman waved his hand to indicate permission) "this gentleman, then, represents our Information Bureau. He gives clients all the information they need, and as our procedure is not very well known

among the populace, a great deal of information is asked
for. He has an answer to every question, if you ever feel
like it you can try him out. But that isn't his only claim to
distinction, he has another, the smartness of his clothes. We
—that's to say the staff—made up our minds that the Clerk
of Inquiries, since he's always dealing with clients and is
the first to see them, must be smartly dressed so as to
create a good first impression. The rest of us, as you must
have noticed at once from myself, are very badly and old-
fashionedly dressed, I'm sorry to say; there isn't much sense
anyhow in spending money on clothes, for we're hardly
ever out of these offices, we even sleep here. But, as I say,
we considered that in his case good clothes were needed.
And as the management, which in this respect is somewhat
peculiar, refused to provide these clothes, we opened a
subscription—some of the clients contributed too—and we
bought him this fine suit and some others as well. Nothing
more would be needed now to produce a good impression,
but he spoils it all again by his laughter which puts people
off." "That's how it is," said the gentleman ironically, "yet
I don't understand, Fräulein, why you should tell this gentleman all our intimate secrets, or rather thrust them on
him, for he doesn't want to hear them at all. Just look at
him, he's obviously much too busy with his own thoughts."
K. felt no inclination even to make a retort, the girl's intentions were no doubt good, probably she merely wanted to
distract him or give him a chance to pull himself together,
but she had not gone the right way about it. "Well, I
needed to explain your laughter to him," the girl said. "It
sounded insulting." "I fancy he would overlook much worse
insults if I would only take him out of here." K. said nothing, he did not even look up, he suffered the two of them
to discuss him as if he were an inanimate object, indeed he
actually preferred that. Then suddenly he felt the man's
hand under one arm and the girl's hand under the other.

"Up you get, you feeble fellow," said the man. "Many thanks to both of you," said K., joyfully surprised, and he got up slowly and himself moved these strangers' hands to the places where he felt most in need of support. "It must seem to you," said the girl softly in K.'s ear as they neared the passage, "as if I were greatly concerned to show the Clerk of Inquiries in a good light, but you can believe me, I only wanted to speak the truth about him. He isn't a hardhearted man. He isn't obliged to help sick people out of here, and yet he does so, as you can see. Perhaps none of us is hardhearted, we should be glad to help everybody, yet as Law Court officials we easily take on the appearance of being hardhearted and of not wishing to help. That really worries me." "Wouldn't you like to sit down here for a little?" asked the Clerk of Inquiries; they were out in the main lobby now and just opposite the client to whom K. had first spoken. K. felt almost ashamed before the man, he had stood so erect before him the first time; now it took a couple of people to hold him up, the Clerk of Inquiries was balancing his hat on the tips of his fingers, his hair was in disorder and hung down over his sweat-drenched forehead. But the client seemed to see nothing of all this, he stood up humbly before the Clerk of Inquiries (who stared through him) and merely sought to excuse his presence. "I know," he said, "that the decision on my affidavits cannot be expected today. But I came all the same, I thought that I might as well wait here, it is Sunday, I have lots of time and here I disturb nobody." "You needn't be so apologetic," replied the Clerk of Inquiries. "Your solicitude is entirely to be commended; you're taking up extra room here, I admit, but so long as you don't inconvenience me, I shan't hinder you at all from following the progress of your case as closely as you please. When one sees so many people who scandalously neglect their duty, one learns to have patience with men like you. You may sit down." "How well he knows how to talk to clients!" whispered the girl. K. nodded, but immediately gave a violent start when the Clerk of Inquiries asked again: "Wouldn't you like to sit down here?" "No," said K. "I don't want a rest." He said this with the utmost possible decision, though in reality he would have been very glad to sit down. He felt as if he were seasick. He felt he was on a ship rolling in heavy seas. It was as if the waters were dashing against the wooden walls, as if the roaring of breaking waves came from the end of the passage, as if the passage itself pitched and rolled and the waiting clients on either side rose and fell with it. All the more incomprehensible, therefore, was the composure of the girl and the man who were escorting him. He was delivered into their hands, if they let him go he must fall like a block of wood. They kept glancing around with their sharp little eyes, K. was aware of their regular advance without himself taking part in it, for he was now being almost carried from step to step. At last he noticed that they were talking to him, but he could not make out what they were saying, he heard nothing but the din that filled the whole place, through which a shrill unchanging note like that of a siren seemed to ring. "Louder," he whispered with bowed head, and he was ashamed, for he knew that they were speaking loudly enough, though he could not make out what they said. Then, as if the wall in front of him had been split in two, a current of fresh air was at last wafted toward him, and he heard a voice near him saying: "First he wants to go, then you tell him a hundred times that the door is in front of him and he makes no move to go." K. saw that he was standing before the outside door, which the girl had opened. It was as if all his energies returned at one bound, to get a foretaste of freedom he set his feet at once on a step of the staircase and from there said good-by to his conductors, who bent their heads down to hear him. "Many thanks," he said several times, then shook hands with them again and again and only left off when he thought he saw that they, accustomed as they were to the office air, felt ill in the relatively fresh air that came up the stairway. They could scarcely answer him and the girl might have fallen if K. had not shut the door with the utmost haste. K. stood still for a moment, put his hair to rights with the help of his pocket mirror, lifted up his hat, which lay on the step below him—the Clerk of Inquiries must have thrown it there—and then leapt down the stairs so buoyantly and with such long strides that he became almost afraid of his own reaction. His usually sound constitution had never provided him with such surprises before. Could his body possibly be meditating a revolution and preparing a new trial for him, since he was withstanding the old one with such ease? He did not entirely reject the idea of going to consult a doctor at the first opportunity, in any case he had made up his mind— and there he could advise himself—to spend all his Sunday mornings in future to better purpose.

CHAPTER FOUR

Fräulein Bürstner's Friend

IN THE next few days K. found it impossible to exchange
even a word with Fräulein Bürstner. He tried to get hold
of her by every means he could think of, but she always
managed to elude him. He went straight home from his
office and sat on the sofa in his room, with the light out
and the door open, concentrating his attention on the entrance hall. If the maid on her way past shut the door of
his apparently empty room, he would get up after a while
and open it again. He rose every morning an hour earlier
than usual on the chance of catching Fräulein Bürstner
alone, before she went to her work. But none of these
stratagems succeeded. Then he wrote a letter to her, send-
ing it both to her office and to her house address, in which
he once more tried to justify his behavior, offered to make
any reparation required, promised never to overstep the
bounds that she should prescribe for him, and begged her
to give him an opportunity of merely speaking to her, more
especially as he could arrange nothing with Frau Grubach

until he had first consulted with her, concluding with the
information that next Sunday he would wait in his room
all day for some sign that she was prepared either to grant
his request or at least to explain why, even though he
was pledging his word to defer to her in everything, she
would not grant it. His letters were not returned, but
neither were they answered. On Sunday, however, he was
given a sign whose meaning was sufficiently clear. In the
early morning K. observed through the keyhole of his door
an unusual commotion in the entrance hall, which soon
explained itself. A teacher of French, she was a German
girl called Montag, a sickly, pale girl with a slight limp
who till now had occupied a room of her own, was apparently moving into Fräulein Bürstner's room. For hours
she kept on trailing through the entrance hall. She seemed
to be always forgetting some article of underwear or a
scrap of drapery or a book that necessitated a special
journey to carry it into the new apartment.

When Frau Grubach brought in his breakfast—ever since
she had angered K. she had devoted herself to performing
even the most trifling services for him—K. could not help
breaking the silence between them for the first time. "Why
is there such a row in the entrance hall today?" he asked
as he poured out his coffee. "Couldn't it be put off to some
other time? Must the place be spring-cleaned on a Sunday?" Although K. did not glance up at Frau Grubach, he
could observe that she heaved a sigh of relief. These questions, though stern, she construed as forgiveness or as an
approach toward forgiveness. "The place is not being
spring-cleaned, Herr K.," she said. "Fräulein Montag is
moving in with Fräulein Bürstner and shifting her things
across." She said no more, waiting first to see how K.
would take it and if he would allow her to go on. But K.
kept her on the rack, reflectively stirring his coffee and re-
maining silent. Then he looked up at her and said: "Have

you given up your previous suspicions of Fräulein Bürstner?" "Herr K.," cried Frau Grubach, who had been merely waiting for this question and now stretched out her clasped hands toward him, "you took a casual remark of mine far too seriously. It never entered my head to offend you or anyone else. You have surely known me long enough, Herr K., to be certain of that. You have no idea how I have suffered during these last few days! I to speak ill of my boarders! And you, Herr K., believed it! And said I should give you notice! Give you notice!" The last ejaculation was already stifled in her sobs, she raised her apron to her face and wept aloud.

"Please don't cry, Frau Grubach," said K., looking out through the window, he was really thinking of Fräulein Bürstner and of the fact that she had taken a strange girl into her room. "Please don't cry," he said again as he turned back to the room and found Frau Grubach still weeping. "I didn't mean what I said so terribly seriously either. We misunderstood each other. That can happen occasionally even between old friends." Frau Grubach took her apron from her eyes to see whether K. was really appeased. "Come now, that's all there was to it," said K., and then ventured to add, since to judge from Frau Grubach's expression her nephew the Captain could not have divulged anything: "Do you really believe that I would turn against you because of a strange girl?" "That's just it, Herr K.," said Frau Grubach, it was her misfortune that as soon as she felt relieved in her mind she immediately said something tactless, "I kept asking myself: Why should Herr K. bother himself so much about Fräulein Bürstner? Why should he quarrel with me because of her, though he knows that every cross word from him makes me lose my sleep? And I said nothing about the girl that I hadn't seen with my own eyes." K. made no reply to this, he should have sent her from the room at the very first word, and he did not

want to do that. He contented himself with drinking his
coffee and leaving Frau Grubach to feel that her presence
was burdensome. Outside he could hear again the trailing
step of Fräulein Montag as she limped from end to end of
the entrance hall. "Do you hear that?" asked K., indicating
the door. "Yes," said Frau Grubach, sighing, "I offered to
help her and to order the maid to help too, but she's self-
willed, she insists on moving everything herself. I'm surprised at Fräulein Bürstner. I often regret having Fräulein
Montag as a boarder, but now Fräulein Bürstner is actually
taking her into her own room." "You mustn't worry about
that," said K., crushing with the spoon the sugar left at
the bottom of his cup. "Does it mean any loss to you?"
"No," said Frau Grubach, "in itself it's quite welcome to
me, I am left with an extra room, and I can put my
nephew, the Captain, there. I've been bothered in case he
might have disturbed you these last few days, for I had
to let him occupy the living room next door. He's not very
considerate." "What an idea!" said K., getting up. "There's
no question of that. You really seem to think I'm hyper-
sensitive because I can't stand Fräulein Montag's trailings
to and fro—there she goes again, coming back this time."
Frau Grubach felt quite helpless. "Shall I tell her, Herr
K., to put off moving the rest of her things until later? If
you like I'll do so at once." "But she's got to move into
Fräulein Bürstner's room!" cried K. "Yes," said Frau Grubach, she could not quite make out what K. meant. "Well
then," said K., "she must surely be allowed to shift her
things there." Frau Grubach simply nodded. Her dumb
helplessness, which outwardly had the look of simple ob-
stinacy, exasperated K. still more. He began to walk up
and down from the window to the door and back again,
and by doing that he hindered Frau Grubach from being
able to slip out of the room, which she would probably
have done.

K. had just reached the door again when there was a knock. It was the maid, who announced that Fräulein Montag would like a word or two with Herr K. and that she accordingly begged him to come to the dining room, where she was waiting for him. K. listened pensively to the message, then he turned an almost mocking eye on the startled Frau Grubach. His look seemed to say that he had long foreseen this invitation of Fräulein Montag's, and that it accorded very well with all the persecution he had had to endure that Sunday morning from Frau Grubach's boarders. He sent the maid back with the information that he would come at once, then went to his wardrobe to change his coat, and in answer to Frau Grubach, who was softly lamenting over the behavior of the importunate Fräulein Montag, had nothing to say but to request her to remove his breakfast tray. "Why, you've scarcely touched anything," said Frau Grubach. "Oh, do take it away," cried K., it seemed to him as if Fräulein Montag were somehow mixed up with the food and made it nauseating.

As he crossed the entrance hall he glanced at the closed door of Fräulein Bürstner's room. Still, he had not been invited there, but to the dining room, where he flung open the door without knocking.

It was a very long narrow room with one large window. There was only enough space in it to wedge two cupboards at an angle on either side of the door, the rest of the room was completely taken up by the long dining table, which began near the door and reached to the very window, making it almost inaccessible. The table was already laid, and for many people too, since on Sunday almost all the boarders had their midday dinner in the house.

When K. entered, Fräulein Montag advanced from the window along one side of the table to meet him. They greeted each other in silence. Then Fräulein Montag said, holding her head very erect as usual: "I don't know if you

know who I am." K. stared at her with contracted brows.
"Of course I do," he said, "you've been staying quite a
long time with Frau Grubach, haven't you?" "But you don't
take much interest in the boarders, I fancy," said Fräulein
Montag. "No," said K. "Won't you take a seat?" asked
Fräulein Montag. In silence they pulled out two chairs at
the very end of the table and sat down opposite each
other. But Fräulein Montag immediately stood up again,
for she had left her little handbag lying on the window sill
and now went to fetch it; she trailed for it along the whole
length of the room. As she came back, swinging the bag
lightly in her hand, she said: "I've been asked by my
friend to say something to you, that's all. She wanted to
come herself, but she is feeling a little unwell today. She
asks you to excuse her and listen to me instead. She would
not have said anything more to you, in any case, than I am
going to say. On the contrary, I fancy that I can actually
tell you more, as I am relatively impartial. Don't you think
so too?"

"Well, what is there to say?" replied K., who was weary
of seeing Fräulein Montag staring so fixedly at his lips. Her
stare was already trying to dominate any words he might
utter. "Fräulein Bürstner evidently refuses to grant me the
personal interview I asked for." "That is so," said Fräulein
Montag, "or rather that isn't it at all, you put it much too
harshly. Surely, in general, interviews are neither deliberately accepted nor refused. But it may happen that one
sees no point in an interview, and that is the case here.
After that last remark of yours I can speak frankly, I take
it. You have begged my friend to communicate with you
by letter or by word of mouth. Now, my friend, at least
that is what I must assume, knows what this conversation
would be about, and is therefore convinced, for reasons of
which I am ignorant, that it would be to nobody's benefit
if it actually took place. To tell the truth, she did not men-

tion the matter to me until yesterday and only in passing, she said among other things that you could not attach very much importance to this interview either, for it could only have been by accident that you hit on the idea, and that even without a specific explanation you would soon come to see how silly the whole affair was, if indeed you didn't see that already. I told her that that might be quite true, but that I considered it advisable, if the matter were to be completely cleared up, that you should receive an explicit answer. I offered myself as an intermediary, and after some hesitation my friend yielded to my persuasions. But I hope that I have served your interests, too, for the slightest uncertainty even in the most trifling matter is always a worry, and when, as in this case, it can be easily dispelled, it is better that that should be done at once."

"Thank you," said K. and he slowly rose to his feet, glanced at Fräulein Montag, then at the table, then out through the window—the sun was shining on the house opposite—and walked to the door. Fräulein Montag followed him for a few steps, as if she did not quite trust him. But at the door they had both to draw back, for it opened and Captain Lanz entered. This was the first time that K. had seen him close at hand. He was a tall man in the early forties with a tanned, fleshy face. He made a slight bow which included K. as well as Fräulein Montag, then went up to her and respectfully kissed her hand. His movements were easy. His politeness toward Fräulein Montag was in striking contrast to the treatment which she had received from K. All the same, Fräulein Montag did not seem to be offended with K., for she actually purposed, K. fancied, to introduce him to the Captain. But K. did not wish to be introduced, he was not in the mind to be polite either to the Captain or to Fräulein Montag, the hand-kissing had in his eyes turned the pair of them into accomplices who, under a cloak of the utmost amiability and

altruism, were seeking to bar his way to Fräulein Bürstner.
Yet he fancied that he could see even more than that, he
recognized that Fräulein Montag had chosen a very good
if somewhat two-edged weapon. She had exaggerated the
importance of the connection between Fräulein Bürstner
and K., she had exaggerated above all the importance of
the interview he had asked for, and she had tried at the
same time so to manipulate things as to make it appear that
it was K. who was exaggerating. She would find that she
was deceived, K. wished to exaggerate nothing, he knew
that Fräulein Bürstner was an ordinary little typist who
could not resist him for long. In coming to this conclusion
he deliberately left out of account what Frau Grubach had
told him about Fräulein Bürstner. He was thinking all this
as he quitted the room with a curt word of leave-taking.
He made straight for his own room, but a slight titter from
Fräulein Montag, coming from the dining room behind him,
put it into his head that perhaps he could provide a surprise for the pair of them, the Captain as well as Fräulein
Montag. He glanced round and listened to make sure that
no interruption was likely from any of the adjacent rooms,
all was still, nothing was to be heard but a murmur of
voices in the dining room and the voice of Frau Grubach
coming from the passage leading to the kitchen. The opportunity seemed excellent, and K. went over to Fräulein
Bürstner's door and knocked softly. When nothing happened he knocked again, but again no answer came. Was
she sleeping? Or was she really unwell? Or was she pretending she wasn't there, knowing that it could only be K.
who was knocking so softly? K. assumed that she was pretending and knocked more loudly, and at last, as his knocking had no result, cautiously opened the door, not without
a feeling that he was doing something wrong and even
more useless than wrong. There was nobody in the room.
Moreover it had scarcely any resemblance now to the room

which K. had seen. Against the wall two beds stood next to each other, three chairs near the door were heaped with dresses and underclothes, a wardrobe was standing open. Fräulein Bürstner had apparently gone out while Fräulein Montag was saying her piece in the dining room. K. was not very much taken aback, he had hardly expected at this stage to get hold of Fräulein Bürstner so easily, he had made this attempt, indeed, mainly to annoy Fräulein Montag. Yet the shock was all the greater when, as he was shutting the door again, he saw Fräulein Montag and the Captain standing talking together in the open door of the dining room. They had perhaps been standing there all the time, they scrupulously avoided all appearance of having been observing him, they talked in low voices, following K.'s movements only with the abstracted gaze one has for people passing when one is deep in conversation. All the same, their glances weighed heavily upon K., and he made what haste he could to his room, keeping close against the wall.

CHAPTER FIVE

The Whipper

A FEW evenings later K. was passing along the Bank corridor from his office to the main staircase—he was almost the last to leave, only two clerks in the dispatch department were still at work by the dim light of a glow lamp—when he heard convulsive sighs behind a door, which he had always taken to be the door of a lumber-room, although he had never opened it. He stopped in astonishment and listened to make sure that he had not been mistaken—all was still, yet in a little while the sighing began again. At first he thought of fetching one of the dispatch clerks, he might need a witness, but then he was seized by such uncontrollable curiosity that he literally tore the door open. It was, as he had correctly assumed, a lumber-room. Bundles of useless old papers and empty earthenware ink bottles lay in a tumbled heap behind the threshold. But in the room itself stood three men, stooping because of the low ceiling, by the light of a candle stuck on a shelf. "What are you doing here?" asked K., in great haste and agitation, but not loud. One of the men, who was clearly in authority over the other two and took the eye first, was sheathed in a sort of dark leather garment which left his throat and a good deal of his chest and the whole of his arms bare. He made no answer. But the other two cried: "Sir! We're to be flogged because you complained about us to the Examining Magistrate." And only then did K. realize that it was actually the warders Franz and Willem, and that the third man was holding a rod in his hand with which to beat them. "Why," said K., staring at them in astonishment, "I never complained, I only said what happened in my rooms. And, after all, your behavior there was not exactly blameless." "Sir," said Willem, while Franz openly tried to take cover behind him from the third man, "if you only knew how badly we are paid, you wouldn't be so hard on us. I have a family to feed and Franz here wants to get married, a man tries to make whatever he can, and you don't get rich on hard work, not even if you work day and night. Your fine shirts were a temptation, of course that kind of thing is forbidden to warders, it was wrong, but it's a tradition that body-linen is the warders' perquisite, it has always been the case, believe me; and it's understandable too, for what importance can such things have for a man who is unlucky enough to be arrested? But if he ventilates it openly, punishment is bound to follow." "I had no idea of all this, nor did I ever demand that you should be punished, I was only defending a principle." "Franz," Willem turned to the other warder, "didn't I tell you that the gentleman never asked for us to be punished? Now you see that he didn't even know we should be punished." "Don't be taken in by what they say," remarked the third man to K., "the punishment is as just as it is inevitable." "Don't listen to him," said Willem, interrupting himself to clap his hand, over which he had got a stinging blow with the rod, to his mouth. "We are only being punished because you accused us; if you hadn't, nothing would have happened, not even if they had discovered what we did. Do you call that justice? Both of us, and especially myself, have a long record of trustworthy service as warders—you must yourself admit that, officially speaking, we guarded you quite well—we had every prospect of advancement and would certainly have been promoted to be Whippers pretty soon, like this man here, who simply had the luck never to be complained of, for a complaint of that kind really happens very seldom indeed. And all is lost now, sir, our careers are done for, we'll be set to do much more menial work than a warder's, and, besides that, we're in for a whipping, and that's horribly painful." "Can that birch-rod cause such terrible pain?" asked K., examining the switch, which the man waved to and fro in front of him. "We'll have to take off all our clothes first," said Willem. "Ah, I see," said K., and he looked more attentively at the Whipper, who was tanned like a sailor and had a brutal, healthy face. "Is there no way of getting these two off their whipping?" K. asked him. "No," said the man, smilingly shaking his head. "Strip," he ordered the warders. And he said to K.: "You mustn't believe all they say, they're so terrified of the whipping that they've already lost what wits they had. For instance, all that this one here"—he pointed to Willem— "says about his possible career is simply absurd. See how fat he is—the first cuts of the birch will be quite lost in fat. Do you know what made him so fat? He stuffs himself with the breakfasts of all the people he arrests. Didn't he eat up your breakfast too? There, you see, I told you so. But a man with a belly like that couldn't ever become a Whipper, it's quite out of the question." "There are Whippers just like me," maintained Willem, loosening his trouser belt. "No," said the Whipper, drawing the switch across his neck so that he winced, "you aren't supposed to be listening, you're to take off your clothes." "I'll reward you well if you'll let them go," said K., and without glancing at the Whipper again—such things should be done with averted eyes on both sides—he drew out his wallet. "So you want to lay a complaint against me too," said the Whipper, "and get me a whipping as well? No, no!" "Do be reasonable," said K. "If I had wanted these two men to be punished, I shouldn't be trying to buy them off now. I could simply leave, shut this door after me, close my eyes and ears, and go home; but I don't want to do that, I really want to see them set free; if I had known that they would be punished or even that they could be punished, I should never have mentioned their names. For in my view they are not guilty. The guilt lies with the organization. It is the high officials who are guilty." "That's so," cried the warders and at once got a cut of the switch over their backs, which were bare now. "If it was one of the high Judges you were flogging," said K., and as he spoke he thrust down the rod which the Whipper was raising again, "I certainly wouldn't try to keep you from laying on with a will, on the contrary I would pay you extra to encourage you in the good work." "What you say sounds reasonable enough," said the man, "but I refuse to be bribed. I am here to whip people, and whip them I shall." The warder Franz, who, perhaps hoping that K.'s intervention might succeed, had thus far kept as much as possible in the background, now came forward to the door clad only in his trousers, fell on his knees, and clinging to K.'s arm whispered: "If you can't get him to spare both of us, try to get me off at least. Willem is older than I am, and far less sensitive too, besides he's had a small whipping already, some years ago, but I've never been in disgrace yet, and I was only following Willem's lead in what I did, he's my teacher, for better or worse. My poor sweetheart is awaiting the outcome at the door of the Bank. I'm so

ashamed and miserable." He dried his tear-wet face on K.'s
jacket. "I can't wait any longer," said the Whipper, grasping the rod with both hands and making a cut at Franz,
while Willem cowered in a corner and secretly watched
without daring to turn his head. Then the shriek rose from
Franz's throat, single and irrevocable, it did not seem to
come from a human being but from some martyred instrument, the whole corridor rang with it, the whole building
must hear it. "Don't," cried K.; he was beside himself, he
stood staring in the direction from which the clerks must
presently come running, but he gave Franz a push, not a
violent one but violent enough nevertheless to make the
half-senseless man fall and convulsively claw at the floor
with his hands; but even then Franz did not escape his
punishment, the birch-rod found him where he was lying,
its point swished up and down regularly as he writhed on
the floor. And now a clerk was already visible in the distance and a few paces behind him another. K. quickly
slammed the door, stepped over to a window close by,
which looked out on the courtyard, and opened it. The
shrieks had completely stopped. To keep the clerks from
approaching any nearer, K. cried: "It's me." "Good evening,
Sir," they called back. "Has anything happened?" "No, no,"
replied K. "It was only a dog howling in the courtyard."
As the clerks still did not budge, he added: "You can go
back to your work." And to keep himself from being involved in any conversation he leaned out of the window.
When after a while he glanced into the corridor again, they
were gone. But he stayed beside the window, he did not
dare to go back into the lumber-room, and he had no wish
to go home either. It was a little square courtyard into
which he was looking down, surrounded by offices, all the
windows were dark now, but the topmost panes cast back
a faint reflection of the moon. K. intently strove to pierce
the darkness of one corner of the courtyard, where several

hand-barrows were jumbled close together. He was deeply disappointed that he had not been able to prevent the whipping, but it was not his fault that he had not succeeded; if Franz had not shrieked—it must have been very painful certainly, but in a crisis one must control oneself —if he had not shrieked, then K., in all probability at least, would have found some other means of persuading the Whipper. If the whole lower grade of this organization were scoundrels, why should the Whipper, who had the most inhuman office of all, turn out to be an exception? Besides, K. had clearly seen his eyes glittering at the sight of the banknote, obviously he had set about his job in earnest simply to raise his price a little higher. And K. would not have been stingy, he was really very anxious to get the warders off; since he had set himself to fight the whole corrupt administration of this Court, it was obviously his duty to intervene on this occasion. But at the moment when Franz began to shriek, any intervention became impossible. K. could not afford to let the dispatch clerks and possibly all sorts of other people arrive and surprise him in a scene with these creatures in the lumber-room. No one could really demand such a sacrifice from him. If a sacrifice had been needed, it would almost have been simpler to take off his own clothes and offer himself to the Whipper as a substitute for the warders.* In any case the Whipper certainly would not have accepted such a substitution, since without gaining any advantage he would have been involved in a grave dereliction of duty, for as long as this trial continued, K. must surely be immune from molestation by the servants of the Court. Though of course ordinary standards might not apply here either. At all events, he could have done nothing but slam the door, though even that action had not shut out all danger. It was a pity that he had given Franz a push at the last moment, the state of agitation he was in was his only excuse.

He heard the steps of the clerks in the distance; so as not to attract their attention he shut the window and began to walk away in the direction of the main staircase. At the door of the lumber-room he stopped for a little and listened. All was silent as the grave. The man might have beaten the warders till they had given up the ghost, they were entirely delivered into his power. K.'s hand was already stretched out to grasp the door-handle when he withdrew it again. They were past help by this time, and the clerks might appear at any moment; but he made a vow not to hush up the incident and to deal trenchantly, so far as lay in his power, with the real culprits, the high officials, none of whom had yet dared show his face. As he descended the outside steps of the Bank he carefully observed all the passers-by, but even in the surrounding streets he could perceive no sign of a girl waiting for anybody. So Franz's tale of a sweetheart waiting for him was simply a lie, venial enough, designed merely to procure more sympathy for him.

All the next day K. could not get the warders out of his head; he was absent-minded and to catch up on his work had to stay in his office even later than the day before. As he passed the lumber-room again on his way out he could not resist opening the door. And what confronted him, instead of the darkness he had expected, bewildered him completely. Everything was still the same, exactly as he had found it on opening the door the previous evening. The files of old papers and the ink bottles were still tumbled behind the threshold, the Whipper with his rod and the warders with all their clothes on were still standing there, the candle was burning on the shelf, and the warders immediately began to wail and cry out: "Sir!" At once K. slammed the door shut and then beat on it with his fists, as if that would shut it more securely. He ran almost weeping to the clerks, who were quietly working at the copying-presses and looked up at him in surprise. "Clear that lumber-room out, can't you?" he shouted. "We're being smothered in dirt!" The clerks promised to do so next day. K. nodded, he could hardly insist on their doing it now, so late in the evening, as he had originally intended. He sat down for a few moments, for the sake of their company, shuffled through some duplicates, hoping to give the impression that he was inspecting them, and then, seeing that the men would scarcely venture to leave the building along with him, went home, tired, his mind quite blank.

CHAPTER SIX

K.'s Uncle · Leni

ONE afternoon—it was just before the day's letters went out and K. was very busy—two clerks bringing him some papers to sign were thrust aside and his Uncle Karl, a small landowner from the country, came striding into the room. K. was the less alarmed by the arrival of his uncle since for a long time he had been shrinking from it in anticipation. His uncle was bound to turn up, he had been convinced of that for about a month past. He had often pictured him just as he appeared now, his back slightly bent, his panama hat crushed in his left hand, stretching out his right hand from the very doorway, and then thrusting it recklessly across the desk, knocking over everything that came in its way. His uncle was always in a hurry, for he was harassed by the disastrous idea that whenever he came to town for the day he must get through all the program he had drawn up for himself, and must not miss either a single chance of a conversation or a piece of business or an entertainment. In all this K., who as his former ward was peculiarly

obliged to him, had to help him as best he could and also
sometimes put him up for the night. "A ghost from the
past," he was in the habit of calling him.

Immediately after his first greetings—he had no time to
sit down in the chair which K. offered him—he begged K.
to have a short talk with him in strict privacy. "It is necessary," he said, painfully gulping, "it is necessary for my
peace of mind." K. at once sent his clerks out of the room
with instructions to admit no one. "What is this I hear,
Joseph?" cried his uncle when they were alone, sitting down
on the desk and making himself comfortable by stuffing several papers under him without looking at them. K. said
nothing, he knew what was coming, but being suddenly
released from the strain of exacting work, he resigned himself for the moment to a pleasant sense of indolence and
gazed out through the window at the opposite side of the
street, of which only a small triangular section could be
seen from where he was sitting, a slice of empty house-
wall between two shopwindows. "You sit there staring out
of the window!" cried his uncle, flinging up his arms. "For
God's sake, Joseph, answer me. Is it true? Can it be true?"
"Dear Uncle," said K., tearing himself out of his reverie.
"I don't know in the least what you mean." "Joseph," said
his uncle warningly, "you've always told the truth, as far
as I know. Am I to take these words of yours as a bad
sign?" "I can guess, certainly, what you're after," said K.
accommodatingly. "You've probably heard something about
my trial." "That is so," replied his uncle, nodding gravely.
"I have heard about your trial." "But from whom?" asked
K. "Erna wrote to me about it," said his uncle. "She doesn't
see much of you, I know, you don't pay much attention to
her, I regret to say, and yet she heard about it. I got the
letter this morning and of course took the first train here. I
had no other reason for coming, but it seems to be a sufficient one. I can read you the bit from her letter that men-

tions you." He took the letter from his wallet. "Here
it is. She writes: 'I haven't seen Joseph for a long time, last
week I called at the Bank, but Joseph was so busy that I
couldn't see him; I waited for almost an hour, but I had to
leave then, for I had a piano lesson. I should have liked
very much to speak to him, perhaps I shall soon have the
chance. He sent me a great big box of chocolates for my
birthday, it was very sweet and thoughtful of him. I forgot
to write and mention it at the time, and it was only your
asking that reminded me. For I may tell you that choco-
late vanishes on the spot in this boarding school, hardly do
you realize that you've been presented with a box when it's
gone. But about Joseph, there is something else that I feel
I should tell you. As I said, I was not able to see him at
the Bank because he was engaged with a gentleman. After
I had waited meekly for a while I asked an attendant if
the interview was likely to last much longer. He said that
that might very well be, for it had probably something to
do with the case which was being brought against the
Chief Clerk. I asked what case, and was he not mistaken,
but he said he was not mistaken, there was a case and a
very serious one too, but more than that he did not know.
He himself would like to help Herr K., for he was a good
and just man, but he did not know how he was to do it,
and he only wished that some influential gentleman would
take the Chief Clerk's part. To be sure, that was certain to
happen and everything would be all right in the end, but
for the time being, as he could see from Herr K.'s state of
mind, things looked far from well. Naturally I did not take
all this too seriously, I tried to reassure the simple fellow
and forbade him to talk about it to anyone else, and I'm
sure it's just idle gossip. All the same, it might be as well
if you, dearest Father, were to inquire into it on your next
visit to town, it will be easy for you to find out the real
state of things, and if necessary to get some of your influ-

ential friends to intervene. Even if it shouldn't be necessary, and that is most likely, at least it will give your daughter an early chance of welcoming you with a kiss, which would please her.' A good child," said K.'s uncle when he had finished reading, wiping a tear from his eye. K. nodded, he had completely forgotten Erna among the various troubles he had had lately, and the story about the chocolates she had obviously invented simply to save his face before his uncle and aunt. It was really touching, and the theater tickets which he now resolved to send her regularly would be a very inadequate return, but he did not feel equal at present to calling at her boarding school and chattering to an eighteen-year-old flapper. "And what have you got to say now?" asked his uncle, who had temporarily forgotten all his haste and agitation over the letter, which he seemed to be rereading. "Yes, Uncle," said K., "it's quite true." "True?" cried his uncle. "What is true? How on earth can it be true? What case is this? Not a criminal case, surely?" "A criminal case," answered K. "And you sit there coolly with a criminal case hanging round your neck?" cried his uncle, his voice growing louder and louder. "The cooler I am, the better in the end," said K. wearily. "Don't worry." "That's a fine thing to ask of me," cried his uncle. "Joseph, my dear Joseph, think of yourself, think of your relatives, think of our good name. You have been a credit to us until now, you can't become a family disgrace. Your attitude," he looked at K. with his head slightly cocked, "doesn't please me at all, that isn't how an innocent man behaves if he's still in his senses. Just tell me quickly what it is all about, so that I can help you. It's something to do with the Bank, of course?" "No," said K., getting up. "But you're talking too loudly, Uncle, I feel pretty certain the attendant is listening at the door, and I dislike the idea. We had better go out somewhere. I'll answer all your questions then as far as I can. I know quite well that I owe the family an explanation." "Right," cried his uncle, "quite right, but hurry, Joseph, hurry!" "I have only to leave some instructions," said K., and he summoned his chief assistant by telephone, who appeared in a few minutes. In his agitation K.'s uncle indicated to the clerk by a sweep of the hand that K. had sent for him, which, of course, was obvious enough. K., standing beside his desk, took up various papers and in a low voice explained to the young man, who listened coolly but attentively, what must be done in his absence. His uncle disturbed him by standing beside him round-eyed and biting his lips nervously; he was not actually listening, but the appearance of listening was disturbing enough in itself. He next began to pace up and down the room, pausing every now and then by the window or before a picture, with sudden ejaculations, such as: "It's completely incomprehensible to me" or "Goodness knows what's to come of this." The young man behaved as if he noticed nothing, quietly heard K.'s instructions to the end, took a few notes, and went, after having bowed both to K. and to his uncle, who, however, had his back to him just then and was gazing out of the window, flinging out his arms, and clutching at curtains. The door had scarcely closed when K.'s uncle cried: "At last that jackass has gone; now we can go too. At last!" Unluckily K. could find no means to make his uncle stop inquiring about the case in the main vestibule, where several clerks and attendants were standing about, while the Assistant Manager himself was crossing the floor. "Come now, Joseph," began his uncle, returning a brief nod to the bows of the waiting clerks, "tell me frankly now what kind of a case this is." K. made a few noncommittal remarks, laughing a little, and only on the staircase explained to his uncle that he had not wanted to speak openly before the clerks. "Right," said his uncle, "but get it off your chest now." He listened with bent head, puffing hastily at a cigar. "The first thing to grasp, Uncle," said K., "is that this is not a case before an ordinary court." "That's bad," said his uncle. "What do you mean?" asked K., looking at his uncle. "I mean that it's bad," repeated his uncle. They were standing on the outside steps of the Bank; as the doorkeeper seemed to be listening, K. dragged his uncle away; they were swallowed up in the street traffic. The uncle, who had taken K.'s arm, now no longer inquired so urgently about the case, and for a while they actually walked on in silence. "But how did this happen?" his uncle asked at last, stopping so suddenly that the people walking behind him shied off in alarm. "Things like this don't occur suddenly, they pile up gradually, there must have been indications. Why did you never write to me? You know I would do anything for you, I'm still your guardian in a sense and till now I have been proud of it. Of course I'll do what I can to help you, only it's very difficult when the case is already under way. The best thing, at any rate, would be for you to take a short holiday and come to stay with us in the country. You've got a bit thinner, I notice that now. You'd get back your strength in the country, that would be all to the good, for this trial will certainly be a severe strain on you. But besides that, in a sense you'd be getting away from the clutches of the Court. Here they have all sorts of machinery which they will automatically set in motion against you, depend on that; but if you were in the country they would have to appoint agents or get at you by letter or telegram or telephone. That would naturally weaken the effect, not that you would escape them altogether, but you'd have a breathing space." "Still, they might forbid me to go away," said K., who was beginning to follow his uncle's line of thought. "I don't think they would do that," said his uncle reflectively, "after all, they wouldn't lose so much by your going away." "I thought," said K., taking his uncle's arm to keep him from standing still, "that you would attach even less importance to this business than I do, and now you are taking it so seriously." "Joseph!" cried his uncle, trying to get his arm free so as to be able to stand still, only K. would not let him, "you're quite changed, you always used to have such a clear brain, and is it going to fail you now? Do you want to lose this case? And do you know what that would mean? It would mean that you would be absolutely ruined. And that all your relatives would be ruined too or at least dragged in the dust. Joseph, pull yourself together. Your indifference drives me mad. Looking at you, one would almost believed the old saying: 'Cases of that kind are always lost.'" "Dear Uncle," said K., "it's no use getting excited, it's as useless on your part as it would be on mine. No case is won by getting excited, you might let my practical experience count for something, look how I respect yours, as I have always done, even when you astonish me. Since you tell me that the family would be involved in any scandal arising from the case—I don't see myself how that could be so, but that's beside the point—I'll submit willingly to your judgment. Only I think going to the country would be inadvisable even from your point of view, for it would look like flight and therefore guilt. Besides, though I'm more hard-pressed here, I can push the case on my own more energetically." "Quite right," said his uncle in a tone of relief, as if he saw their minds converging at last, "I only made the suggestion because I thought your indifference would endanger the case while you stayed here, and that it might be better if I took it up for you instead. But if you intend to push it energetically yourself, that of course would be far better." "We're agreed on that, then," said K. "And now can you suggest what my first step should be?" "I'll have to do a bit of thinking about it, naturally," said his uncle, "you must consider that I have lived in the country for twenty years almost without a break, and my flair for such matters can't be so good as it was. Various connections of mine with influential persons who would probably know better than I how to tackle this affair have slackened in the course of time. I'm a bit isolated in the country, as you know yourself. Actually it's only in emergencies like this that one becomes aware of it. Besides, this affair of yours has come on me more or less unexpectedly, though strangely enough, after Erna's letter, I guessed at something of the kind, and as soon as I saw you today I was almost sure of it. Still that doesn't matter, the important thing now is to lose no time." Before he had finished speaking he was already on tiptoe waiting for a taxi, and now, shouting an address to the driver, he dragged K. into the car after him. "We'll drive straight to Huld, the lawyer," he said. "He was at school with me. You know his name, of course? You don't? That is really extraordinary. He has quite a considerable reputation as a defending counsel and a poor man's lawyer. But it's as a human being that I'm prepared to pin my faith to him." "I'm willing to try anything you suggest," said K., though the hasty headlong way in which his uncle was dealing with the matter caused him some perturbation. It was not very flattering to be driven to a poor man's lawyer as a petitioner. "I did not know," he said, "that in a case like this one could employ a lawyer." "But of course," said his uncle. "That's obvious. Why not? And now tell me everything that has happened up to now, so that I have some idea where we stand." K. at once began his story and left out no single detail, for absolute frankness was the only protest he could make against his uncle's assumption that the case was a terrible disgrace. Fräulein Bürstner's name he mentioned only once and in passing, but that did not detract from his frankness, since Fräulein Bürstner had no connection with the case. As he told his story he gazed out through the window and noted that they were approaching the very suburb where the Law Court had its attic offices; he drew his uncle's attention to this fact, but his uncle did not seem to be particularly struck by the coincidence. The taxi stopped before a dark house. His uncle rang the bell of the first door on the ground floor; while they were waiting he bared his great teeth in a smile and whispered: "Eight o'clock, an unusual time for clients to call. But Huld won't take it amiss from me." Behind a grille in the door two great dark eyes appeared, gazed at the two visitors for a moment, and then vanished again; yet the door did not open. K. and his uncle assured each other that they had really seen a pair of eyes. "A new maid, probably afraid of strangers," said K.'s uncle and knocked again. Once more the eyes appeared and now they seemed almost sad, yet that might have been an illusion created by the naked gas jet which burned just over their heads and kept hissing shrilly but gave little light. "Open the door!" shouted K.'s uncle, banging upon it with his fists, "we're friends of Herr Huld." "Herr Huld is ill," came a whisper from behind them. A door had opened at the other end of the little passage and a man in a dressing gown was standing there imparting this information in a hushed voice. K.'s uncle, already furious at having had to wait so long, whirled round shouting: "Ill? You say he's ill?" and bore down almost threateningly on the man as if he were the alleged illness in person. "The door has been opened," said the man, indicated the lawyer's door, caught his dressing gown about him, and disappeared. The door really was open, a young girl—K. recognized the dark, somewhat protuberant eyes—was standing in the entrance hall in a long white apron, holding a candle in her hand. "Next time be a little smarter in opening the door," K.'s uncle threw at her instead of a greeting, while she sketched a curtsy. "Come on, Joseph," he cried to K., who was slowly insinuating himself past the girl. "Herr Huld is ill," said the girl, as K.'s uncle, without any hesitation, made toward an inner door. K. was still glaring at the girl,

who turned her back on him to bolt the house door; she
had a doll-like rounded face; not only were her pale cheeks
and her chin quite round in their modeling, but her temples
and the line of her forehead as well. "Joseph!" K.'s uncle
shouted again, and he asked the girl: "Is it his heart?" "I
think so," said the girl, she had now found time to precede
him with the candle and open the door of a room. In one
corner, which the candlelight had not yet reached, a face
with a long beard was raised from a pillow. "Leni, who is
it?" asked the lawyer, who, blinded by the candlelight,
could not recognize his visitors. "It's your old friend Albert,"
said K.'s uncle. "Oh, Albert," said the lawyer, sinking back
on his pillow again, as if there were no need to keep up
appearances before this visitor. "Are you really in a bad
way?" asked K.'s uncle, sitting down on the edge of the
bed. "I can't believe it. It's one of your heart attacks and
it'll pass over like all the others." "Maybe," said the lawyer
in a faint voice, "but it's worse than it's ever been before.
I find it difficult to breathe, can't sleep at all, and am losing
strength daily." "I see," said K.'s uncle, pressing his panama
hat firmly against his knee with his huge hand. "That's bad
news. But are you being properly looked after? And it's so
gloomy in here, so dark. It's a long time since I was here
last, but it looked more cheerful then. And this little maid
of yours doesn't seem to be very bright, or else she's concealing the fact." The girl was still standing near the door
with her candle; as far as one could make out from the
vague flicker of her eyes, she seemed to be looking at K.
rather than at his uncle, even while the latter was speaking
about her. K. was leaning against a chair which he had
pushed near her. "When a man is as ill as I am," said the
lawyer, "he must have quiet. I don't find it gloomy." After
a slight pause he added: "And Leni looks after me well,
she's a good girl." * But this could not convince K.'s uncle,
who was visibly prejudiced against the nurse, and though

he made no reply to the sick man he followed her with a
stern eye as she went over to the bed, set down the candle
on the bedside table, bent over her patient, and whispered
to him while she rearranged the pillows. K.'s uncle, almost
forgetting that he was in a sick-room, jumped to his feet
and prowled up and down behind the girl; K. would not
have been surprised if he had seized her by the skirts and
dragged her away from the bed. K. himself looked on with
detachment, the illness of the lawyer was not entirely unwelcome to him, he had not been able to oppose his uncle's
growing ardor for his cause, and he thankfully accepted
the situation, which had deflected that ardor without any
connivance from him. Then his uncle, perhaps only with
the intention of offending the nurse, cried out: "Fräulein,
please be so good as to leave us alone for a while; I want
to consult my friend on some personal business." The girl,
who was still bending down over the sick man smoothing
the sheet beside the wall, merely turned her head and said
quite calmly, in striking contrast to the furious stuttering
and frothing of K.'s uncle: "You see that my master is ill;
he cannot be consulted about business." She had probably
reiterated the phrase from sheer indolence; all the same it
could have been construed as mockery even by an un-
prejudiced observer, and K.'s uncle naturally flared up as if
he had been stung. "You damned—" he spluttered, but he
was so furious as to be hardly intelligible. K. started up in
alarm, though he had expected some such outburst, and
rushed over to his uncle with the firm intention of clapping
both hands over his mouth and so silencing him. Fortunately the patient raised himself up in bed behind the girl.
K.'s uncle made a wry grimace as if he were swallowing
some nauseous draught and he said in a smoother voice:
"I assure you we aren't altogether out of our senses; if what
I ask were impossible I should not ask it. Please go away
now." The girl straightened herself beside the bed, turning

full toward K.'s uncle, but with one hand, at least so K. surmised, she was patting the lawyer's hand. "You can discuss anything before Leni," said the lawyer in a voice of sheer entreaty. "This does not concern myself," said K.'s uncle, "it is not my secret." And he turned away as if washing his hands of the matter, although willing to give the lawyer a moment for reconsideration. "Then whom does it concern?" asked the lawyer in an exhausted voice, lying down again. "My nephew," said K.'s uncle, "I have brought him here with me." And he presented his nephew: Joseph K., Chief Clerk. "Oh," said the sick man with much more animation, stretching out his hand to K., "forgive me, I didn't notice you. Go now, Leni," he said to the nurse, clasping her by the hand as if saying good-by to her for a long time, and she went submissively enough. "So you haven't come," he said at last to K.'s uncle, who was now appeased and had gone up to the bed again, "to pay me a sick visit; you've come on business." It was as if the thought of a sick visit had paralyzed him until now, so rejuvenated did he look as he supported himself on his elbow, which must itself have been something of a strain; and he kept combing with his fingers a strand of hair in the middle of his beard. "You look much better already," said K.'s uncle, "since that witch went away." He broke off, whispered: "I bet she's listening," and sprang to the door. But there was no one behind the door and he returned again, not so much disappointed, since her failure to listen seemed to him an act of sheer malice, as embittered. "You are unjust to her," said the lawyer, without adding anything more in defense of his nurse; perhaps by this reticence he meant to convey that she stood in no need of defense. Then in a much more friendly tone he went on: "As for this case of your nephew's I should certainly consider myself very fortunate if my strength proved equal to such an excessively arduous task; I'm very much afraid that it will not do so, but at any

rate I shall make every effort; if I fail, you can always call
in someone else to help me. To be quite honest, the case
interests me too deeply for me to resist the opportunity of
taking some part in it. If my heart does not hold out, here
at least it will find a worthy obstacle to fail against." K.
could not fathom a single word of all this, he glanced at
his uncle, hoping for some explanation, but with the candle
in his hand his uncle was sitting on the bedside table, from
which a medicine-bottle had already rolled on to the carpet,
nodding assent to everything and now and then casting a
glance at K. which demanded from him a like agreement.
Could his uncle have told the lawyer all about the case
already? But that was impossible, the course of events ruled
it out. "I don't understand—" he therefore began. "Oh, perhaps I have misunderstood you?" asked the lawyer, just as
surprised and embarrassed as K. "Perhaps I have been too
hasty. Then what do you want to consult me about? I
thought it concerned your case?" "Of course it does," said
K.'s uncle, turning to K. with the question: "What's bothering you?" "Well, but how do you come to know about me
and my case?" asked K. "Oh, that's it," said the lawyer,
smiling. "I'm a lawyer, you see, I move in legal circles
where all the various cases are discussed, and the more
striking ones are bound to stick in my mind, especially one
that concerns the nephew of an old friend of mine. Surely
that's not so extraordinary." "What's bothering you?" K.'s
uncle repeated. "You're all nerves." "So you move in those
legal circles?" asked K. "Yes," replied the lawyer. "You ask
questions like a child," said K.'s uncle. "Whom should I
associate with if not with men of my own profession?"
added the lawyer. It sounded incontrovertible and K. made
no answer. But you're attached to the Court in the Palace
of Justice, not to the one in the attics, he wanted to say,
yet could not bring himself actually to say it. "You must
consider," the lawyer continued in the tone of one per-

functorily explaining something that should be self-evident, "you must consider that this intercourse enables me to benefit my clients in all sorts of ways, some of which cannot even be divulged. Of course I'm somewhat handicapped now because of my illness, but in spite of that, good friends of mine from the Law Courts visit me now and then and I learn lots of things from them. Perhaps more than many a man in the best of health who spends all his days in the Courts. For example, there's a dear friend of mine visiting me at this very moment," and he waved a hand toward a dark corner of the room. "Where?" asked K., almost rudely, in his first shock of astonishment. He looked round uncertainly; the light of the small candle did not nearly reach the opposite wall. And then some form or other in the dark corner actually began to stir. By the light of the candle, which his uncle now held high above his head, K. could see an elderly gentleman sitting there at a little table. He must have been sitting without even drawing breath, to have remained for so long unnoticed. Now he got up fussily, obviously displeased to have his presence made known. With his hands, which he flapped like short wings, he seemed to be deprecating all introductions or greetings, trying to show that the last thing he desired was to disturb the other gentlemen, and that he only wanted to be transported again to the darkness where his presence might be forgotten. But that privilege could no longer be his. "I may say you took us by surprise," said the lawyer in explanation, and he waved his hand to encourage the gentleman to approach, which he did very slowly and glancing around him hesitantly, but with a certain dignity. "The Chief Clerk of the Court—oh, I beg your pardon, I have not introduced you—this is my friend Albert K., this is his nephew Joseph K., and this is the Chief Clerk of the Court—who, to return to what I was saying, has been so good as to pay me a visit. The value of such a visit can really be appreciated

only by the initiated who know how dreadfully the Clerk
of the Court is overwhelmed with work. Yet he came to see
me all the same, we were talking here peacefully, as far
as my ill health permitted, we didn't actually forbid Leni to
admit visitors, it was true, for we expected none, but we
naturally thought that we should be left in peace, and then
came your furious tattoo, Albert, and the Clerk of the Court
withdrew into the corner with his chair and his table, but
now it seems we have the chance, that is, if you care to
take it, of making the discussion general, since this case
concerns us all, and so we can get together.—Please, my
dear Sir," he said with a bow and an obsequious smile,
indicating an armchair near the bed. "Unfortunately I can
only stay for a few minutes longer," said the Chief Clerk
of the Court affably, seating himself in the chair and looking at his watch, "my duties call me. But I don't want to
miss this opportunity of becoming acquainted with a friend
of my friend here." He bowed slightly to K.'s uncle, who
appeared very flattered to make this new acquaintance, yet,
being by nature incapable of expressing reverent feelings,
requited the Clerk of the Court's words with a burst of
embarrassed but raucous laughter. An ugly sight! K. could
observe everything clamly, for nobody paid any attention
to him. The Chief Clerk of the Court, now that he had
been brought into prominence, seized the lead, as seemed
to be his usual habit. The lawyer, whose first pretense of
weakness had probably been intended simply to drive away
his visitors, listened attentively, cupping his hand to his ear.
K.'s uncle as candlebearer—he was balancing the candle on
his thigh, the lawyer often glanced at it in apprehension—
had soon rid himself of his embarrassment and was now de-
lightedly absorbed in the Clerk of the Court's eloquence
and the delicate wavelike gestures of the hand with which
he accompanied it. K., leaning against the bedpost, was
completely ignored by the Clerk of the Court, perhaps by

deliberate intention, and served merely as an audience to the old gentleman. Besides, he could hardly follow the conversation and was thinking first of the nurse and the rude treatment she had received from his uncle, and then wondering if he had not seen the Clerk of the Court before, perhaps actually among the audience during his first interrogation. He might be mistaken, yet the Clerk of the Court would have fitted excellently into the first row of the audience, the elderly gentlemen with the brittle beards.

Then a sound from the entrance hall as of breaking crockery made them all prick up their ears. "I'll go and see what has happened," said K., and he went out, rather slowly, to give the others a chance to call him back. Hardly had he reached the entrance hall and was beginning to grope his way in the darkness, when a hand much smaller than his own covered the hand with which he was still holding the door and gently drew the door shut. It was the nurse, who had been waiting there. "Nothing has happened," she whispered. "I simply flung a plate against the wall to bring you out." K. said in his embarrassment: "I was thinking of you too." "That's all the better," said the nurse. "Come this way." A step or two brought them to a door paneled with thick glass, which she opened. "In here," she said. It was evidently the lawyer's office; as far as one could see in the moonlight, which brilliantly lit up a small square section of the floor in front of each of the two large windows, it was fitted out with solid antique furniture. "Here," said the nurse, pointing to a dark chest with a carved wooden back. After he had sat down K. still kept looking round the room, it was a lofty, spacious room, the clients of this "poor man's lawyer" must feel lost in it.* K. pictured to himself the timid, short steps with which they would advance to the huge table. But then he forgot all this and had eyes only for the nurse, who was sitting very close to him, almost squeezing him against the arm of the bench. "I thought," she said, "you would come out of your own accord, without waiting till I had to call you out. A queer way to behave. You couldn't keep your eyes off me from the very moment you came in, and yet you leave me to wait. And you'd better just call me Leni," she added quickly and abruptly, as if there were not a moment to waste. "I'll be glad to," said K. "But as for my queer behavior, Leni, that's easy to explain. In the first place I had to listen to these old men jabbering. I couldn't simply walk out and leave them without any excuse, and in the second place I'm not in the least a bold young man, but rather shy, to tell the truth, and you too, Leni, really didn't look as if you were to be had for the asking." "It isn't that," said Leni, laying her arm along the back of the seat and looking at K. "But you didn't like me at first and you probably don't like me even now." Liking is a feeble word," said K. evasively. "Oh!" she said, with a smile, and K.'s remark and that little exclamation gave her a certain advantage over him. So K. said nothing more for a while. As he had grown used to the darkness in the room, he could now distinguish certain details of the furnishings. He was particularly struck by a large picture which hung to the right of the door, and bent forward to see it more clearly. It represented a man in a Judge's robe; he was sitting on a high thronelike seat, and the gilding of the seat stood out strongly in the picture. The strange thing was that the Judge did not seem to be sitting in dignified composure, for his left arm was braced along the back and the side-arm of his throne, while his right arm rested on nothing, except for the hand, which clutched the other arm of the chair; it was as if in a moment he must spring up with a violent and probably wrathful gesture to make some decisive observation or even to pronounce sentence. The accused might be imagined as standing on the lowest step leading up to the chair of justice; the top steps, which were covered with a yellowish carpet,

were shown in the picture. "Perhaps that is my Judge," said
K., pointing with his finger at the picture. "I know him,"
said Leni, and she looked at the picture too. "He often
comes here. That picture was painted when he was young,
but it could never have been in the least like him, for he's
a small man, almost a dwarf. Yet in spite of that he had
himself drawn out to that length in the portrait, for he's
madly vain like everybody else here. But I'm a vain person,
too, and very much upset that you don't like me in the
least." To this last statement K. replied merely by putting
his arm around her and drawing her to him; she leaned
her head against his shoulder in silence. But to the rest of
her remarks he answered: "What's the man's rank?" "He is
an Examining Magistrate," she said, seizing the hand with
which K. held her and beginning to play with his fingers.
"Only an Examining Magistrate again," said K. in disappointment. "The higher officials keep themselves well
hidden. But he's sitting in a chair of state." "That's all invention," said Leni, with her face bent over his hand.
"Actually he is sitting on a kitchen chair, with an old horse-
rug doubled under him. But must you eternally be brooding
over your case?" she queried slowly. "No, not at all," said
K. "In fact I probably brood far too little over it." "That
isn't the mistake you make," said Leni. "You're too unyielding, that's what I've heard." "Who told you that?"
asked K.; he could feel her body against his breast and
gazed down at her rich, dark, firmly knotted hair. "I should
give away too much if I told you that," replied Leni.
"Please don't ask me for names, take my warning to heart
instead, and don't be so unyielding in future, you can't fight
against this Court, you must confess to guilt. Make your
confession at the first chance you get. Until you do that,
there's no possibility of getting out of their clutches, none
at all. Yet even then you won't manage it without help
from outside, but you needn't trouble your head about that,

I'll see to it myself." "You know a great deal about this
Court and the intrigues that prevail in it!" said K., lifting
her on to his knee, for she was leaning too heavily against
him. "That's better," she said, making herself at home on
his knee by smoothing her skirt and pulling her blouse
straight. Then she clasped both her hands round his neck,
leaned back, and looked at him for a long time. "And if I
don't make a confession of guilt, then you can't help me?"
K. asked experimentally. I seem to recruit women helpers,
he thought almost in surprise; first Fräulein Bürstner, then
the wife of the usher, and now this little nurse who appears
to have some incomprehensible desire for me. She sits there
on my knee as if it were the only right place for her! "No,"
said Leni, shaking her head slowly, "then I can't help you.
But you don't in the least want my help, it doesn't matter
to you, you're stiff-necked and never will be convinced."
After a while she asked: "Have you got a sweetheart?"
"No," said K. "Oh, yes, you have," she said. "Well, yes, I
have," said K. "Just imagine it, I have denied her existence
and yet I am actually carrying her photograph in my
pocket." At her entreaty he showed her Elsa's photograph;
she studied it, curled up on his knee. It was a snapshot
taken of Elsa as she was finishing a whirling dance such
as she often gave at the cabaret, her skirt was still flying
round her like a fan, her hands were planted on her firm
hips, and with her chin thrown up she was laughing over
her shoulder at someone who did not appear in the photograph. "She's very tightly laced," said Leni, indicating the
place where in her opinion the tight lacing was evident. "I
don't like her, she's rough and clumsy. But perhaps she's
soft and kind to you, one might guess that from the photograph. Big strong girls like that often can't help being soft
and kind. But would she be capable of sacrificing herself
for you?" "No," said K. "She is neither soft nor kind, nor
would she be capable of sacrificing herself for me. And up

till now I have demanded neither the one thing nor the other from her. In fact I've never even examined this photograph as carefully as you have." "So she doesn't mean so very much to you," said Leni. "She isn't your sweetheart after all." "Oh, yes," replied K. "I refuse to take back my words." "Well, granted that she's your sweetheart," said Leni, "you wouldn't miss her very much, all the same, if you were to lose her or exchange her for someone else, me, for instance?" "Certainly," said K., smiling, "that's conceivable, but she has one great advantage over you, she knows nothing about my case, and even if she knew she wouldn't bother her head about it. She wouldn't try to get me to be less unyielding." "That's no advantage," said Leni. "If that's all the advantage she has over me I shan't give up hope. Has she any physical defect?" "Any physical defect?" asked K. "Yes," said Leni. "For I have a slight one. Look." She held up her right hand and stretched out the two middle fingers, between which the connecting web of skin reached almost to the top joint, short as the fingers were. In the darkness K. could not make out at once what she wanted to show him, so she took his hand and made him feel it. "What a freak of nature!" said K. and he added, when he had examined the whole hand: "What a pretty little paw!" Leni looked on with a kind of pride while K. in astonishment kept pulling the two fingers apart and then putting them side by side again, until at last he kissed them lightly and let them go. "Oh!" she cried at once. "You have kissed me!" She hastily scrambled up until she was kneeling open-mouthed on his knees. K. looked up at her almost dumfounded; now that she was so close to him she gave out a bitter exciting odor like pepper; she clasped his head to her, bent over him, and bit and kissed him on the neck, biting into the very hairs of his head. "You have exchanged her for me," she cried over and over again. "Look, you have exchanged her for me after all!" Then her knees slipped,

with a faint cry she almost fell on the carpet, K. put his
arms round her to hold her up and was pulled down to her.
"You belong to me now," she said.

"Here's the key of the door, come whenever you like,"
were her last words, and as he took his leave a final aimless
kiss landed on his shoulder. When he stepped out on to the
pavement a light rain was falling; he was making for the
middle of the street so as perhaps to catch a last glimpse
of Leni at her window, but a car which was waiting before
the house and which in his distraction he had not even
noticed suddenly emitted his uncle, who seized him by the
arms and banged him against the house door as if he
wanted to nail him there. "Joseph!" he cried, "how could
you do it! You have damaged your case badly, which was
beginning to go quite well. You hide yourself away with a
filthy little trollop, who is obviously the lawyer's mistress
into the bargain, and stay away for hours. You don't even
seek any pretext, you conceal nothing, no, you're quite
open, you simply run off to her and stay beside her. And all
this time we three sit there, your uncle, who is doing his
best for you, the lawyer, who has to be won over to your
side, above all the Chief Clerk of the Court, a man of importance, who is actually in charge of your case at its present stage. There we sit, consulting how to help you, I have
to handle the lawyer circumspectly, and the lawyer in turn
the Clerk of the Court, and one might think you had every
reason to give me at least some support. Instead of which
you absent yourself. You were away so long that there was
no concealing it; of course the two gentlemen, being men
of the world, didn't talk about it, they spared my feelings,
but finally even they could no longer ignore it, and as
they couldn't mention it they said nothing at all. We sat
there for minutes on end in complete silence, listening for
you to come back at last. And all in vain. Finally the Chief
Clerk of the Court, who had stayed much longer than he

intended, got up and said good night, evidently very sorry for me without being able to help me, his kindness was really extraordinary, he stood waiting for a while longer at the door before he left. And I was glad when he went, let me tell you; by that time I felt hardly able to breathe. And the poor sick lawyer felt it even more, the good man couldn't utter a word as I took leave of him. In all probability you have helped to bring about his complete collapse and so hastened the death of a man on whose good offices you are dependent. And you leave me, your uncle, to wait here in the rain for hours and worry myself sick, just feel, I'm wet through and through!"

CHAPTER SEVEN

Lawyer · Manufacturer · Painter

ONE winter morning—snow was falling outside the window in a foggy dimness—K. was sitting in his office, already exhausted in spite of the early hour. To save his face before his subordinates at least, he had given his clerk instructions to admit no one, on the plea that he was occupied with an important piece of work. But instead of working he twisted in his chair, idly rearranged the things lying on his writing-table, and then, without being aware of it, let his outstretched arm rest on the table and went on sitting motionless with bowed head.

The thought of his case never left him now. He had often considered whether it would not be better to draw up a written defense and hand it in to the Court. In this defense he would give a short account of his life, and when he came to an event of any importance explain for what reasons he had acted as he did, intimate whether he approved or condemned his way of action in retrospect, and adduce grounds for the condemnation or approval. The advantages

113

of such a written defense, as compared with the mere advocacy of a lawyer who himself was not impeccable, were undoubted. K. had no idea what the lawyer was doing about the case; at any rate it did not amount to much, it was more than a month since Huld had sent for him, and at none of the previous consultations had K. formed the impression that the man could do much for him. To begin with, he had hardly cross-questioned him at all. And there were so many questions to put. To ask questions was surely the main thing. K. felt that he could draw up all the necessary questions himself. But the lawyer, instead of asking questions, either did all the talking or sat quite dumb opposite him, bent slightly forward over his writing-table, probably because of his hardness of hearing, stroking a strand of hair in the middle of his beard and gazing at the carpet, perhaps at the very spot where K. had lain with Leni. Now and then he would give K. some empty admonitions such as people hand out to children. Admonitions as useless as they were wearisome, for which K. did not intend to pay a penny at the final reckoning. After the lawyer thought he had humbled him sufficiently, he usually set himself to encourage him slightly again. He had already, so he would relate, won many similar cases either outright or partially. Cases which, though in reality not quite so difficult, perhaps, as this one, had been outwardly still more hopeless. He had a list of these cases in a drawer of his desk—at this he tapped one of them—but he regretted he couldn't show it, as it was a matter of official secrecy. Nevertheless the vast experience he had gained through all these cases would now redound to K.'s benefit. He had started on K.'s case at once, of course, and the first plea was almost ready for presentation. That was very important, for the first impression made by the Defense often determined the whole course of subsequent proceedings. Though, unfortunately, it was his duty to warn K., it sometimes happened that the

first pleas were not read by the Court at all. They simply
filed them among the other papers and pointed out that for
the time being the observation and interrogation of the accused were more important than any formal petition. If
the petitioner pressed them, they generally added that before the verdict was pronounced all the material accumu-
lated, including, of course, every document relating to the
case, the first plea as well, would be carefully examined.
But unluckily even that was not quite true in most cases,
the first plea was often mislaid or lost altogether and, even
if it were kept intact till the end, was hardly ever read;
that was of course, the lawyer admitted, merely a rumor.
It was all very regrettable, but not wholly without justification. K. must remember that the proceedings were not
public; they could certainly, if the Court considered it necessary, become public, but the Law did not prescribe that
they must be made public. Naturally, therefore, the legal
records of the case, and above all the actual charge-sheets,
were inaccessible to the accused and his counsel, consequently one did not know in general, or at least did not
know with any precision, what charges to meet in the first
plea; accordingly it could be only by pure chance that it
contained really relevant matter. One could draw up gen-
uinely effective and convincing pleas only later on, when
the separate charges and the evidence on which they were
based emerged more definitely or could be guessed at from
the interrogations. In such circumstances the Defense was
naturally in a very ticklish and difficult position. Yet that,
too, was intentional. For the Defense was not actually
countenanced by the Law, but only tolerated, and there
were differences of opinion even on that point, whether the
Law could be interpreted to admit such tolerance at all.
Strictly speaking, therefore, none of the counsels for the
Defense was recognized by the Court, all who appeared
before the Court as counsels being in reality merely in the

position of pettifogging lawyers. That naturally had a very humiliating effect on the whole profession, and the next time K. visited the Law Court offices he should take a look at the lawyers' room, just for the sake of having seen it once in his life. He would probably be horrified by the kind of people he found assembled there. The very room, itself small and cramped, showed the contempt in which the Court held them. It was lit only by a small skylight, which was so high up that if you wanted to look out, you had to get some colleague to hoist you on his back, and even then the smoke from the chimney close by choked you and blackened your face. To give only one more example of the state the place was in—there had been for more than a year now a hole in the floor, not so big that you could fall through the floor, but big enough to let a man's leg slip through. The lawyers' room was in the very top attic, so that if you stumbled through the hole your leg hung down into the lower attic, into the very corridor where the clients had to wait. It wasn't saying too much if the lawyers called these conditions scandalous. Complaints to the authorities had not the slightest effect, and it was strictly forbidden for the lawyers to make any structural repairs or alterations at their own expense. Still, there was some justification for this attitude on the part of the authorities. They wanted to eliminate defending counsel as much as possible; the whole onus of the Defense must be laid on the accused himself. A reasonable enough point of view, yet nothing could be more erroneous than to deduce from this that accused persons had no need of defending counsel when appearing before this Court. On the contrary, in no other Court was legal assistance so necessary. For the proceedings were not only kept secret from the general public, but from the accused as well. Of course only so far as this was possible, but it had proved possible to a very great extent. For even the accused had no access to the Court records, and to

guess from the course of an interrogation what documents
the Court had up its sleeve was very difficult, particularly
for an accused person, who was himself implicated and
had all sorts of worries to distract him. Now here was where
defending counsel stepped in. Generally speaking, he was
not allowed to be present during the examination, consequently he had to cross-question the accused immediately
after an interrogation, if possible at the very door of the
Court of Inquiry, and piece together from the usually confused reports he got anything that might be of use for the
Defense. But even that was not the most important thing,
for one could not elicit very much in that way, though of
course here as elsewhere a capable man could elicit more
than others. The most important thing was counsel's personal connection with officials of the Court; in that lay the
chief value of the Defense. Now K. must have discovered
from experience that the very lowest grade of the Court
organization was by no means perfect and contained venal
and corrupt elements, whereby to some extent a breach was
made in the water-tight system of justice. This was where
most of the petty lawyers tried to push their way in, by
bribing and listening to gossip, in fact there had actually
been cases of purloining documents, at least in former times.
It was not to be gainsaid that these methods could achieve
for the moment surprisingly favorable results for the accused, on which the petty lawyers prided themselves,
spreading them out as a lure for new clients, but they had
no effect on the further progress of the case, or only a bad
effect. Nothing was of any real value but respectable personal connections with the higher officials, that was to say
higher officials of subordinate rank, naturally. Only through
these could the course of the proceedings be influenced,
imperceptibly at first, perhaps, but more and more strongly
as the case went on. Of course very few lawyers had such
connections, and here K.'s choice had been a very fortu-

nate one. Perhaps only one or two other lawyers could boast of the same connections as Dr. Huld. These did not worry their heads about the mob in the lawyers' room and had nothing whatever to do with them. But their relations with the Court officials were all the more intimate. It was not even necessary that Dr. Huld should always attend the Court, wait in the Anteroom of the Examining Magistrates till they chose to appear, and be dependent on their moods for earning perhaps a delusive success or not even that. No, as K. had himself seen, the officials, and very high ones among them, visited Dr. Huld of their own accord, voluntarily providing information with great frankness or at least in broad enough hints, discussing the next turn of the various cases; more, even sometimes letting themselves be persuaded to a new point of view. Certainly one should not rely too much on their readiness to be persuaded, for definitely as they might declare themselves for a new standpoint favorable to the Defense, they might well go straight to their offices and issue a statement in the directly contrary sense, a verdict far more severe on the accused than the original intention which they claimed to have renounced completely. Against that, of course, there was no remedy, for what they said to you in private was simply said to you in private and could not be followed up in public, even if the Defense were not obliged for other reasons to do its utmost to retain the favor of these gentlemen. On the other hand it had also to be considered that these gentlemen were not moved by mere human benevolence or friendly feeling in paying visits to defending counsel—only to experienced counsel, of course; they were in a certain sense actually dependent on the Defense. They could not help feeling the disadvantages of a judiciary system which insisted on secrecy from the start. Their remoteness kept the officials from being in touch with the populace; for the average case they were excellently equipped, such a case pro-

ceeded almost mechanically and only needed a push now
and then; yet confronted with quite simple cases, or particularly difficult cases, they were often utterly at a loss,
they did not have any right understanding of human relations, since they were confined day and night to the workings of their judicial system, whereas in such cases a
knowledge of human nature itself was indispensable. Then
it was that they came to the lawyers for advice, with a
servant behind them carrying the papers that were usually
kept so secret. In that window over there many a gentleman one would never have expected to encounter had sat
gazing out hopelessly into the street, while the lawyer at
his desk examined his papers in order to give him good
advice. And it was on such occasions as these that one
could perceive how seriously these gentlemen took their
vocation and how deeply they were plunged into despair
when they came upon obstacles which the nature of things
kept them from overcoming. In other ways, too, their position was not easy, and one must not do them an injustice
by regarding it as easy. The ranks of officials in this judiciary system mounted endlessly, so that not even the initiated could survey the hierarchy as a whole. And the
proceedings of the Courts were generally kept secret from
subordinate officials, consequently they could hardly ever
quite follow in their further progress the cases on which
they had worked; any particular case thus appeared in their
circle of jurisdiction often without their knowing whence it
came, and passed from it they knew not whither. Thus the
knowledge derived from a study of the various single stages
of the case, the final verdict and the reasons for that verdict
lay beyond the reach of these officials. They were forced
to restrict themselves to that stage of the case which was
prescribed for them by the Law, and as for what followed,
in other words the results of their own work, they generally
knew less about it than the Defense, which as a rule re-

mained in touch with the accused almost to the end of the case. So in that respect, too, they could learn much that was worth knowing from the Defense. Should it surprise K., then, keeping all this in mind, to find that the officials lived in a state of irritability which sometimes expressed itself in offensive ways when they dealt with their clients? That was the universal experience. All the officials were in a constant state of irritation, even when they appeared calm. Naturally the petty lawyers were most liable to suffer from it. The following story, for example, was current, and it had all the appearance of truth. An old official, a well-meaning, quiet man, had a difficult case in hand which had been greatly complicated by the lawyer's petitions, and he had studied it continuously for a whole day and night—the officials were really more conscientious than anyone else. Well, toward morning, after twenty-four hours of work with probably very little result, he went to the entrance door, hid himself behind it, and flung down the stairs every lawyer who tried to enter. The lawyers gathered down below on the landing and took counsel what they should do; on the one hand they had no real claim to be admitted and consequently could hardly take any legal action against the official, and also, as already mentioned, they had to guard against antagonizing the body of officials. But on the other hand every day they spent away from the Court was a day lost to them, and so a great deal depended on their getting in. At last they all agreed that the best thing to do was to tire out the old gentleman. One lawyer after another was sent rushing upstairs to offer the greatest possible show of passive resistance and let himself be thrown down again into the arms of his colleagues. That lasted for about an hour, then the old gentleman—who was exhausted in any case by his work overnight—really grew tired and went back to his office. The lawyers down below would not believe it at first and sent one of their number up to peep behind the door and assure himself that the place was actually vacant. Only then were they able to enter, and probably they did not dare even to grumble. For although the pettiest lawyer might be to some extent capable of analyzing the state of things in the Court, it never occurred to the lawyers that they should suggest or insist on any improvements in the system, while—and this was very characteristic—almost every accused man, even quite simple people among them, discovered from the earliest stages a passion for suggesting reforms which often wasted time and energy that could have been better employed in other directions. The only sensible thing was to adapt oneself to existing conditions. Even if it were possible to alter a detail for the better here or there—but it was simple madness to think of it—any benefit arising from that would profit clients in the future only, while one's own interests would be immeasurably injured by attracting the attention of the ever-vengeful officials. Anything rather than that! One must lie low, no matter how much it went against the grain, and try to understand that this great organization remained, so to speak, in a state of delicate balance, and that if someone took it upon himself to alter the disposition of things around him, he ran the risk of losing his footing and falling to destruction, while the organization would simply right itself by some compensating reaction in another part of its machinery—since everything interlocked—and remain unchanged, unless, indeed, which was very probable, it became still more rigid, more vigilant, severer, and more ruthless. One must really leave the lawyers to do their work, instead of interfering with them. Reproaches were not of much use, particularly when the offender was unable to perceive the full scope of the grounds for them; all the same, he must say that K. had very greatly damaged his case by his discourtesy to the Chief Clerk of the Court. That influential man could already almost be eliminated

from the list of those who might be got to do something
for K. He now ignored clearly on purpose even the slightest
reference to the case. In many ways the functionaries were
like children. Often they could be so deeply offended by
the merest trifle—unfortunately, K.'s behavior could not be
classed as a trifle—that they would stop speaking even to
old friends, give them the cold shoulder, and work against
them in all imaginable ways. But then, suddenly, in the
most surprising fashion and without any particular reason,
they would be moved to laughter by some small jest which
you only dared to make because you felt you had nothing
to lose, and then they were your friends again. In fact it
was both easy and difficult to handle them, you could
hardly lay down any fixed principles for dealing with them.
Sometimes you felt astonished to think that one single ordinary lifetime sufficed to gather all the knowledge needed
for a fair degree of success in such a profession. There were
dark hours, of course, such as came to everybody, in which
you thought you had achieved nothing at all, in which it
seemed to you that only the cases predestined from the start
to succeed came to a good end, which they would have
reached in any event without your help, while every one
of the others was doomed to fail in spite of all your ma-
neuvers, all your exertions, all the illusory little victories on
which you plumed yourself. That was a frame of mind, of
course, in which nothing at all seemed certain, and so you
could not positively deny when questioned that your intervention might have sidetracked some cases which would
have run quite well on the right lines had they been left
alone. A desperate kind of self-assurance, to be sure, yet it
was the only kind available at such times. These moods—
for of course they were only moods, nothing more—afflicted
lawyers more especially when a case which they had conducted satisfactorily to the desired point was suddenly
taken out of their hands. That was beyond all doubt the

worst thing that could happen to a lawyer. Not that a client
ever dismissed his lawyer from a case, such a thing was
not done, an accused man, once having briefed a lawyer,
must stick to him whatever happened. For how could he
keep going by himself, once he had called in someone to
help him? So that never happened, but it did sometimes
happen that the case took a turn where the lawyer could
no longer follow it. The case and the accused and everything were simply withdrawn from the lawyer; then even
the best connections with officials could no longer achieve
any result, for even they knew nothing. The case had simply reached the stage where further assistance was ruled
out, it was being conducted in remote, inaccessible Courts,
where even the accused was beyond the reach of a lawyer.
Then you might come home some day and find on your
table all the countless pleas relating to the case, which you
had drawn up with such pains and such high hopes;
they had been returned to you because in the new stage of
the trial they were not admitted as relevant; they were
mere waste paper. It did not follow that the case was lost,
by no means, at least there was no decisive evidence for
such an assumption; you simply knew nothing more about
the case and would never know anything more about it.
Now, very luckily, such occurrences were exceptional, and
even if K.'s case were a case of that nature, it still had a
long way to go before reaching that stage. For the time
being, there were abundant opportunities for legal labor,
and K. might rest assured that they would be exploited to
the utmost. The first plea, as before mentioned, was not yet
handed in, but there was no hurry; far more important
were the preliminary consultations with the relevant officials, and they had already taken place. With varying success, as must be frankly admitted. It would be better for
the time being not to divulge details which might have a
bad influence on K. by elating or depressing him unduly,

yet this much could be asserted, that certain officials had expressed themselves very graciously and had also shown great readiness to help, while others had expressed themselves less favorably, but in spite of that had by no means refused their collaboration. The result on the whole was therefore very gratifying, though one must not seek to draw any definite conclusion from that, since all preliminary negotiations began in the same way and only in the course of further developments did it appear whether they had real value or not. At any rate nothing was yet lost, and if they could manage to win over the Chief Clerk of the Court in spite of all that had happened—various moves had already been initiated toward that end—then, to use a surgeon's expression, this could be regarded as a clean wound and one could await further developments with an easy mind.

In such and similar harangues K.'s lawyer was inexhaustible. He reiterated them every time K. called on him. Progress had always been made, but the nature of the progress could never be divulged. The lawyer was always working away at the first plea, but it had never reached a conclusion, which at the next visit turned out to be an advantage, since the last few days would have been very inauspicious for handing it in, a fact which no one could have foreseen. If K., as sometimes happened, wearied out by the lawyer's volubility, remarked that, even taking into account all the difficulties, the case seemed to be getting on very slowly, he was met with the retort that it was not getting on slowly at all, although they would have been much further on by now had K. come to the lawyer in time. Unfortunately he had neglected to do so and that omission was likely to keep him at a disadvantage, and not merely a temporal disadvantage, either.

The one welcome interruption to these visits was Leni, who always so arranged things that she brought in the lawyer's tea while K. was present. She would stand behind K.'s chair, apparently looking on, while the lawyer stooped with a kind of miserly greed over his cup and poured out and sipped his tea, but all the time she was letting K. surreptitiously hold her hand. There was total silence. The lawyer sipped, K. squeezed Leni's hand, and sometimes Leni ventured to caress his hair. "Are you still here?" the lawyer would ask, after he had finished. "I wanted to take the tea tray away," Leni would answer, there would follow a last handclasp, the lawyer would wipe his mouth and begin again with new energy to harangue K.

Was the lawyer seeking to comfort him or to drive him to despair? K. could not tell, but he soon held it for an established fact that his defense was not in good hands. It might be all true, of course, what the lawyer said, though his attempts to magnify his own importance were transparent enough and it was likely that he had never till now conducted such an important case as he imagined K.'s to be. But his continual bragging of his personal connections with the officials was suspicious. Was it so certain that he was exploiting these connections entirely for K.'s benefit? The lawyer never forgot to mention that these officials were subordinate officials, therefore officials in a very dependent position, for whose advancement certain turns in the various cases might in all probability be of some importance. Could they possibly employ the lawyer to bring about such turns in the case, turns which were bound, of course, to be unfavorable to the accused? Perhaps they did not always do that, it was hardly likely, there must be occasions on which they arranged that the lawyer should score a point or two as a reward for his services, since it was to their own interest for him to keep up his professional reputation. But if that were really the position, into which category were they likely to put K.'s case, which, as the lawyer maintained, was a very difficult, therefore important case, and had roused great interest in the Court from the very beginning? There could not be very much doubt what they would do. A clue was already provided by the fact that the first plea had not yet been handed in, though the case had lasted for months, and that according to the lawyer all the proceedings were still in their early stages, words which were obviously well calculated to lull the accused and keep him in a helpless state, in order suddenly to overwhelm him with the verdict or at least with the announcement that the preliminary examination had been concluded in his disfavor and the case handed over to higher authorities.

It was absolutely necessary for K. to intervene personally. In states of intense exhaustion, such as he experienced this winter morning, when all these thoughts kept running at random through his head, he was particularly incapable of resisting this conviction. The contempt which he had once felt for the case no longer obtained. Had he stood alone in the world he could easily have ridiculed the whole affair, though it was also certain that in that event it could never have arisen at all. But now his uncle had dragged him to this lawyer, family considerations had come in; his position was no longer quite independent of the course the case took, he himself, with a certain inexplicable complacence, had imprudently mentioned it to some of his acquaintances, others had come to learn of it in ways unknown to him, his relations with Fräulein Bürstner seemed to fluctuate with the case itself—in short, he hardly had the choice now to accept the trial or reject it, he was in the middle of it and must fend for himself. To give in to fatigue would be dangerous.

Yet there was no need for exaggerated anxiety at the moment. In a relatively short time he had managed to work himself up to his present high position in the Bank and to maintain himself in that position and win recognition from everybody; surely if the abilities which had made this possible were to be applied to the unraveling of his own case, there was no doubt that it would go well. Above all, if he were to achieve anything, it was essential that he should banish from his mind once and for all the idea of possible guilt. There was no such guilt. This legal action was nothing more than a business deal such as he had often concluded to the advantage of the Bank, a deal within which, as always happened, lurked various dangers which must simply be obviated. The right tactics were to avoid letting one's thoughts stray to one's own possible short-comings, and to cling as firmly as one could to the thought of one's advantage. From this standpoint the conclusion was inevitable that the case must be withdrawn from Dr. Huld as soon as possible, preferably that very evening. According to him that was something unheard of, it was true, and very likely an insult, but K. could not endure that his efforts in the case should be thwarted by moves possibly originating in the office of his own representative. Once the lawyer was shaken off, the petition must be sent in at once and the officials be urged daily, if possible, to give their attention to it. This would never be achieved by sitting meekly in the attic lobby like the others with one's hat under the seat. K. himself, or one of the women, or some other messenger must keep at the officials day after day and force them to sit down at their desks and study K.'s papers instead of gaping out into the lobby through the wooden rails. These tactics must be pursued unremit-tingly, everything must be organized and supervised; the Court would encounter for once an accused man who knew how to stick up for his rights.

Yet even though K. believed he could manage all this, the difficulty of drawing up the petition seemed overwhelming. At one time, not more than a week ago, he had regarded the possibility of having to draw up his own plea with merely a slight feeling of shame; it never even occurred to him that there might be difficulties in the way. He could remember that one of those mornings, when he was up to his ears in work, he had suddenly pushed everything aside and seized his jotting-pad with the idea of drafting the plan of such a plea and handing it to Dr. Huld by way of egging him on, but just at that moment the door of the Manager's room opened and the Assistant Manager came in laughing uproariously. That had been a very painful moment for K., though, of course, the Assistant Manager had not been laughing at the plea, of which he knew nothing, but at a funny story from the Stock Exchange which he had just heard, a story which needed illustrating for the proper appreciation of the point, so that the Assistant Manager, bending over the desk, took K.'s pencil from his hand and drew the required picture on the page of the jotting-pad which had been intended for the plea.

Today K. was no longer hampered by feelings of shame; the plea simply had to be drawn up. If he could find no time for it in his office, which seemed very probable, then he must draft it in his lodgings by night. And if his nights were not enough, then he must ask for furlough. Anything but stop halfway, that was the most senseless thing one could do in any affair, not only in business. No doubt it was a task that meant almost interminable labor. One did not need to have a timid and fearful nature to be easily persuaded that the completion of this plea was a sheer impossibility. Not because of laziness or obstructive malice, which could only hinder Dr. Huld, but because to meet an unknown accusation, not to mention other possible charges arising out of it, the whole of one's life would have to be recalled to mind, down to the smallest actions and accidents, clearly formulated and examined from every angle. And besides, how dreary such a task would be! It would do well enough, perhaps, as an occupation for one's second childhood in years of retirement, when the long days needed filling up. But now, when K. should be devoting his mind entirely to work, when every hour was hurried and crowded—for he was still in full career and rapidly becoming a rival even to the Assistant Manager—when his evenings and nights were all too short for the pleasures of a bachelor life, this was the time when he must sit down to such a task! Once more his train of thought had led him into self-pity. Almost involuntarily, simply to make an end of it, he put his finger on the button which rang the bell in the waiting-room. While he pressed it he glanced at the clock. It was eleven o'clock, he had wasted two hours in dreaming, a long stretch of precious time, and he was, of course, still wearier than he had been before. Yet the time had not been quite lost, he had come to decisions which might prove valuable. The attendants brought in several letters and two cards from gentlemen who had been waiting for a considerable time. They were, in fact, extremely important clients of the Bank who should on no account have been kept waiting at all. Why had they come at such an unsuitable hour?—and why, they might well be asking in their turn behind the door, did the assiduous K. allow his private affairs to usurp the best time of the day? Weary of what had gone before and wearily awaiting what was to come, K. got up to receive the first of his clients.

This was a jovial little man, a manufacturer whom K. knew well. He regretted having disturbed K. in the middle of important work and K. on his side regretted that he had kept the manufacturer waiting for so long. But his very regret he expressed in such a mechanical way, with such a lack of sincerity in his tone of voice, that the manufacturer could not have helped noticing it, had he not been so engrossed by the business in hand. As it was, he tugged papers covered with statistics out of every pocket, spread them before K., explained various entries, corrected a trifling error which his eye had caught even in this hasty survey, reminded K. of a similar transaction which he had concluded with him about a year before, mentioned casually that this time another bank was making great sacrifices to secure the deal, and finally sat in eager silence waiting for K.'s comments. K. had actually followed the man's argument quite closely in its early stages—the thought of such an important piece of business had its attractions for him too—but unfortunately not for long; he had soon ceased to listen and merely nodded now and then as the manufacturer's claims waxed in enthusiasm, until in the end he forgot to show even that much interest and confined himself to staring at the other's bald head bent over the papers and asking himself when the fellow would begin to realize that all his eloquence was being wasted. When the manufacturer stopped speaking, K. actually thought for a moment that the pause was intended to give him the chance of confessing that he was not in a fit state to attend to business. And it was with regret that he perceived the intent look on the manufacturer's face, the alertness, as if prepared for every objection, which indicated that the interview would have to continue. So he bowed his head as at a word of command and began slowly to move his pencil point over the papers, pausing here and there to stare at some figure. The manufacturer suspected K. of looking for flaws in the scheme, perhaps the figures were merely tentative, perhaps they were not the decisive factors in the deal, at any rate he laid his hand over them and shifting closer to K. began to expound the general policy behind the transaction. "It's difficult," said K., pursing his lips, and now that the papers, the only things he had to hold on to, were covered up, he sank weakly against the arm of his chair. He glanced up slightly, but only slightly, when the door of the Manager's room opened, disclosed the Assistant Manager, a blurred figure who looked as if veiled in some kind of gauze. K. did not

seek for the cause of this apparition, but merely registered
its immediate effect, which was very welcome to him. For
the manufacturer at once bounded from his chair and
rushed over to the Assistant Manager, though K. could
have wished him to be ten times quicker, since he was
afraid the apparition might vanish again. His fear was
superfluous, the two gentlemen met each other, shook
hands, and advanced together toward K.'s desk. The manufacturer lamented that his proposals were being cold-
shouldered by the Chief Clerk, indicating K., who under the
Assistant Manager's eye had once more bent over the
papers. Then as the two of them leaned against his desk,
and the manufacturer set himself to win the newcomer's
approval for his scheme, it seemed to K. as though two
giants of enormous size were negotiating above his head
about himself. Slowly, lifting his eyes as far as he dared,
he peered up to see what they were about, then picked one
of the documents from the desk at random, laid it flat on
his open palm, and gradually raised it, himself rising with
it, to their level. In doing so he had no definite purpose,
but merely acted with the feeling that this was how he
would have to act when he had finished the great task of
drawing up the plea which was to acquit him completely.
The Assistant Manager, who was giving his full attention
to the conversation, merely glanced at the paper without
even reading what was on it—for anything that seemed
important to the Chief Clerk was unimportant to him—
took it from K.'s hand, said: "Thanks, I know all that already," and quietly laid it back on the desk again. K.
darted a bitter look at him, but the Assistant Manager did
not notice that, or, if he did, was only amused; he laughed
loudly several times, visibly disconcerted the manufacturer
by a quick retort, only to counter it immediately himself,
and finally invited the man into his private office, where
they could complete the transaction together. "It is a very

important proposal," he said to the manufacturer, "I entirely agree. And the Chief Clerk"—even in saying this he went on addressing himself only to the manufacturer—"will I am sure be relieved if we take it off his shoulders. This business needs thinking over. And he seems to be overburdened today; besides, there are some people who have been waiting for him in the anteroom for hours." K. had still enough self-command to turn away from the Assistant Manager and address his friendly but somewhat fixed smile solely to the manufacturer; except for this he did not intervene, supporting himself with both hands on the desk, bending forward a little like an obsequious clerk, and looked on while the two men, still talking away, gathered up the papers and disappeared into the Manager's room. In the very doorway, the manufacturer turned round to remark that he would not say good-by yet, for of course he would report the result of the interview to the Chief Clerk; besides, there was another little matter he had to mention.

At last K. was alone. He had not the slightest intention of interviewing any more clients and vaguely realized how pleasant it was that the people waiting outside believed him to be still occupied with the manufacturer, so that nobody, not even the attendant, could disturb him. He went over to the window, perched on the sill, holding on to the latch with one hand, and looked down on the square below. The snow was still falling, the sky had not yet cleared.

For a long time he sat like this, without knowing what really troubled him, only turning his head from time to time with an alarmed glance toward the anteroom, where he fancied, mistakenly, that he heard a noise. But as no one came in he recovered his composure, went over to the washbasin, washed his face in cold water, and returned to his place at the window with a clearer mind. The decision to take his defense into his own hands seemed now more grave to him than he had originally fancied. So long as the lawyer was responsible for the case it had not come really home to him, he had viewed it with a certain detachment and kept beyond reach of immediate contact with it, he had been able to supervise it whenever he liked, but could also withdraw whenever he liked. Now, on the other hand, if he were to conduct his own defense he would be putting himself completely in the power of the Court, at least for the time being, a policy which would eventually bring about his absolute and definite acquittal, but would meanwhile, provisionally at least, involve him in far greater dangers than before. If he had ever doubted that, his state of mind today in his encounter with the Assistant Manager and the manufacturer would have been more than enough to convince him. What a stupor had overcome him, merely because he had decided to conduct his own defense! And what would develop later on? What days were lying in wait for him? Would he ever find the right path through all these difficulties? To put up a thoroughgoing defense—and any other kind would be a waste of time—to put up a thoroughgoing defense, did that not involve cutting himself off from every other activity? Would he be able to carry that through? And how was he to conduct his case from a Bank office? It was not merely the drawing up of a plea; that might be managed on a few weeks' furlough, though to ask for leave of absence just now would be decidedly risky; but a whole trial was involved, whose duration it was impossible to foresee. What an obstacle had suddenly arisen to block K.'s career!

And this was the moment when he was supposed to work for the Bank? He looked down at his desk. This the time to interview clients and negotiate with them? While his case was unfolding itself, while up in the attics the Court officials were poring over the charge papers, was he to devote his attention to the affairs of the Bank? It looked like a kind of torture sanctioned by the Court, arising from his case and concomitant with it. And would allowances be made for his peculiar position when his work in the Bank came to be judged? Never, and by nobody. The existence of his case was not entirely unknown in the Bank, though it was not quite clear who knew of it and how much they knew. But apparently the rumor had not yet reached the Assistant Manager, otherwise K. could hardly have failed to perceive it, since the man would have exploited his knowledge without any scruples as a colleague or as a human being. And the Manager himself? He was certainly well disposed to K. and as soon as he heard of the case would probably be willing enough to lighten K.'s duties as far as lay in his power, but his good intentions would be checkmated, for K.'s waning prestige was no longer sufficient to counterbalance the influence of the Assistant Manager, who was gaining a stronger hold on the Manager and exploiting the latter's invalid condition to his own advantage.* So what had K. to hope? It might be that he was only sapping his powers of resistance by harboring these thoughts; still, it was necessary to have no illusions and to view the position as clearly as the moment allowed.

Without any particular motive, merely to put off returning to his desk, he opened the window. It was difficult to open, he had to push the latch with both hands. Then there came into the room through the great window a blend of fog and smoke, filling it with a faint smell of burning soot. Some snowflakes fluttered in too. "An awful autumn," came the voice of the manufacturer from behind K.; returning from his colloquy with the Assistant Manager, he had entered the room unobserved. K. nodded and shot an apprehensive glance at the man's attaché case, from which doubtless he would now extract all his papers in order to inform K. how the negotiations had gone. But the manufacturer, catching K.'s eye, merely tapped his attaché case

without opening it and said: "You would like to know how
it turned out? The final settlement is as good as in my pocket.
A charming fellow, your Assistant Manager, but dangerous
to reckon with." He laughed and shook K. by the hand,
trying to make him laugh too. But now K.'s suspicions
seized on the fact that the manufacturer had not offered to
show him the papers, and he found nothing to laugh at.
"Herr K.," said the manufacturer, "you're under the weather
today. You look so depressed." "Yes," said K., putting his
hand to his brow, "a headache, family troubles." "Ah, yes,"
said the manufacturer, who was a hasty man and could
never listen quietly to anybody, "we all have our troubles."
K. had involuntarily taken a step toward the door, as if to
show the manufacturer out, but the latter said: "Herr K.,
there's another little matter I should mention to you. I'm
afraid this isn't exactly the moment to bother you with it,
but the last two times I've been here I forgot to mention it.
And if I put off mentioning it any longer it will probably
lose its point altogether. And that would be a pity, since
my information may have some real value for you." Before
K. had time to make any reply the man stepped up close
to him, tapped him with one finger on the chest, and said
in a low voice: "You're involved in a case, aren't you?" K.
started back, crying out: "The Assistant Manager told you
that." "Not at all," said the manufacturer. "How should the
Assistant Manager know anything about it?" "How do you
know about it?" asked K., pulling himself together. "I pick
up scraps of information about the Court now and then,"
said the manufacturer, "and that accounts for what I have
to mention." "So many people seem to be connected with
the Court!" said K. with a bowed head, as he led the manufacturer back to the desk. They sat down as before and the
manufacturer began: "Unfortunately it isn't much that I
can tell you. But in these affairs one shouldn't leave the
smallest stone unturned. Besides, I feel a strong desire to

help you, no matter how modest the help. We have always been good business friends till now, haven't we? Well, then." K. wanted to excuse himself for his behavior that morning, but the manufacturer would not hear of it, pushed his attaché case firmly under his arm to show that he was in a hurry to go, and continued: "I heard of your case from a man called Titorelli. He's a painter, Titorelli is only his professional name, I don't know at all what his real name is. For years he has been in the habit of calling at my office from time to time, bringing little paintings for which I give him a sort of alms—he's almost a beggar. And they're not bad pictures, moors and heaths and so on. These deals—we have got into the way of them—pass off quite smoothly. But there was a time when he turned up too frequently for my taste, I told him so, we fell into conversation, I was curious to know how he could keep himself going entirely by his painting, and I discovered to my astonishment that he really earned his living as a portrait painter. He worked for the Court, he said. For what Court, I asked. And then he told me about this Court. With your experience you can well imagine how amazed I was at the tales he told me. Since then he brings me the latest news from the Court every time he arrives, and in this way I have gradually acquired a considerable insight into its workings. Of course Titorelli wags his tongue too freely, and I often have to put a stopper on him, not only because he's certainly a liar, but chiefly because a businessman like myself has so many troubles of his own that he can't afford to bother much about other people's. That's only by the way. Perhaps—I thought to myself—Titorelli might be of some use to you, he knows many of the Judges, and even if he can hardly have much influence himself, he can at least advise you how to get in touch with influential men. And even if you can't take him as an oracle, still it seems to me that in your hands his information might become important. For you are almost as good as a lawyer yourself. I'm always saying: The Chief Clerk is almost a lawyer. Oh, I have no anxiety about your case. Well, would you care to go and see Titorelli? On my recommendation he will certainly do all he can for you; I really think you should go. It needn't be today, of course, some time, any time will do. Let me add that you needn't feel bound to go just because I advise you to, not in the least. No, if you think you can dispense with Titorelli, it's certainly better to leave him entirely out of it. Perhaps you've a detailed plan of your own already drawn up and Titorelli might spoil it. Well, in that case you'd much better not go to see him. And it would certainly mean swallowing one's pride to go to such a fellow for advice. Anyhow, do just as you like. Here is my letter of recommendation and here is the address."

K. took the letter, feeling dashed, and stuck it in his pocket. Even in the most favorable circumstances the advantages which this recommendation could procure him must be outweighed by the damage implied in the fact that the manufacturer knew about his trial and that the painter was spreading news of it. He could hardly bring himself to utter a few words of thanks to the manufacturer, who was already on his way out. "I'll go to see the man," he said as he shook hands at the door, "or write to him to call here, since I'm so busy." "I knew," said the manufacturer, "that you could be depended on to find the best solution. Though I must say I rather thought you would prefer to avoid receiving people like this Titorelli at the Bank, to discuss your case with him. Besides, it's not always advisable to let such people get their hands on letters of yours. But I'm sure you've thought it all over and know what you can do." K. nodded and accompanied the manufacturer a stage farther, through the waiting room. In spite of his outward composure he was horrified at his own lack of sense. His suggestion of writing to Titorelli had been made merely to

show the manufacturer that he appreciated the recommendation and meant to lose no time in making contact with the
painter, but, left to himself, he would not have hesitated to
write to Titorelli had he regarded the man's assistance as
important. Yet it needed the manufacturer to point out the
dangers lurking in such an action. Had he really lost his
powers of judgment to that extent already? If it were possible for him to think of explicitly inviting a questionable
character to the Bank in order to ask for advice about his
case with only a door between him and the Assistant Manager, was it not also possible and even extremely probable
that he was overlooking other dangers as well, or blindly
running into them? There wasn't always someone at his
side to warn him. And this was the moment, just when he
intended to concentrate all his energies on the case, this was
the moment for him to start doubting the alertness of his
faculties! Must the difficulties he was faced with in carrying
out his office work begin to affect the case as well? At all
events he simply could not understand how he could ever
have thought of writing to Titorelli and inviting him to
come to the Bank.

He was still shaking his head over this when the attendant came up to him and indicated three gentlemen sitting
on a bench in the waiting room. They had already waited
for a long time to see K. Now that the attendant accosted
K. they sprang to their feet, each one of them eager to seize
the first chance of attracting K.'s attention. If the Bank
officials were inconsiderate enough to make them waste their
time in the waiting room, they felt entitled in their turn to
behave with the same lack of consideration. "Herr K.," one
of them began. But K. had sent for his overcoat and said to
all three of them while the attendant helped him into it:
"Forgive me, gentlemen, I'm sorry to tell you that I have
no time to see you at present. I do apologize, but I have to
go out on urgent business and must leave the building at

once. You have seen for yourselves how long I have been held up by my last caller. Would you be so good as to come back tomorrow or at some other time? Or could we talk the matter over on the telephone, perhaps? Or perhaps you could inform me now, briefly, what your business is, and I shall give you a detailed answer in writing? Though it would certainly be much better if you made an appointment for some other time." These suggestions threw the three men, whose time had thus been wasted to no purpose at all, into such astonishment that they gazed at each other dumbly. "That's settled, then?" asked K., turning to the attendant, who was bringing him his hat. Through the open door of his room he could see that the snow was now falling more thickly. Consequently he put up his coat collar and buttoned it high round his neck.

At that very moment the Assistant Manager stepped out of the next room, glanced smilingly at K. in his overcoat talking to the clients, and asked: "Are you going out, Herr K.?" "Yes," said K., straightening himself, "I have to go out on business." But the Assistant Manager had already turned to the three clients. "And these gentlemen?" he asked. "I believe they have already been waiting a long time." "We have settled what we are to do," said K. But now the clients could no longer be held in check, they clustered round K. protesting that they would not have waited for hours unless their business had been important, not to say urgent, necessitating immediate discussion at length, and in private at that. The Assistant Manager listened to them for a moment or two, meanwhile observing K., who stood holding his hat and dusting it spasmodically, then he remarked: "Gentlemen, there is a very simple solution. If you will accept me, I will gladly place myself at your disposal instead of the Chief Clerk. Your business must, of course, be attended to at once. We are businessmen like yourselves and know how valuable time is to a businessman. Will you be so good as to come with me?" And he opened the door which led to the waiting room of his own office.

How clever the Assistant Manager was at poaching on the preserves which K. was forced to abandon! But was not K. abandoning more than was absolutely needful? While with the vaguest and—he could not but admit it—the faintest of hopes, he was rushing away to see an unknown painter, his prestige in the Bank was suffering irreparable injury. It would probably be much better for him to take off his overcoat again and conciliate at least the two clients waiting next door for their turn to receive the Assistant Manager's attention. K. might actually have attempted this if he had not at that moment caught sight of the Assistant Manager himself in K.'s own room, searching through his files as if they belonged to him. In great agitation K. approached the doorway of the room and the Assistant Manager exclaimed: "Oh, you're not gone yet." He turned his face toward K.—the deep lines scored upon it seemed to speak of power rather than old age—and immediately resumed his search. "I'm looking for a copy of an agreement," he said, "which the firm's representative says should be among your papers. Won't you help me to look?" K. took a step forward, but the Assistant Manager said: "Thanks, now I've found it," and carrying a huge package of documents, which obviously contained not only the copy of the agreement but many other papers as well, he returned to his office.

"I'm not equal to him just now," K. told himself, "but once my personal difficulties are settled he'll be the first to feel it, and I'll make him suffer for it, too." Somewhat soothed by this thought, K. instructed the attendant, who had been holding open the corridor door for a long time, to inform the Manager at any convenient time that he had gone out on a business call, and then, almost elated at the thought of being able to devote himself entirely to his case for a while, he left the Bank.

He drove at once to the address where the painter lived, in a suburb which was almost at the diametrically opposite end of the town from the offices of the Court. This was an even poorer neighborhood, the houses were still darker, the streets filled with sludge oozing about slowly on top of the melting snow. In the tenement where the painter lived only one wing of the great double door stood open, and beneath the other wing, in the masonry near the ground, there was a gaping hole of which, just as K. approached, issued a disgusting yellow fluid, steaming hot, from which some rats fled into the adjoining canal. At the foot of the stairs an infant lay face down on the ground bawling, but one could scarcely hear its shrieks because of the deafening din that came from a tinsmith's workshop at the other side of the entry. The door of the workshop was open; three apprentices were standing in a half-circle round some object on which they were beating with their hammers. A great sheet of tin hanging on the wall cast a pallid light, which fell between two of the apprentices and lit up their faces and aprons. K. flung only a fleeting glance at all this, he wanted to finish off here as quickly as possible, he would merely ask the painter a few searching questions and return at once to the Bank. His work at the Bank for the rest of the day would benefit should he have any luck at all on this visit. When he reached the third floor he had to moderate his pace, he was quite out of breath, both the stairs and the stories were disproportionately high, and the painter was said to live quite at the top, in an attic. The air was stifling; there was no well for these narrow stairs, which were enclosed on either side by blank walls, showing only at rare intervals a tiny window very high up. Just as K. paused to take breath, several young girls rushed out of one of the flats and laughingly raced past him up the stairs. K. slowly followed them, catching up with one who had stumbled and been left behind, and as they ascended together he asked her: "Does a painter called Titorelli live here?" The girl, who was slightly hunchbacked and seemed scarcely thirteen years old, nudged him with her elbow and peered up at him knowingly. Neither her youth nor her deformity had saved her from being prematurely debauched. She did not even smile, but stared unwinkingly at K. with shrewd, bold eyes. K. pretended not to have noticed her behavior and asked: "Do you know the painter Titorelli?" She nodded and asked in her turn: "What do you want him for?" K. thought it a good chance to find out a little more about Titorelli while he still had time: "I want him to paint my portrait," he said. "To paint your portrait?" she repeated, letting her jaw fall open, then she gave K. a little slap as if he had said something extraordinarily unexpected or stupid, lifted her abbreviated skirts with both hands, and raced as fast as she could after the other girls, whose shrieks were already dying away in the distance. Yet at the very next turn of the stair K. ran into all of them. Obviously the hunchback had reported K.'s intention, and they were waiting there for him. They stood lined up on either side of the stairway, squeezing against the walls to leave room for K. to pass, and smoothing their skirts down with their hands. All their faces betrayed the same mixture of childishness and depravity which had prompted this idea of making him run the gauntlet between them. At the top end of the row of girls, who now closed in behind K. with spurts of laughter, stood the hunchback ready to lead the way. Thanks to her, he was able to make straight for the right door. He had intended to go on up the main stairs, but she indicated a side-stair that branched off toward Titorelli's dwelling. This stairway was extremely narrow, very long, without any turning, could thus be surveyed in all its length, and was abruptly terminated by Titorelli's door. In contrast to the rest of the stairway this door was relatively brightly lit by a little fan-light set on an angle above it, and was made of unpainted planks on which sprawled the name

Titorelli in red, traced in sweeping brush-strokes. K. with his escort was hardly more than halfway up the stairs when someone above, obviously disturbed by the clatter of so many feet, opened the door a little way, and a man who seemed to be wearing nothing but a nightshirt appeared in the opening. "Oh!" he cried when he saw the approaching mob, and promptly vanished. The hunchback clapped her hands in joy, and the other girls crowded K. from behind to urge him on faster.

Yet they were still mounting toward the top when the painter flung the door wide open and with a deep bow invited K. to enter. As for the girls, he turned them off, he would not admit one of them, eagerly as they implored and hard as they tried to enter by force if not by permission. The hunchback alone managed to slip in under his outstretched arm, but he rushed after her, seized her by the skirts, whirled her once round his head, and then set her down before the door among the other girls, who had not dared meanwhile, although he had quitted his post, to cross the threshold. K. did not know what to make of all this, for they seemed to be on the friendliest terms together. The girls outside the door, craning their necks behind one another, shouted various jocular remarks at the painter which K. did not understand, and the painter was laughing too as he almost hurled the hunchback through the air. Then he shut the door, bowed once more to K., held out his hand, and said in introduction: "I'm the painter Titorelli." K. pointed at the door, behind which the girls were whispering, and said: "You seem to be a great favorite here." "Oh, those brats!" said the painter, trying unsuccessfully to button his nightshirt at the neck. He was barefooted and besides the nightshirt had on only a pair of wide-legged yellow linen trousers girt by a belt with a long end flapping to and fro. "Those brats are a real nuisance," he went on, while he desisted from fiddling with his nightshirt—since the top button had just come off—fetched a chair, and urged K. to sit down. "I painted one of them once—not any of those you saw—and since then they've all persecuted me. When I'm here myself they only come in if I let them, but whenever I go away there's always at least one of them here. They've had a key made for my door, and they lend it round. You can hardly imagine what a nuisance that is. For instance, if I bring a lady here whom I want to paint, I unlock the door with my own key and find, say, the hunchback over there at the table, reddening her lips with my paint brushes, while her little sisters, whom she's supposed to keep an eye on, are scampering over the whole place and messing up every corner of the room. Or, and this actually happened last night, I come home very late—by the way, that's why I'm in this state of disrepair, and the room too, please excuse it—I come home late, then, and start climbing into bed and something catches me by the leg; I look under the bed and haul out another of these pests. Why they should make such a set at me I don't know, you must have noticed yourself that I don't exactly encourage them. And, of course, all this disturbs me in my work. If it hadn't been that I have free quarters in this studio I should have cleared out long ago." Just then a small voice piped behind the door with anxious cajolery: "Titorelli, can we come in now?" "No," replied the painter. "Not even me?" the voice asked again. "Not even you," said the painter, and he went to the door and locked it.

Meanwhile K. had been looking round the room; it would never have occurred to him that anyone could call this wretched little hole a studio. You could scarcely take two strides in any direction. The whole room, floor, walls, and ceiling, was a box of bare wooden planks with cracks showing between them. Opposite K., against a wall, stood a bed with a variegated assortment of coverings. In the middle of the room an easel supported a canvas covered by a shirt whose sleeves dangled on the floor. Behind K. was the window, through which in the fog one could not see farther than the snow-covered roof of the next house.

The turning of the key in the lock reminded K. that he had not meant to stay long. Accordingly he fished the manufacturer's letter from his pocket, handed it to the painter, and said: "I heard of you from this gentleman, an acquaintance of yours, and have come here at his suggestion." The painter hastily read the letter through and threw it on the bed. If the manufacturer had not so explicitly claimed acquaintance with Titorelli as a poor man dependent on his charity, one might actually have thought that Titorelli did not know the manufacturer or at least could not remember him. On top of this he now asked: "Have you come to buy pictures or to have your portrait painted?" K. stared at him in amazement. What could have been in the letter? He had assumed as a matter of course that the manufacturer would tell Titorelli that he had come for no other purpose than to inquire about his case. He had been altogether too rash and reckless in rushing to this man. But he must make a relevant reply of some kind, and so he said with a glance at the easel: "You're working on a painting just now?" "Yes," said Titorelli, stripping the shirt from the easel and throwing it on the bed after the letter. "It's a portrait. A good piece of work, but not quite finished yet." K. was apparently in luck, the opportunity to mention the Court was being literally thrown at his head, for this was obviously the portrait of a Judge. Also it strikingly resembled the portrait hanging in the lawyer's office. True, this was quite a different Judge, a stout man with a black bushy beard which reached far up on his cheeks on either side; moreover the other portrait was in oils, while this was lightly and indistinctly sketched in pastel. Yet everything else showed a close resemblance, for here too the Judge seemed to be on the point of rising menacingly from his high seat, bracing himself firmly on the arms of it. "That must be a Judge," K. felt like saying at once, but he checked himself for the time being and approached the picture as if he wished to study the detail. A large figure rising in the middle of the picture from the high back of the chair he could not identify, and he asked the painter whom it was intended to represent. It still needed more detail, the painter replied, and fetched a crayon from a table, armed with which he worked a little at the outline of the figure, but without making it any more recognizable to K. "It is Justice," said the painter at last. "Now I can recognize it," said K. "There's the bandage over the eyes, and here are the scales. But aren't there wings on the figure's heels, and isn't it flying?" "Yes," said the painter, "my instructions were to paint it like that; actually it is Justice and the goddess of Victory in one." "Not a very good combination, surely," said K., smiling. "Justice must stand quite still, or else the scales will waver and a just verdict will become impossible." "I had to follow my client's instructions," said the painter. "Of course," said K., who had not wished to give any offense by his remark. "You have painted the figure as it actually stands above the high seat." "No," said the painter, "I have neither seen the figure nor the high seat, that is all invention, but I am told what to paint and I paint it." "How do you mean?" asked K., deliberately pretending that he did not understand. "It's surely a Judge sitting on his seat of justice?" "Yes," said the painter, "but it is by no means a high Judge and he has never sat on such a seat in his life." "And yet he has himself painted in that solemn posture? Why, he sits there as if he were the actual President of the Court." "Yes, they're very vain, these gentlemen," said the painter. "But their superiors give them permission to get themselves painted like that. Each one of them gets precise instructions how he may have his portrait painted. Only you can't judge the detail of the costume and the seat itself from this picture, unfortunately, pastel is

really unsuited for this kind of thing." "Yes," said K., "it's
curious that you should have used pastel." "My client
wished it," said the painter, "he intends the picture for a
lady." The sight of the picture seemed to have roused his
ardor, he rolled up his shirt-sleeves, took several crayons in
his hand, and as K. watched the delicate crayon-strokes a
reddish shadow began to grow round the head of the Judge,
a shadow which tapered off in long rays as it approached
the edge of the picture. This play of shadow bit by bit surrounded the head like a halo or a high mark of distinction.
But the figure of Justice was left bright except for an almost
imperceptible touch of shadow; that brightness brought the
figure sweeping right into the foreground and it no longer
suggested the goddess of Justice, or even the goddess of
Victory, but looked exactly like a goddess of the Hunt in
full cry. The painter's activities absorbed K. against his will,
and in the end he began to reproach himself for having
stayed so long without even touching on the business that
brought him. "What is the name of this Judge?" he asked
suddenly. "I'm not allowed to tell," replied the painter,
stooping over the picture and ostentatiously ignoring the
guest whom at first he had greeted with such consideration.
K. put this down to caprice and was annoyed that his time
should be wasted in such a manner. "You're in the confidence of the Court, I take it?" he asked. The painter laid
down his crayons at once, straightened himself, rubbed his
hands, and looked at K. with a smile. "Come out with the
truth," he said. "You want to find out something about the
Court, as your letter of recommendation told me, I may say,
and you started talking about my paintings only to win me
over. But I don't take that ill, you could hardly know that
that wasn't the right way to tackle me. Oh, please don't
apologize!" he said sharply, as K. tried to make some excuse. And then he continued: "Besides, you were quite right
in what you said; I am in the confidence of the Court." He

paused, as if he wanted to give K. time to digest this fact.
Now they could hear the girls behind the door again. They
seemed to be crowding round the keyhole, perhaps they
could see into the room through the cracks in the door as
well. K. abandoned any attempt at apology, for he did not
want to deflect the conversation, nor did he want the painter
to feel too important, and so become in a sense inaccessible,
accordingly he asked: "Is your position an official appointment?" "No," said the painter curtly, as if the question had
cut him short. K., being anxious to keep him going, said:
"Well, such unrecognized posts often carry more influence
with them than the official ones." "That is just how it is
with me," said the painter, knitting his brow and nodding.
"The manufacturer mentioned your case to me yesterday,
he asked me if I wouldn't help you; I said to him: 'Let the
man come and see me some time,' and I'm delighted to see
you here so soon. The case seems to lie very near your heart,
which, of course, is not in the least surprising. Won't you
take off your coat for a moment?" Although K. had it in
mind to stay only for a short time, this request was very
welcome to him. He had begun to feel the air in the room
stifling, several times already he had eyed with amazement
a little iron stove in the corner which did not seem even to
be working; the sultry heat in the place was inexplicable.
He took off his overcoat, unbuttoning his jacket as well, and
the painter said apologetically: "I must have warmth. It's
very cozy in here, isn't it? I'm well enough off in that respect." K. said nothing to this, for it was not the warmth
that made him so uncomfortable, it was rather the stuffy,
oppressive atmosphere; the room could not have been aired
for a long time. His discomfort was still more intensified
when the painter begged him to sit down on the bed, while
he himself took the only chair in the room, which stood
beside the easel. Titorelli also seemed to misunderstand K.'s
reasons for sitting on the extreme edge of the bed, he urged

him to make himself comfortable and actually pushed the reluctant K. deep down among the bedclothes and pillows. Then he returned to his chair again and at last put his first serious question, which made K. forget everything else. "Are you innocent?" he asked. "Yes," said K. The answering of this question gave him a feeling of real pleasure, particularly as he was addressing a private individual and therefore need fear no consequences. Nobody else had yet asked him such a frank question. To savor his elation to the full, he added: "I am completely innocent." "I see," said the painter, bending his head as if in thought. Suddenly he raised it again and said: "If you are innocent, then the matter is quite simple." K.'s eyes darkened, this man who said he was in the confidence of the Court was talking like an ignorant child. "My innocence doesn't make the matter any simpler," said K. But after all he could not help smiling, and then he slowly shook his head. "I have to fight against countless subtleties in which the Court indulges. And in the end, out of nothing at all, an enormous fabric of guilt will be conjured up." "Yes, yes, of course," said the painter, as if K. were needlessly interrupting the thread of his ideas. "But you're innocent all the same?" "Why, yes," said K. "That's the main thing," said the painter. He was not to be moved by argument, yet in spite of his decisiveness it was not clear whether he spoke out of conviction or out of mere indifference. K. wanted first to be sure of this, so he said: "You know the Court much better than I do, I feel certain, I don't know much more about it than what I've heard from all sorts and conditions of people. But they all agree on one thing, that charges are never made frivolously, and that the Court, once it has brought a charge against someone, is firmly convinced of the guilt of the accused and can be dislodged from that conviction only with the greatest difficulty." "The greatest difficulty?" cried the painter, flinging one hand in the air. "The Court can never be dislodged from that conviction. If I were to paint all the Judges in a row on one canvas and you were to plead your case before it, you would have more hope of success than before the actual Court." "I see," said K. to himself, forgetting that he merely wished to pump the painter.

Again a girl's voice piped from behind the door: "Tito-relli, won't he be going away soon now?" "Quiet, there!" cried the painter over his shoulder. "Can't you see that I'm engaged with this gentleman?" But the girl, not to be put off, asked: "Are you going to paint him?" And when the painter did not reply she went on: "Please don't paint him, such an ugly man as that." The others yelled agreement in a confused jabbering. The painter made a leap for the door, opened it a little—K. could see the imploring, outstretched, clasped hands of the girls—and said: "If you don't stop that noise I'll fling you all down the stairs. Sit down here on the steps and see that you keep quiet." Apparently they did not obey him at once, for he had to shout in an imperious voice: "Down with you on the steps!" After that all was still.

"Excuse me," said the painter, returning to K. again. K. had scarcely glanced toward the door, he had left it to the painter to decide whether and in what manner he was to be protected. Even now he scarcely made a movement when the painter bent down to him and whispered in his ear, so that the girls outside might not hear: "These girls belong to the Court too." "What?" cried K., screwing his head round to stare at the painter. But Titorelli sat down again on his chair and said half in jest, half in explanation: "You see, everything belongs to the Court." "That's something I hadn't noticed," said K. shortly; the painter's general statement stripped his remark about the girls of all its disturbing significance. Yet K. sat gazing for some time at the door, behind which the girls were now sitting quietly on the stairs. One of them had thrust a blade of straw through a crack between the planks and was moving it slowly up and down.

"You don't seem to have any general idea of the Court yet," said the painter, stretching his legs wide in front of him and tapping with his shoes on the floor. "But since you're innocent you won't need it anyhow. I shall get you off all by myself." "How can you do that?" asked K. "For you told me yourself a few minutes ago that the Court was quite impervious to proof." "Impervious only to proof which one brings before the Court," said the painter, raising one finger as if K. had failed to perceive a fine distinction. "But it is quite a different matter with one's efforts behind the scenes; that is, in the consulting-rooms, in the lobbies or, for example, in this very studio." What the painter now said no longer seemed incredible to K., indeed it agreed in the main with what he had heard from other people. More, it was actually hopeful in a high degree. If a judge could really be so easily influenced by personal connections as the lawyer insisted, then the painter's connections with these vain functionaries were especially important and certainly not to be undervalued. That made the painter an excellent recruit to the ring of helpers which K. was gradually gathering round him. His talent for organization had once been highly praised in the Bank, and now that he had to act entirely on his own responsibility this was his chance to prove it to the uttermost. Titorelli observed the effect his words had produced upon K. and then said with a slight uneasiness: "Perhaps it strikes you that I talk almost like a jurist? It's my uninterrupted association with the gentlemen of the Court that has made me grow like that. I have many advantages from it, of course, but I'm losing a great deal of my *élan* as an artist." "How did you come in contact with the Judges to begin with?" asked K.; he wanted to win the painter's confidence first, before actually enlisting him in his service. "That was quite simple," said the painter. "I inherited the connection. My father was the Court painter before me. It's a hereditary post. New people are of no use for it. There are so many complicated and various and above all secret rules laid down for the painting of the different grades of functionaries that a knowledge of them is confined to certain families. Over there in that drawer, for instance, I keep all my father's drawings, which I never show to anyone. And only a man who has studied them can possibly paint the Judges. Yet even if I were to lose them, I have enough rules tucked away in my head to make my post secure against all comers. For every Judge insists on being painted as the great old Judges were painted, and nobody can do that but me." "Yours is an enviable situation," said K., who was thinking of his own post in the Bank. "So your position is unassailable?" "Yes, unassailable," replied the painter, proudly bracing his shoulders. "And for that reason, too, I can venture to help a poor man with his trial now and then." "And how do you do it?" asked K., as if it were not himself who had just been described as a poor man. But Titorelli refused to be sidetracked and went on: "In your case, for instance, as you are completely innocent, this is the line I shall take." The repeated mention of his innocence was already making K. impatient. At moments it seemed to him as if the painter were offering his help on the assumption that the trial would turn out well, which made his offer worthless. But in spite of his doubts K. held his tongue and did not interrupt the man. He was not prepared to renounce Titorelli's assistance, on that point he was decided; the painter was no more questionable as an ally than the lawyer. Indeed he very much preferred the painter's offer of assistance, since it was made so much more ingenuously and frankly.

Titorelli drew his chair closer to the bed and continued in a low voice: "I forgot to ask you first what sort of acquittal you want. There are three possibilities, that is, definite acquittal, ostensible acquittal, and indefinite postponement. Definite acquittal is, of course, the best, but I haven't the slightest influence on that kind of verdict. As far as I know, there is no single person who could influence the verdict of definite acquittal. The only deciding factor seems to be the innocence of the accused. Since you're innocent, of course it would be possible for you to ground your case on your innocence alone. But then you would require neither my help nor help from anyone."

This lucid explanation took K. aback at first, but he replied in the same subdued voice as the painter: "It seems to me that you're contradicting yourself." "In what way?" asked the painter patiently, leaning back with a smile. The smile awoke in K. a suspicion that he was now about to expose contradictions not so much in the painter's statements as in the Court procedure itself. However, he did not retreat, but went on: "You made the assertion earlier that the Court is impervious to proof, later you qualified that assertion by confining it to the public sessions of the Court, and now you actually say that an innocent man requires no help before the Court. That alone implies a contradiction. But, in addition, you said at first that the Judges can be moved by personal intervention, and now you deny that definite acquittal, as you call it, can ever be achieved by personal intervention. In that lies the second contradiction." "These contradictions are easy to explain," said the painter. "We must distinguish between two things: what is written in the Law, and what I have discovered through personal experience; you must not confuse the two. In the code of the Law, which admittedly I have not read, it is of course laid down on the one hand that the innocent shall be acquitted, but it is not stated on the other hand that the Judges are open to influence. Now, my experience is diametrically opposed to that. I have not met one case of definite acquittal, and I have met many cases of influential intervention. It is possible, of course, that in all the cases known to me there was none in which the accused was really innocent. But is not that improbable? Among so many cases no single case of innocence? Even as a child I used to listen carefully to my father when he spoke of cases he had heard about; the Judges, too, who came to his studio were always telling stories about the Court, in our circle it is in fact the sole topic of discussion; no sooner did I get the chance to attend the Court myself than I took full advantage of it; I have listened to countless cases in their most crucial stages, and followed them as far as they could be followed, and yet—I must admit it—I have never encountered one case of definite acquittal." "Not one case of acquittal, then," said K. as if he were speaking to himself and his hopes, "but that merely confirms the opinion that I have already formed of this Court. It is a pointless institution from any point of view. A single executioner could do all that is needed." "You mustn't generalize," said the painter in displeasure. "I have only quoted my own experience." "That's quite enough," said K. "Or have you ever heard of acquittals in earlier times?" "Such acquittals," replied the painter, "are said to have occurred. Only it is very difficult to prove the fact. The final decisions of the Court are never recorded, even the Judges can't get hold of them, consequently we have only legendary accounts of ancient cases. These legends certainly provide instances of acquittal; actually the majority of them are about acquittals, they can be believed, but they cannot be proved. All the same, they shouldn't be entirely left out of account, they must have an element of truth in them, and besides they are very beautiful. I myself have painted several pictures founded on such legends." "Mere legends cannot alter my opinion," said K., "and I fancy that one cannot appeal to such legends before the Court?" The painter laughed. "No, one can't do that," he said. "Then there's no use talking about them," said K., willing for the time being to accept the painter's opinions, even where they seemed improbable or contradicted other reports he had heard. He had no time now to inquire into the truth of all the painter said, much less contradict it, the utmost he could hope to do was to get the man to help him in some way, even should the help prove inconclusive. Accordingly he said: "Let us leave definite acquittal out of account, then; you mentioned two other possibilities as well." "Ostensible acquittal and postponement. These are the only possibilities," said the painter. "But won't you take off your jacket before we go on to speak of them? You look very hot." "Yes," said K., who had been paying no attention to anything but the painter's expositions, but now that he was reminded of the heat found his forehead drenched in sweat. "It's almost unbearable." The painter nodded as if he comprehended K.'s discomfort quite well. "Couldn't we open the window?" asked K. "No," replied the painter. "It's only a sheet of glass let into the roof, it can't be opened." Now K. realized that he had been hoping all the time that either the painter or he himself would suddenly go over to the window and fling it open. He was prepared to gulp down even mouthfuls of fog if he could only get air. The feeling of being completely cut off from the fresh air made his head swim. He brought the flat of his hand down on the feather bed and said in a feeble voice: "That's both uncomfortable and unhealthy." "Oh, no," said the painter in defense of his window. "Because it's hermetically sealed it keeps the warmth in much better than a double window, though it's only a simple pane of glass. And if I want to air the place, which isn't really necessary, for the air comes in everywhere through the chinks, I can always open one of the doors or even both of them." Somewhat reassured by this explanation, K. glanced round to discover the second door. The painter saw what he was doing and said: "It's behind you, I had to block it up by putting the bed in front of it." Only now did K. see the little door in the wall. "This is really too small for a studio," said the painter, as if to forestall K.'s criticisms. "I had to manage as best I could. Of course it's a bad place for a bed, just in front of that door. The Judge whom I'm painting just now, for instance, always comes in by that door, and I've had to give him a key for it so that he can wait for me in the studio if I happen to be out. Well, he usually arrives early in the morning, while I'm still asleep. And of course however fast asleep I am, it wakes me with a start when the door behind my bed suddenly opens. You would lose any respect you have for the Judges if you could hear the curses that welcome him when he climbs over my bed in the early morning. I could certainly take the key away from him again, but that would only make things worse. It is easy enough to burst open any of the doors here." All during these exchanges K. kept considering whether he should take off his jacket, but at last he realized that if he did not he would be incapable of staying any longer in the room, so he took it off, laying it, however, across his knee, to save time in putting it on again whenever the interview was finished. Scarcely had he taken off his jacket when one of the girls cried: "He's taken off his jacket now," and he could hear them all crowding to peer through the cracks and view the spectacle for themselves. "The girls think," said the painter, "that I'm going to paint your portrait and that's why you are taking off your jacket." "I see," said K., very little amused, for he did not feel much better than before, although he was now sitting in his shirt-sleeves. Almost morosely he asked: "What did you say the other two possibilities were?" He had already forgotten what they were called. "Ostensible acquittal and indefinite postponement," said the painter. "It lies with you to choose between them. I can help you to either of them, though not without taking some trouble, and, as far as that is concerned, the difference between them is that ostensible acquittal demands temporary concentration, while postponement taxes your strength

less but means a steady strain. First, then, let us take
ostensible acquittal. If you decide on that, I shall write
down on a sheet of paper an affidavit of your innocence.
The text for such an affidavit has been handed down to me
by my father and is unassailable. Then with this affidavit I
shall make a round of the Judges I know, beginning, let us
say, with the Judge I am painting now, when he comes for
his sitting tonight. I shall lay the affidavit before him,
explain to him that you are innocent, and guarantee your
innocence myself. And that is not merely a formal guarantee
but a real and binding one." In the eyes of the painter there
was a faint suggestion of reproach that K. should lay upon
him the burden of such a responsibility. "That would be
very kind of you," said K. "And the Judge would believe
you and yet not give me a definite acquittal?" "As I have
already explained," replied the painter. "Besides, it is not in
the least certain that every Judge will believe me; some
Judges, for instance, will ask to see you in person. And then
I should have to take you with me to call on them. Though
when that happens the battle is already half won, particularly as I should tell you beforehand, of course, exactly
what line to take with each Judge. The real difficulty comes
with the Judges who turn me away at the start—and that's
sure to happen too. I shall go on petitioning them, of
course, but we shall have to do without them, though one
can afford to do that, since dissent by individual Judges
cannot affect the result. Well then, if I get a sufficient
number of Judges to subscribe to the affidavit, I shall then
deliver it to the Judge who is actually conducting your trial.
Possibly I may have secured his signature too, then everything will be settled fairly soon, a little sooner than usual.
Generally speaking, there should be no difficulties worth
mentioning after that, the accused at this stage feels su-
premely confident. Indeed it's remarkable, but true, that
people's confidence mounts higher at this stage than after

their acquittal. There's no need for them to do much more. The Judge is covered by the guarantees of the other Judges subscribing to the affidavit, and so he can grant an acquittal with an easy mind, and though some formalities will remain to be settled, he will undoubtedly grant the acquittal to please me and his other friends. Then you can walk out of the Court a free man." "So then I'm free," said K. doubtfully. "Yes," said the painter, "but only ostensibly free, or more exactly, provisionally free. For the Judges of the lowest grade, to whom my acquaintances belong, haven't the power to grant a final acquittal, that power is reserved for the highest Court of all, which is quite inaccessible to you, to me, and to all of us. What the prospects are up there we do not know and, I may say in passing, do not even want to know. The great privilege, then, of absolving from guilt our Judges do not possess, but they do have the right to take the burden of the charge off your shoulders. That is to say, when you are acquitted in this fashion the charge is lifted from your shoulders for the time being, but it continues to hover above you and can, as soon as an order comes from on high, be laid upon you again. As my connection with the Court is such a close one, I can also tell you how in the regulations of the Law Court offices the distinction between definite and ostensible acquittal is made manifest. In definite acquittal the documents relating to the case are said to be completely annulled, they simply vanish from sight, not only the charge but also the records of the case and even the acquittal are destroyed, everything is destroyed. That's not the case with ostensible acquittal. The documents remain as they were, except the affidavit is added to them and a record of the acquittal and the grounds for granting it. The whole dossier continues to circulate, as the regular official routine demands, passing on to the higher Courts, being referred to the lower ones again, and thus swinging backwards and forwards with greater or smaller oscillations, longer or shorter delays. These peregrinations are incalculable. A detached observer might sometimes fancy that the whole case had been forgotten, the documents lost, and the acquittal made absolute. No one really acquainted with the Court could think such a thing. No document is ever lost, the Court never forgets anything. One day—quite unexpectedly—some Judge will take up the documents and look at them attentively, recognize that in this case the charge is still valid, and order an immediate arrest. I have been speaking on the assumption that a long time elapses between the ostensible acquittal and the new arrest; that is possible and I have known of such cases, but it is just as possible for the acquitted man to go straight home from the Court and find officers already waiting to arrest him again. Then, of course, all his freedom is at an end." "And the case begins all over again?" asked K. almost incredulously. "Certainly," said the painter. "The case begins all over again, but again it is possible, just as before, to secure an ostensible acquittal. One must again apply all one's energies to the case and never give in." These last words were probably uttered because he noticed that K. was looking somewhat collapsed. "But," said K., as if he wanted to forestall any more revelations, "isn't the engineering of a second acquittal more difficult than the first?" "On that point," said the painter, "one can say nothing with certainty. You mean, I take it, that the second arrest might influence the Judges against the accused? That is not so. Even while they are pronouncing the first acquittal the Judges foresee the possibility of the new arrest. Such a consideration, therefore, hardly comes into question. But it may happen, for hundreds of reasons, that the Judges are in a different frame of mind about the case, even from a legal viewpoint, and one's efforts to obtain a second acquittal must consequently be adapted to the changed circumstances, and in general must be every whit as energetic as those that secured the first one." "But this second acquittal isn't final either," said K., turning away his head in repudiation. "Of course not," said the painter. "The second acquittal is followed by the third arrest, the third acquittal by the fourth arrest, and so on. That is implied in the very conception of ostensible acquittal." K. said nothing. "Ostensible acquittal doesn't seem to appeal to you," said the painter. "Perhaps postponement would suit you better. Shall I explain to you how postponement works?" K. nodded. The painter was lolling back in his chair, his nightshirt gaped open, he had thrust one hand inside it and was lightly fingering his breast. "Postponement," he said, gazing in front of him for a moment as if seeking a completely accurate explanation, "postponement consists in preventing the case from ever getting any further than its first stages. To achieve that it is necessary for the accused and his agent, but more particularly his agent, to remain continuously in personal touch with the Court. Let me point out again that this does not demand such intense concentration of one's energies as an ostensible acquittal, yet on the other hand it does require far greater vigilance. You daren't let the case out of your sight, you visit the Judge at regular intervals as well as in emergencies and must do all that is in your power to keep him friendly; if you don't know the Judge personally, then you must try to influence him through other Judges whom you do know, but without giving up your efforts to secure a personal interview. If you neglect none of these things, then you can assume with fair certainty that the case will never pass beyond its first stages. Not that the proceedings are quashed, but the accused is almost as likely to escape sentence as if he were free. As against ostensible acquittal postponement has this advantage, that the future of the accused is less uncertain, he is secured from the terrors of sudden arrest and doesn't need to fear having to undergo—perhaps at a most inconvenient moment—the

strain and agitation which are inevitable in the achievement
of ostensible acquittal. Though postponement, too, has cer-
tan drawbacks for the accused, and these must not be mini-
mized. In saying this I am not thinking of the fact that the
accused is never free; he isn't free either, in any real sense,
after the ostensible acquittal. There are other drawbacks.
The case can't be held up indefinitely without at least some
plausible grounds being provided. So as a matter of form a
certain activity must be shown from time to time, various
measures have to be taken, the accused is questioned, evidence is collected, and so on. For the case must be kept
going all the time, although only in the small circle to which
it has been artificially restricted. This naturally involves the
accused in occasional unpleasantness, but you must not
think of it as being too unpleasant. For it's all a formality,
the interrogations, for instance, are only short ones; if you
have neither the time nor the inclination to go, you can
excuse yourself; with some Judges you can even plan your
interviews a long time ahead, all that it amounts to is a
formal recognition of your status as an accused man by
regular appearances before your Judge." Already while
these last words were being spoken K. had taken his jacket
across his arm and got up. "He's getting up now," came the
cry at once from behind the door. "Are you going already?"
asked the painter, who had also got up. "I'm sure it's the
air here that is driving you away. I'm sorry about it. I had
a great deal more to tell you. I have had to express myself
very briefly. But I hope my statements were lucid enough."
"Oh, yes," said K., whose head was aching with the strain
of forcing himself to listen. In spite of K.'s confirmation, the
painter went on to sum up the matter again, as if to give
him a last word of comfort: "Both methods have this in
common, that they prevent the accused from coming up
for sentence." "But they also prevent an actual acquittal,"
said K. in a low voice, as if embarrassed by his own per-

spicacity. "You have grasped the kernel of the matter," said the painter quickly. K. laid his hand on his overcoat, but could not even summon the resolution to put on his jacket. He would have liked best of all to bundle them both together and rush out with them into the fresh air. Even the thought of the girls could not move him to put on his garments, although their voices were already piping the premature news that he was doing so. The painter was anxious to guess K.'s intentions, so he said: "I take it that you haven't come to any decision yet on my suggestions. That's right. In fact, I should have advised you against it had you attempted an immediate decision. It's like splitting hairs to distinguish the advantages and disadvantages. You must weigh everything very carefully. On the other hand you mustn't lose too much time either." "I'll come back again soon," said K., in a sudden fit of resolution putting on his jacket, flinging his overcoat across his shoulders, and hastening to the door, behind which the girls at once began shrieking. K. felt he could almost see them through the door. "But you must keep your word," said the painter, who had not followed him, "or else I'll have to come to the Bank myself to make inquiries." "Unlock this door, will you?" said K., tugging at the handle, which the girls, as he could tell from the resistance, were hanging on to from outside. "You don't want to be bothered by the girls, do you?" asked the painter. "You had better take this way out," and he indicated the door behind the bed. K. was perfectly willing and rushed back to the bed. But instead of opening the bedside door the painter crawled right under the bed and said from down there: "Wait just a minute. Wouldn't you like to see a picture or two that you might care to buy?" K. did not want to be discourteous, the painter had really taken an interest in him and promised to help him further, also it was entirely owing to K.'s distractedness that the matter of a fee for the painter's services had not been

mentioned, consequently he could not turn aside his offer
now, and so he consented to look at the pictures, though
he was trembling with impatience to be out of the place.
Titorelli dragged a pile of unframed canvases from under
the bed; they were so thickly covered with dust that when
he blew some of it from the topmost, K. was almost blinded
and choked by the cloud that flew up. "Wild Nature, a
heathscape," said the painter, handing K. the picture. It
showed two stunted trees standing far apart from each
other in darkish grass. In the background was a many-hued
sunset. "Fine," said K., "I'll buy it." K.'s curtness had been
unthinking and so he was glad when the painter, instead of
being offended, lifted another canvas from the floor. "Here's
the companion picture," he said. It might be intended as a
companion picture, but there was not the slightest difference that one could see between it and the other, here were
the two trees, here the grass, and there the sunset. But K.
did not bother about that. "They're fine prospects," he said.
"I'll buy both of them and hang them up in my office."
"You seem to like the subject," said the painter, fishing out
a third canvas. "By a lucky chance I have another of these
studies here." But it was not merely a similar study, it was
simply the same wild heathscape again. The painter was
apparently exploiting to the full this opportunity to sell off
his old pictures. "I'll take that one as well," said K. "How
much for the three pictures?" "We'll settle that next time,"
said the painter. "You're in a hurry today and we're going
to keep in touch with each other anyhow. I may say I'm
very glad you like these pictures and I'll throw in all the
others under the bed as well. They're heathscapes every
one of them, I've painted dozens of them in my time. Some
people won't have anything to do with these subjects because they're too somber, but there are always people like
yourself who prefer somber pictures." But by now K. had
no mind to listen to the professional pronouncements of the

peddling painter. "Wrap the pictures up," he cried, interrupting Titorelli's garrulity, "my attendant will call tomorrow and fetch them." "That isn't necessary," said the
painter. "I think I can manage to get you a porter to take
them along with you now." And at last he reached over the
bed and unlocked the door. "Don't be afraid to step on the
bed," he said. "Everybody who comes here does that." K.
would not have hesitated to do it even without his invitation, he had actually set one foot plump on the middle of
the feather bed, but when he looked out through the open
door he drew his foot back again. "What's this?" he asked
the painter. "What are you surprised at?" returned the
painter, surprised in his turn. "These are the Law Court
offices. Didn't you know that there were Law Court offices
here? There are Law Court offices in almost every attic,
why should this be an exception? My studio really belongs
to the Law Court offices, but the Court has put it at my
disposal." It was not so much the discovery of the Law
Court offices that startled K.; he was much more startled at
himself, at his complete ignorance of all things concerning
the Court. He accepted it as a fundamental principle for an
accused man to be always forearmed, never to let himself
be caught napping, never to let his eyes stray unthinkingly
to the right when his judge was looming up on the left—
and against that very principle he kept offending again and
again. Before him stretched a long passage, from which was
wafted an air compared to which the air in the studio was
refreshing. Benches stood on either side of the passage,
just as in the lobby of the offices that were handling K.'s
case. There seemed, then, to be exact regulations for the
interior disposition of these offices. At the moment there
was no great coming and going of clients. A man was half
sitting, half reclining on a bench, his face was buried in
his arms and he seemed to be asleep; another man was
standing in the dusk at the end of the passage. K. now

stepped over the bed, the painter following him with the pictures. They soon found an usher—by this time K. recognized these men from the gold button added to the buttons on their ordinary civilian clothing—and the painter gave him instructions to accompany K. with the pictures. K. tottered rather than walked, keeping his handkerchief pressed to his mouth. They had almost reached the exit when the girls came rushing to meet them, so K. had not been spared even that encounter. The girls had obviously seen the second door of the studio opening and had made a detour at full speed, in order to get in. "I can't escort you any farther," cried the painter laughingly, as the girls surrounded him. "Till our next meeting. And don't take too long to think it over!" K. did not even look back. When he reached the street he hailed the first cab that came along. He must get rid of the usher, whose gold button offended his eyes, even though, likely enough, it escaped everyone else's attention. The usher, zealously dutiful, got up beside the coachman on the box, but K. made him get down again. Midday was long past when K. reached the Bank. He would have liked to leave the pictures in the cab, but was afraid that some day he might be required to recall himself to the painter by their means. So he had them carried into his office and locked them in the bottom drawer of his desk, to save them for the next few days at least from the eyes of the Assistant Manager.

CHAPTER EIGHT

Block, the Tradesman · Dismissal of the Lawyer

AT LONG last K. had made up his mind to take his case out of the lawyer's hands. He could not quite rid himself of doubts about the wisdom of this step, but his conviction of its necessity prevailed. To screw himself up to the decision cost him a lot of energy, on the day when he resolved to visit the lawyer his work lagged behind, he had to stay very late in the office, and so he did not reach the lawyer's door until well past ten o'clock. Before actually ringing the bell he thought it over once again; it might be better to dismiss the lawyer by telephone or by letter, a personal interview was bound to prove painful. Still, he did not want to lose the advantage of a personal interview, any other mode of dismissal would be accepted in silence or with a few formal words of acknowledgment, and unless he were to extract information from Leni he would never learn how the lawyer had reacted to the dismissal and what consequences for himself were likely to ensue according to the lawyer's opinion, which was not entirely negligible. Face to face with the lawyer, one could spring the dismissal on him as a surprise, and however guarded the man might be, K. would be easily able to learn from his demeanor all that he wanted to know. It was even possible that he might perceive the wisdom of leaving the case in the lawyer's hands after all and might withdraw his ultimatum.

The first ring at the lawyer's door produced, as usual, no result. Leni could be a little quicker, thought K. But it was enough to be thankful for that no third party had come nosing in, as usually happened, the man in the dressing-gown, for instance, or some other interfering creature. K. glanced at the farther door as he pressed the button a second time, but on this occasion both doors remained firmly shut. At last a pair of eyes appeared at the peephole in the lawyer's door, but they were not Leni's eyes. Someone shot back the bolt, but still blocked the way as a preliminary measure, calling back into the house: "It's him," and only then flinging the door open. K. had been pushing against the door, for he could already hear a key being hastily turned in the neighboring lock, and when it suddenly opened he was literally precipitated into the hall and caught a glimpse of Leni, for whom the warning cry must have been intended, rushing down the lobby in her shift. He peered after her for a moment and then turned to see who had opened the door. It was a dried-up little man with a long beard, he was holding a candle in one hand. "Are you employed here?" asked K. "No," said the man, "I don't belong to the house, I'm only the lawyer's client, I've come here on business." "In your shirt-sleeves?" asked K., indicating the man's inadequate attire. "Oh, excuse me," said the man, peering at himself by the light of the candle as if he had been unaware of his condition. "Is Leni your mistress?" inquired K. curtly. He was straddling his legs slightly, his hands, in which he was holding his hat, clasped behind his back. The mere possession of a thick greatcoat gave him a feeling of superiority over the meager little fellow. "Oh, God," said the other, raising one hand before his face in horrified repudiation, "no, no, what are you thinking of?" "You look an honest man," said K., smiling, "but all the same—come along." He waved him on with his hat, urging him to go first. "What's your name?" K. asked as they were proceeding. "Block, a tradesman," said the little man, turning round to introduce himself, but K. would not suffer him to remain standing. "Is that your real name?" went on K. "Of course," came the answer, "why should you doubt it?" "I thought you might have some reason for concealing your name," said K. He was feeling at ease now, at ease as one is when speaking to an inferior in some foreign country, keeping one's own affairs to oneself and discussing with equanimity the other man's interests, which gain consequence for the attention one bestows on them yet can be dismissed at will. As they came to the lawyer's study K. halted, opened the door, and called to the fellow, who was meekly advancing along the lobby: "Not so fast, show a light here." K. fancied that Leni might have hidden herself in the study; he made the tradesman shine the candle into all the corners, but the room was empty. In front of the Judge's portrait K. caught the fellow from behind by the braces and pulled him back. "Do you know who that is?" he asked, pointing upward at the picture. The man raised the candle, blinked up at the picture, and said: "It's a Judge." "A high Judge?" asked K., stationing himself beside the other to observe what impression the portrait made on him. The man gazed up with reverence. "It is a high Judge," he said. "You haven't much insight," said K., "that's the lowest of the low among the examining Judges." "Now I remember," said the man, letting the candle sink. "I've been told that before." "But of course," cried K., "how could I forget, of course you must have heard it before." "But why,

why must I?" asked the man, moving toward the door, for
K. was propelling him from behind. When they were out in
the lobby, K. said: "I suppose you know where Leni's hiding?" "Hiding?" said he. "No, she should be in the kitchen
making soup for the lawyer." "Why didn't you tell me that
at first?" asked K. "I was going to take you there, but you
called me back," answered the man, as if bewildered by
these contradictory demands. "You fancy you're being very
sly," said K., "lead the way then!" K. had never yet been in
the kitchen, and it was surprisingly large and well furnished.
The cooking-stove alone was three times the size of an
ordinary stove; the rest of the fittings could not be seen in
detail since the sole light came from a small lamp hanging
near the door. Leni was standing by the stove in a white
apron, as usual, emptying eggs into a pan that stood over an
alcohol flame. "Good evening, Joseph," she said, glancing
over her shoulder. "Good evening," said K., waving the
tradesman to a chair some distance away, on which the man
obediently sat down. Then K. went quite close up behind
Leni, leaned over her shoulder, and asked: "Who's this
man?" Leni put her disengaged arm round K., stirring the
soup with the other, and pulled him forward. "He's a miserable creature," she said, "a poor tradesman called Block.
Just look at him." They both glanced round. The tradesman
was sitting in the chair K. had indicated for him; having
blown out the candle, which was no longer needed, he was
snuffing the wick with his fingers. "You were in your shift,"
said K., turning Leni's head forcibly to the stove. She made
no answer. "Is he your lover?" asked K. She reached for the
soup pan, but K. imprisoned both her hands and said: "Give
me an answer!" She said: "Come into the study and I'll
explain everything." "No," said K., "I want you to tell me
here." She slipped her arm into his and tried to give him a
kiss, but K. fended her off, saying: "I don't want you to kiss
me now." "Joseph," said Leni, gazing at him imploringly and

yet frankly, "surely you're not jealous of Herr Block?" Then
she turned to the tradesman and said: "Rudi, come to the
rescue, you can see that I'm under suspicion, put that
candle down." One might have thought that he had been
paying no attention, but he knew at once what she meant.
"I can't think what you have to be jealous about either," he
said, with no great acumen. "Nor can I, really," replied K.,
regarding him with a smile. Leni laughed outright and
profited by K.'s momentary distraction to hook herself on to
his arm, whispering: "Leave him alone now, you can see the
kind of creature he is. I've shown him a little kindness because he's one of the lawyer's best clients, but that was the
only reason. What about yourself? Do you want to see the
lawyer tonight? He's far from well today; all the same, if
you like I'll tell him you're here. But you're certainly going
to spend the night with me. It's such a long time since you
were here last, even the lawyer has been asking after you.
It won't do to neglect your case! And I've got some information for you, too, things I've found out. But the first thing
is to get your coat off." She helped him out of his coat, took
his hat from him, ran into the hall to hang them up, and
then ran back to keep an eye on the soup. "Shall I announce you first or give him his soup first?" "Announce me
first," said K. He felt irritated, for he had originally intended
to discuss the whole case thoroughly with Leni, especially
the question of dismissing the lawyer, and the tradesman's
being there spoiled the situation. But again it struck him
that his affairs were too important to allow of decisive inter-
ference by a petty tradesman, and so he called back Leni,
who was already out in the lobby. "No, let him have his
soup first," he said, "it'll strengthen him for his interview
with me, and he'll need it." "So you're one of the lawyer's
clients too," said the tradesman quietly from his corner, as
if confirming a statement. His comment was but ill received.
"What's that got to do with you?" said K., and Leni put in:

"You be quiet." To K. Leni said: "Well, then, I'll take him his soup first," and she poured the soup into a bowl. "Only there's a risk that he might go to sleep immediately, he always falls asleep after food." "What I have to say to him will keep him awake all right," said K., who wanted to let it be known that his interview with the lawyer promised to be momentous; he wanted Leni to question him about it and only then would he ask her advice. But Leni merely followed out to the letter the orders he gave her. As she passed him with the bowl of soup she deliberately nudged him and whispered: "I'll announce you the minute he's finished his soup, so that I can have you back as soon as possible." "Get along," said K., "get along with you." "Don't be so cross," she said, turning right round in the doorway, soup bowl and all.

K. stood gazing after her; now it was definitely settled that he would dismiss the lawyer, and it was just as well that he should have no chance of discussing it beforehand with Leni; the whole affair was rather beyond her scope and she would certainly have tried to dissuade him, possibly she might even have prevailed on him to put it off this time, and he would have continued to be a prey to doubts and fears until in the long run he carried out his resolve, since it was too imperative a resolve to be dropped. But the sooner it was carried out the less he would suffer. Perhaps, after all, the tradesman might be able to throw some light on the subject.

K. turned toward the man, who immediately gave a start as if to jump to his feet. "Keep your seat," said K., drawing a chair up beside him. "You're an old client of the lawyer's, aren't you?" "Yes," said the tradesman, "a very old client." "How long has he been in charge of your affairs?" asked K. "I don't quite know what affairs you mean," said the tradesman; "in my business affairs—I'm a grain dealer—the lawyer has been my representative since the very beginning, that must be for the past twenty years, and in my private case, which is probably what you are thinking of, he has been my lawyer also from the beginning, which is more than five years ago. Yes, well over five years now," he confirmed, drawing out an old wallet. "I have it all written down here. I can give you the exact dates if you like. It's difficult to keep them in one's head. My case probably goes back further than I said, it began just after my wife's death, certainly more than five and a half years ago." K. moved his chair closer to the man. "So the lawyer has an ordinary practice as well?" he asked. This alliance between Court and jurisprudence seemed to him uncommonly reassuring. "Of course," said the tradesman, adding in a whisper: "They even say that he's better at ordinary law than at the other kind." Then apparently he regretted having ventured so far, for he laid a hand on K.'s shoulder and said: "Don't give me away, I implore you." K. patted him soothingly on the thigh and said: "No, I'm not an informer." "He's vindictive, you see," said Block. "Surely he wouldn't harm a faithful client like you?" said K. "Oh, yes," said Block, "once he's roused he draws no distinctions; besides, I'm not really faithful to him." "How is that?" asked K. "Perhaps I oughtn't to tell you," said Block doubtfully. "I think you can risk it," said K. "Well," said Block, "I'll tell you a certain amount, but in your turn you must tell me one of your secrets, so that we each have a hold over the other." "You're very cautious," said K., "but I'll entrust you with a secret that will allay all your suspicions. In what way, then, are you unfaithful to the lawyer?" "Well," said the tradesman hesitatingly, as if confessing something dishonorable, "I have other lawyers as well as him." "That's nothing very dreadful," said K., somewhat disappointed. "It's supposed to be," said the tradesman, who had breathed freely since making his confession, but now gained a little confidence from K.'s rejoinder. "It's not allowed. And least of all is it allowed to consult pettifogging lawyers when one is the client of an official lawyer. And that's exactly what I've been doing, I have five pettifogging lawyers besides him." "Five!" cried K., amazed at the mere number, "five lawyers besides this one?" Block nodded: "I'm even negotiating with a sixth one." "But what do you need so many for?" asked K. "I need every one of them," said Block. "Tell me why, will you?" asked K. "With pleasure," said the tradesman. "To begin with, I don't want to lose my case, as you can well understand. And so I daren't ignore anything that might help me; if there's even the faintest hope of an advantage for myself I daren't reject it. That's why I've spent every penny I possess on this case of mine. For instance, I've drawn all the money out of my business; my business offices once filled nearly a whole floor of the building where now I need only a small back room and an apprentice. Of course it's not only the withdrawal of my money that has brought the business down, but the withdrawal of my energies. When you're trying to do anything you can to help your case along you haven't much energy to spare for other things." "So you've been working on your own behalf as well," interrupted K., "that's precisely what I wanted to ask you about." "There's not much to tell you," said the trades-man. "I did try my hand at it in the beginning, but I soon had to give it up. It's too exhausting, and the results are disappointing. Merely attending the Court to keep an eye on things proved too much, for me, at least. It makes you feel limp even to sit about and wait your turn. But you know yourself what the air's like." "How do you know I was ever up there?" asked K. "I happened to be in the lobby when you were passing through." "What a coincidence!" cried K., quite carried away and completely forgetting the ridiculous figure the tradesman had cut in his estimation. "So you saw me! You were in the lobby when I passed through. Yes, I did pass through the lobby once." "It's not such a coincidence as all that," said the tradesman, "I'm up there nearly every day." "I'm likely to be up there, too, often enough after this," said K., "only I can hardly expect to be received with such honor as on that occasion. Everyone stood up. I suppose they took me for a Judge." "No," said the tradesman, "it was the usher we stood up for. We knew you were an accused man. News of that kind spreads rapidly." "So you knew that already," commented K., "then perhaps you thought me somewhat high and mighty. Did no one comment on it?" "Not unfavorably," said the tradesman. "But it's all nonsense." "What's nonsense?" asked K. "Why do you insist on asking?" said the tradesman, irritably. "Apparently you don't know the people there yet and you might take it up wrongly. You must remember that in these proceedings things are always coming up for discussion that are simply beyond reason, people are too tired and distracted to think and so they take refuge in superstition. I'm as bad as anyone myself. And one of the superstitions is that you're supposed to tell from a man's face, especially the line of his lips, how his case is going to turn out. Well, people declared that judging from the expression of your lips you would be found guilty, and in the near future too. I tell you, it's a silly superstition and in most cases completely belied by the facts, but if you live among these people it's difficult to escape the prevailing opinion. You can't imagine what a strong effect such superstitions have. You spoke to a man up there, didn't you? And he could hardly utter a word in answer. Of course there's many a reason for being bewildered up there, but one of the reasons why he couldn't bring out an answer was the shock he got from looking at your lips. He said afterwards that he saw on your lips the sign of his own condemnation." "On my lips?" asked K., taking out a pocket mirror and studying them. "I can't see anything peculiar about my lips. Do you?" "I don't either," said the tradesman, "not in the least." "How superstitious these people are!" cried K. "Didn't I tell you?" asked the other. "Do they meet each other so frequently, then, and exchange all these ideas?" queried K., "I've never had anything to do with them myself." "As a rule they don't mix much," said the tradesman, "it would be hardly possible, there are too many of them. Besides, they have few interests in common. Occasionally a group believes it has found a common interest, but it soon finds out its mistake. Combined action against the Court is impossible. Each case is judged on its own merits, the Court is very conscientious about that, and so common action is out of the question. An individual here and there may score a point in secret, but no one hears it until afterwards, no one knows how it has been done. So there's no real community, people come across each other in the lobbies, but there's not much conversation. The superstitious beliefs are an old tradition and increase automatically." "I saw all the people in the lobby," remarked K., "and thought how pointless it was for them to be hanging about." "It's not pointless at all," said Block, "the only pointless thing is to try taking independent action. As I told you, I have five lawyers besides this one. You might think—as I did once—that I could safely wash my hands of the case. But you would be wrong. I have to watch it more carefully than if I had only one lawyer. I suppose you don't understand that?" "No," said K., laying his hand appealingly on the other's to keep him from talking so fast, "I would only like to beg you to speak more slowly, all these things are extremely important to me and I can't follow so quickly." "I'm glad you reminded me," said the tradesman; "of course you're a newcomer, you're young in the matter. Your case is six months old, isn't it? Yes, I've heard about it. An infant of a case! But I've had to think these things out I don't know how many times, they've become second nature to me." "I suppose you're thankful to think that your case is so far advanced," asked K., not liking to make a direct inquiry how the tradesman's case stood. But he received no direct answer either. "Yes, I've carried my burden for five long years," said Block, drooping his head, "it's no small achievement, that." Then he sat silent for a little. K. listened to hear if Leni were coming back. On the one hand he did not want her to come in just then, for he had many questions still to ask, nor did he want her to find him so deep in intimate conversation with the tradesman, but on the other hand he was annoyed because she was spending so much time with the lawyer while he was in the house, much more time than was needed for handing over a bowl of soup. "I can still remember exactly," the tradesman began again, and K. was at once all attention, "the days when my case was at much the same stage as yours is now. I had only this lawyer then, and I wasn't particularly satisfied with him." Now I'm going to find out everything, thought K., nodding his head eagerly, as if that would encourage the tradesman to bring out all the right information. "My case," Block continued, "wasn't making any progress; there were of course interrogations, and I attended every one of them, I collected evidence, I even laid all my account books before the Court, which wasn't necessary at all, as I discovered later. I kept running to the lawyer, he presented various petitions—" "Various petitions?" asked K. "Yes, certainly," said Block. "That's an important point for me," said K., "for in my case he's still working on the first petition. He's done nothing at all yet. Now I see how scandalously he's neglecting me." "There might be several excellent reasons why the petition isn't ready yet," said Block. "Let me tell you that my petitions turned out later to be quite worthless. I even had a look at one of them, thanks to the kindness of a Court official. It was very learned but it said nothing of any consequence. Crammed with Latin in the first place, which I don't understand, and then whole pages of general appeals to the Court, then flattering references to

particular officials, who weren't actually named but were
easy enough for anyone versed in these matters to recognize, then self-praise of the lawyer himself, in the course of
which he addressed the Court with a crawling humility,
ending up with an analysis of various cases from ancient
times that were supposed to resemble mine. I must say that
this analysis, in so far as I could follow it, was very careful
and thorough. You mustn't think that I'm passing judgment
on the lawyer's work; that petition, after all, was only one
of many; but at any rate, and this is what I'm coming to,
I couldn't see that my case was making any progress."
"What kind of progress did you expect to see?" asked K.
"A good question," said the tradesman with a smile, "it's
very rarely that progress in these cases is visible at all. But
I didn't know that then. I'm a businessman, and I was much
more of a businessman then than now, I wanted to see
palpable results, the whole negotiation should be coming to
a finish, I thought, or taking a regular upward course.
Instead of that there were only ceremonial interviews, one
after another, mostly of the same tenor, where I could reel
off the responses like a litany; several times a week Court
messengers came to my place of business or to my house or
wherever I was to be found, and that, of course, was a
nuisance (today I'm much better off in that respect, for
telephone calls bother me less); and besides all that, rumors
about my case began to spread among my business friends,
but especially among my relatives, so that I was being
injured on all sides without the slightest sign of any intention on the part of the Court to begin legal proceedings in
the near future. So I went to the lawyer and made my
complaint. He treated me to a lengthy explanation, but refused utterly to take action in my sense of the word, saying
that nobody could influence the Court to appoint a day for
hearing a case, and that to urge anything of the kind in a
petition—as I wanted him to do—was simply unheard of

and would only ruin myself and him. I thought: what this lawyer won't or can't do, another will and can. So I looked round for other lawyers. I may as well tell you now that not one of them ever petitioned the Court to fix a day for the trial of my case, or managed to obtain such a trial; it is really an impossibility—with one qualification that I shall explain later—and the lawyer had not misled me there, although I found no cause for regretting having called in the other lawyers. I suppose Dr. Huld has told you plenty of things about the pettifogging lawyers, he has probably described them as contemptible creatures, and so they are, in a sense. All the same, in speaking of them and contrasting himself and his colleagues with them he always makes a small mistake, which I may as well call your attention to in passing. He always refers to the lawyers of his own circle as the 'great lawyers,' by way of contrast. Now that's untrue; any man can call himself 'great,' of course, if he pleases, but in this matter the Court tradition must decide. And according to the Court tradition, which recognizes both small and great lawyers outside the hole-and-corner lawyers, our lawyer and his colleagues rank only among the small lawyers, while the really great lawyers, whom I have merely heard of and never seen, stand as high above the small lawyers as these above the despised pettifogging lawyers." "The really great lawyers?" asked K. "Who are they, then? How does one get to them?" "So you've never heard of them," said Block. "There's hardly an accused man who doesn't spend some time dreaming of them after hearing about them. Don't you give way to that temptation. I have no idea who the great lawyers are and I don't believe they can be got at. I know of no single instance in which it could be definitely asserted that they had intervened. They do defend certain cases, but one cannot achieve that oneself. They only defend those whom they wish to defend, and they never take action, I should think, until the case is

already beyond the province of the lower Court. In fact, it's
better to put them out of one's mind altogether, or else one
finds interviews with ordinary lawyers so stale and stupid,
with their niggling counsels and proposals—I have experienced it myself—that one feels like throwing the whole
thing up and taking to bed with one's face to the wall. And
of course that would be stupider still, for even in bed one
wouldn't find peace." "So you didn't entertain the thought
of going to the great lawyers?" asked K. "Not for long,"
said Block, smiling again; "unfortunately one can never
quite forget about them, especially during the night. But at
that time I was looking for immediate results, and so I
went to the pettifogging lawyers."

"How close you've got!" cried Leni, who had come back
with the soup bowl and was standing in the doorway. They
were indeed sitting so close to each other that they must
have bumped their heads together at the slightest movement; Block, who was not only a small man but stooped
forward as he sat, spoke so low that K. was forced to bend
down to hear every word he said. "Give us a moment or
two," cried K., warning Leni off; the hand which he still
kept on the tradesman's hand twitched with irritation. "He
wanted me to tell him about my case," the tradesman said
to Leni. "Well, go on telling him," said she. Her tone in
speaking to Block was kind but a little condescending.
That annoyed K.; the man, after all, as he had discovered,
possessed a certain value, he had experiences and knew
how to communicate them. Leni at least probably misjudged him. To K.'s further annoyance Leni removed the
candle, which he had been grasping all this time, wiped his
hand with her apron, and knelt down to scratch off some
tallow which had dripped on his trousers. "You were going
to tell me about pettifogging lawyers," said K., pushing
Leni's hand away without comment. "What do you think
you're doing?" she asked, giving K. a small slap and re-

suming her task. "Yes, the pettifogging lawyers," said Block, passing his hand over his brow as if in reflection. K. wanted to help him out and added: "You were looking for immediate results and so you went to the pettifogging lawyers." "That's right," said Block, but he did not continue. Perhaps he doesn't want to talk of it before Leni, thought K., suppressing his impatience to hear the rest of the story at once and not urging the man any more.

"Did you announce me?" he asked Leni instead. "Of course," she said, "and the lawyer's waiting for you. Leave Block alone now, you can talk to him later, for he's staying here." K. still hesitated. "Are you staying here?" he asked the tradesman; he wanted the man to speak for himself, he disliked the way Leni discussed him as if he were absent, he was filled with obscure irritation today against Leni. And again it was Leni who did the speaking: "He often sleeps here." "Sleeps here?" cried K.; he had thought that the tradesman was waiting only till the interview with the lawyer was brought to a speedy conclusion, and that then they would go off together to discuss the whole business thoroughly in private. "Yes," said Leni, "everyone isn't like you, Joseph, getting an interview with the lawyer at any hour they choose. It doesn't even seem to strike you as surprising that a sick man like the lawyer should agree to see you at eleven o'clock at night. You take all that your friends do for you far too much as a matter of course. Well, your friends, or I at least, like doing things for you. I don't ask for thanks and I don't need any thanks, except that I want you to be fond of me." Fond of you? thought K., and only after framing the words did it occur to him: But I am fond of her. Yet he said, ignoring the rest of her remarks: "He receives me because I'm his client. If I needed the help of others even to get an interview with my lawyer, I'd have to be bowing and scraping at every turn." "How difficult he is today, isn't he?" said Leni to the tradesman.

Now it's my turn to be treated as if I were absent, thought K., and his irritation extended to the tradesman too when the latter, copying Leni's discourtesy, remarked: "But the lawyer has other reasons for agreeing to see him. His is a much more interesting case than mine. Besides, it's only beginning, probably still at a hopeful stage, and so the lawyer likes handling it. You'll see a difference later on." "Yes, yes," said Leni, regarding the tradesman laughingly, "what a tongue-wagger!" Here she turned to K. and went on: "You mustn't believe a word he says. He's a nice fellow but his tongue wags far too much. Perhaps that's why the lawyer can't bear him. Anyhow, he never consents to see him unless he's in a good mood. I've tried my best to change that, but it can't be done. Only fancy, sometimes I tell the lawyer Block is here and he puts off seeing him for three days together. And then if Block isn't on the spot when he's called for, his chance is gone and I have to announce him all over again. That's why I let Block sleep here, for it has happened before now that he has been rung for in the middle of the night. So Block has to be ready night and day. It sometimes happens, too, that the lawyer changes his mind, once he has discovered that Block actually is on the spot, and refuses the interview." K. threw a questioning glance at the tradesman, who nodded and said, with the same frankness as before, or perhaps merely discomposed by a feeling of shame: "Yes, one becomes very dependent on one's lawyer in the course of time." "He's just pretending to complain," said Leni, "for he likes sleeping here, as he has often told me." She went over to a small door and pushed it open. "Would you like to see his bedroom?" she asked. K. followed her and gazed from the threshold into a low-roofed chamber with no window which had room only for a narrow bed. One had to climb over the bedposts to get into the bed. At the head of it, in a recess in the wall, stood a candle, an ink well, and a pen,

carefully arranged beside a bundle of papers, probably documents concerning the case. "So you sleep in the maid's
room?" asked K., turning to the tradesman. "Leni lets me
have it," said he, "it's very convenient." K. gave him a long
look; the first impression he had had of the man was perhaps, after all, the right one; Block was a man of experience, certainly, since his case had lasted for years, yet
he had paid dearly for his experience. Suddenly K. could
no longer bear the sight of him. "Put him to bed," he cried
to Leni, who seemed not to comprehend what he meant.
Yet what he wanted was to get away to the lawyer and
dismiss from his life not only Huld but Leni and the tradesman too. Before he could reach the room, however, Block
spoke to him in a low voice: "Herr K." K. turned round
angrily. "You've forgotten your promise," said the tradesman, reaching out imploringly toward K. "You were going
to tell me one of your secrets." "True," said K., casting a
glance also at Leni, who was regarding him attentively,
"well, listen then, though it's almost an open secret by this
time. I'm going to the lawyer now to dismiss him from my
case." "Dismiss him!" exclaimed the tradesman; he sprang
from his seat and rushed round the kitchen with upraised
arms, crying as he ran: "He's dismissing the lawyer!" Leni
made a grab at K. but Block got in her way, and she requited him with her fists. Still clenching her fists, she chased
after K., who was well ahead of her. He got inside the
lawyer's room before she caught up with him; he tried to
close the door behind him, but Leni put one foot in the
crack and reached through it to grab his arm and haul him
back. K. caught her wrist and squeezed it so hard that she
had to loose her hold with a whimper. She did not dare to
force her way right in, but K. made certain by turning the
key in the lock.*

"I've been waiting a long time for you," said the lawyer
from his bed, laying on the table a document which he had

been reading by the light of a candle, and putting on a pair of spectacles through which he scrutinized K. sharply. Instead of apologizing K. said: "I shan't detain you long." This remark, as it was no apology, the lawyer ignored, saying: "I shall not see you again at such a late hour." "That agrees with my intentions," retorted K. The lawyer gave him a questioning look and said: "Sit down." "Since you ask me to," said K., pulling up a chair to the bedside table and seating himself. "I fancied I heard you locking the door," said the lawyer. "Yes," said K., "that was because of Leni." He was not thinking of shielding anyone, but the lawyer went on: 'Has she been pestering you again?" "Pestering me?" asked K. "Yes," said the lawyer, chuckling until stopped by a fit of coughing, after which he began to chuckle once more. "I suppose you can't have helped noticing that she pesters you?" he asked, patting K.'s hand, which in his nervous distraction he had put on the bedside table and now hastily withdrew. "You don't attach much importance to it," went on the lawyer as K. remained silent. "So much the better. Or else I might have had to apologize for her. It's a peculiarity of hers, which I have long forgiven her and which I wouldn't mention now had it not been for your locking the door. This peculiarity of hers, well, you're the last person I should have to explain it to, but you're looking so bewildered that I feel I must, this peculiarity of hers consists in her finding nearly all accused men attractive. She makes up to all of them, loves them all, and is evidently also loved in return; she often tells me about these affairs to amuse me, when I allow her. It doesn't surprise me so much as it seems to surprise you. If you have the right eye for these things, you can see that accused men are often attractive. It's a remarkable phenomenon, almost a natural law. For of course the fact of being accused makes no alteration in a man's appearance that is immediately obvious and recognizable. These cases are not like ordinary criminal cases, most of the defendants continue in their usual vocations, and if they are in the hands of a good lawyer their interests don't suffer much. And yet those who are experienced in such matters can pick out one after another all the accused men in the largest of crowds. How do they know them? you will ask. I'm afraid my answer won't seem satisfactory. They know them because accused men are always the most attractive. It cannot be guilt that makes them attractive, for—it behooves me to say this as a lawyer, at least—they aren't all guilty, and it can't be the justice of the penance laid on them that makes them attractive in anticipation, for they aren't all going to be punished, so it must be the mere charge preferred against them that in some way enhances their attraction. Of course some are much more attractive than others. But they are all attractive, even that wretched creature Block."

By the time the lawyer finished this harangue K. had completely regained his composure, he had even nodded as if in complete agreement with the last words, whereas he was really confirming his own long-cherished opinion that the lawyer invariably attempted, as now, to bring in irrelevant generalizations in order to distract his attention from the main question, which was: how much actual work had been achieved in furthering the case? Presumably the lawyer felt that K. was more hostile than usual, for now he paused to give him the chance of putting in a word, and then asked, since K. remained silent: "Did you come here this evening for some specific reason?" "Yes," said K., shading the light of the candle a little with one hand so as to see the lawyer better. "I came to tell you that I dispense with your services as from today." "Do I understand you rightly?" asked the lawyer, half propping himself up in bed with one hand on the pillows. "I expect so," said K., sitting bolt upright as if on guard. "Well, that's a plan we can at least discuss," said the lawyer after a pause. "It's no plan, it's a fact," said K. "Maybe," said the lawyer, "but we mustn't be in too much of a hurry." He used the word "we" as if he had no intention of letting K. detach himself, as if he meant to remain at least K.'s adviser if not his official agent. "It's not a hurried decision," said K., slowly getting up and retreating behind his chair, "I have thought it well over, perhaps even for too long. It is my final decision." "Then allow me a few comments," said the lawyer, throwing off his feather quilt and sitting on the edge of the bed. His bare legs, sprinkled with white hairs, trembled with cold. He asked K. to hand him a rug from the sofa. K. fetched the rug and said: "It's quite unnecessary for you to expose yourself to a chill." "I have grave enough reasons for it," said the lawyer, wrapping the bed quilt round his shoulders and tucking the rug round his legs. "Your uncle is a friend of mine, and I've grown fond of you, too, in the course of time. I admit it freely. It's nothing to be ashamed of." This outburst of sentiment from the old man was most unwelcome to K., for it compelled him to be more explicit in his statements, which he would have liked to avoid, and disconcerted him too, as he frankly admitted to himself, although without in the least affecting his decision. "I am grateful for your friendly attitude," he said, "and I appreciate that you have done all you could do for what you thought to be my advantage. But for some time now I have been growing convinced that your efforts are not enough. I shall not, of course, attempt to thrust my opinions on a man so much older and more experienced than myself; if I have unwittingly seemed to do so, please forgive me, but I have grave enough reasons for it, to use your own phrase, and I am convinced that it is necessary to take much more energetic steps in this case of mine than have been taken so far." "I understand you," said the lawyer, "you are feeling impatient." "I'm not impatient," said K., a little irritated and therefore less careful in his choice of words, "you must have noticed on my very first visit here, when I came with my uncle, that I did not take my case very seriously; if I wasn't forcibly reminded of it, so to speak, I forgot it completely. Still my uncle insisted on my engaging you as my representative, and I did so to please him. One would naturally have expected the case to weigh even less on my conscience after that, since after all one engages a lawyer to shift the burden a little on to his shoulders. But the very opposite of that resulted. I was never so much plagued by my case as I have been since engaging you to represent me. When I stood alone I did nothing at all, yet it hardly bothered me; after acquiring a lawyer, on the other hand, I felt that the stage was set for something to happen, I waited with unceasing and growing expectancy for your intervention, and you did nothing whatever. I admit that you gave me information about the Court which I probably could not have obtained elsewhere. But that is hardly adequate assistance for a man who feels this thing secretly encroaching upon him and literally touching him to the quick." K. had pushed the chair away and now stood upright, his hands in his jacket pockets. "After a certain stage in one's practice," said the lawyer quietly in a low voice, "nothing really new ever happens. How many of my clients have reached the same point in their cases and stood before me in exactly the same frame of mind as you and said the same things!" "Well," said K., "then they were all as much in the right as I am. That doesn't counter my arguments." "I wasn't trying to counter them," said the lawyer, "but I should like to add that I expected you to show more judgment than the others, especially as I have given you more insight into the workings of the Court and my own procedure than I usually give my clients. And now I cannot help seeing that in spite of everything you haven't enough confidence in me. You don't make things very easy for me." How the lawyer was humbling himself before K.! And without any regard for his professional dignity, which was surely most sensitive on this very point. Why was he doing it? If appearances spoke truly he was in great demand as a lawyer and wealthy as well, the loss of K. as a client or the loss of his fees could not mean much to such a man. Besides, he was an invalid and should himself have contemplated the advisability of losing clients. Yet he was clinging to K. with an insistence! Why? Was it personal affection for K.'s uncle, or did he really regard the case as so extraordinary that he hoped to win prestige either from defending K. or—a possibility not to be excluded—from pandering to his friends in the Court? His face provided no clue, searchingly as K. scrutinized it. One could almost suppose that he was deliberately assuming a blank expression, while waiting for the effect of his words. But he was obviously putting too favorable an interpretation on K.'s silence when he went on to say: "You will have noticed that although my office is large enough I don't employ any assistants. That wasn't so in former years, there was a time when several young students of the Law worked for me, but today I work alone. This change corresponds in part to the change in my practice, for I have been confining myself more and more to cases like yours, and in part to a growing conviction that has been borne in upon me. I found that I could not delegate the responsibility for these cases to anyone else without wronging my clients and imperiling the tasks I had undertaken. But the decision to cover all the work myself entailed the natural consequences: I had to refuse most of the cases brought to me and apply myself only to those which touched me closely —and I can tell you there's no lack of wretched creatures even in this very neighborhood, ready to fling themselves on any crumb I choose to throw them. And then I broke down under stress of overwork. All the same, I don't regret my decision, perhaps I ought to have taken a firmer

stand and refused more cases, but the policy of devoting myself singlemindedly to the cases I did accept has proved both absolutely necessary and has been justified by the results. I once read a very finely worded description of the difference between a lawyer for ordinary legal rights and a lawyer for cases like these. It ran like this: the one lawyer leads his client by a slender thread until the verdict is reached, but the other lifts his client on his shoulders from the start and carries him bodily without once letting him down until the verdict is reached, and even beyond it. That is true. But it is not quite true to say that I do not at all regret devoting myself to this great task. When, as in your case, my labors are so completely misunderstood, then, yes, then and only then, I come near to regretting it." *
This speech, instead of convincing K., only made him impatient. He fancied that the very tone of the lawyer's voice suggested what was in store for him should he yield; the same old exhortations would begin again, the same references to the progress of the petition, to the more gracious mood of this or that official, while not forgetting the enormous difficulties that stood in the way—in short, the same stale platitudes would be brought out again either to delude him with vague false hopes or to torment him with equally vague menaces. That must be stopped once and for all, so he said: "What steps do you propose to take in my case if I retain you as my representative?" The lawyer meekly accepted even this insulting question and replied: "I should continue with those measures that I have already begun." "I knew it," said K., "well, it's a waste of time to go on talking." "I'll make one more attempt," said the lawyer, as if it were K. who was at fault and not himself. "I have an idea that what makes you so wrongheaded not only in your judgment of my legal assistance but also in your general behavior is the fact that you have been treated too well, although you are an accused man, or

rather, more precisely, that you have been treated with negligence, with apparent negligence. There's a reason for the negligence, of course; it's often better to be in chains than to be free. But I'd like to show you how other accused men are treated, and perhaps you may learn a thing or two. I shall now send for Block; you'd better unlock the door and sit here beside the bed table." "With pleasure," said K., fulfilling these injunctions; he was always ready to learn. As a precaution, however, he asked once more: "You realize that I am dispensing with your services?" "Yes," said the lawyer, "but you may change your mind about it yet." He lay back in bed again, drew the quilt up to his chin, and turned his face to the wall. Then he rang the bell.

Almost at the same moment Leni was on the spot, darting quick glances to learn what was happening; she seemed to find it reassuring that K. was sitting so quietly beside the lawyer's bed. She nodded to him with a smile, but he gazed at her blankly. "Fetch Block," said the lawyer. Instead of fetching Block, however, she merely went to the door, called out: "Block! The lawyer wants you!" and then, probably because the lawyer had his face turned to the wall and was paying no attention to her, insinuated herself behind K., where she distracted him during all the rest of the proceedings by leaning over the back of his chair or running her fingers, gently and cautiously enough, through his hair and over his temples. In the end K. sought to prevent her by holding on to her hand, which after a little resistance she surrendered to him.

Block had answered the summons immediately, yet he hesitated outside the door, apparently wondering whether he was to come in or not. He raised his eyebrows and cocked his head as if listening for the summons to be repeated. K. could have encouraged the man to come in, but he was determined to make a final break not only with

the lawyer but with all the persons in the house, and so he
remained motionless. Leni too was silent. Block noticed
that at least no one was turning him away, and he tiptoed
into the room with anxious face, and hands clutched behind
him, leaving the door open to secure his retreat. He did not
once look at K., but kept his eyes fixed on the humped-up
quilt beneath which the lawyer was not even visible, since
he had shifted close up to the wall. A voice, however, came
from the bed, saying: "Is that Block?" This question acted
like a blow upon Block, who had advanced a goodish way;
he staggered, as if he had been hit on the chest and then
beaten on the back, and, bowing deeply, stood still, answering: "At your service." "What do you want?" asked the
lawyer. "You've come at the wrong time." "Wasn't I called
for?" said Block, more to himself than to the lawyer,
thrusting out his hands as if to guard himself, and preparing to back out. "You were called for," said the lawyer,
"and yet you've come at the wrong time." After a pause he
added: "You always come at the wrong time." From the
moment when the lawyer's voice was heard Block averted
his eyes from the bed and stood merely listening, gazing
into a far corner, as if the sight of the lawyer were too
dazzling to bear. But it was difficult for him even to listen,
since the lawyer was speaking close to the wall and in a
voice both low and quick. "Do you want me to go away?"
asked Block. "Well, since you're here," said the lawyer,
"stay!" One might have fancied that instead of granting
Block his desire the lawyer had threatened to have him
beaten, for the fellow now began to tremble in earnest.
"Yesterday," said the lawyer, "I saw my friend the Third
Judge and gradually worked the conversation round to
your case. Would you like to know what he said?" "Oh,
please," said Block. Since the lawyer made no immediate
reply, Block implored him again and seemed on the point
of getting down on his knees. But K. intervened with a

shout: "What's that you're doing?" Leni had tried to stifle
his shout and so he gripped her other hand as well. It was
no loving clasp in which he held her; she sighed now and
then and struggled to free herself. But it was Block who
paid the penalty for K.'s outburst; the lawyer shot the question at him: "Who is your lawyer?" "You are," said Block.
"And besides me?" asked the lawyer. "No one besides you,"
said Block. "Then pay no heed to anyone else," said the
lawyer. Block took the full force of these words; he gave
K. an angry glare and shook his head violently at him. If
these gestures had been translated into speech they would
have made a tirade of abuse. And this was the man with
whom K. had wished to discuss his own case in all friendliness! "I shan't interfere again," said K., leaning back in
his chair. "Kneel on the floor or creep on all fours if you
like, I shan't bother." Yet Block had some self-respect left,
at least where K. was concerned, for he advanced upon
him flourishing his fists and shouting as loudly as he dared
in the lawyer's presence: "You're not to talk to me in that
tone, it isn't allowed. What do you mean by insulting me?
Before the lawyer, too, who admits us here, both of us,
you and me, only out of charity? You're no better than I
am, you're an accused man too and are involved in a case
like me. If nonetheless you're a gentleman as well, let me
tell you I'm as great a gentleman as you, if not greater.
And I'll have you address me as such, yes, you especially.
For if you think you have the advantage of me because
you're allowed to sit there at your ease and watch me
creeping on all fours, as you put it, let me remind you of
the old maxim: people under suspicion are better moving
than at rest, since at rest they may be sitting in the balance
without knowing it, being weighed together with their
sins." K. said not a word, he merely stared in unwinking
astonishment at this madman. What a change had come
over the fellow in the last hour! Was it his case that agi-

tated him to such an extent that he could not distinguish
friend from foe? Did he not see that the lawyer was deliberately humiliating him, for no other purpose on this
occasion than to make a display of his power before K.
and so perhaps cow K. into acquiescence as well? Yet if
Block were incapable of perceiving this, or if he were so
afraid of the lawyer that he could not allow himself to
perceive it, how did it come about that he was sly enough
or brave enough to deceive the lawyer and deny that he
was having recourse to other lawyers? And how could he
be so foolhardy as to attack K., knowing that K. might
betray his secret? His foolhardiness went even further, he
now approached the lawyer's bed and laid a complaint
against K. "Dr. Huld," he said, "did you hear what this
man said to me? His case is only a few hours old compared with mine, and yet, though I have been five years
involved in my case, he takes it on himself to give me
advice. He even abuses me. Knows nothing at all and
abuses me, me, who has studied as closely as my poor
wits allow every precept of duty, piety, and tradition."
"Pay no heed to anyone," said the lawyer, "and do what
seems right to yourself." "Certainly," said Block, as if to
give himself confidence, and then with a hasty side-glance
knelt down close beside the bed. "I'm on my knees, Dr.
Huld," he said. But the lawyer made no reply.* Block cautiously caressed the quilt with one hand. In the silence
that now reigned Leni said, freeing herself from K.:
"You're hurting me. Let go. I want to be with Block." She
went over and sat on the edge of the bed. Block was
greatly pleased by her coming; he made lively gestures,
though in dumb show, imploring her to plead his cause
with the lawyer. Obviously he was urgently in need of any
information which the lawyer might give, but perhaps he
only wanted to hand it on to his other lawyers for exploita-
tion. Leni apparently knew exactly the right way to coax

the lawyer; she pointed to his hand and pouted her lips as if giving a kiss. Block immediately kissed the hand, repeating the performance twice at Leni's instigation. But the lawyer remained persistently unresponsive. Then Leni, displaying the fine lines of her taut figure, bent over close to the old man's face and stroked his long white hair. That finally evoked an answer. "I hesitate to tell him," said the lawyer, and one could see him shaking his head, perhaps only the better to enjoy the pressure of Leni's hand. Block listened with downcast eyes, as if he were breaking a law by listening. "Why do you hesitate?" asked Leni. K. had the feeling that he was listening to a well-rehearsed dialogue which had been often repeated and would be often repeated and only for Block would never lose its novelty. "How has he been behaving today?" inquired the lawyer instead of answering. Before providing this information Leni looked down at Block and watched him for a moment as he raised his hands toward her and clasped them appealingly together. At length she nodded gravely, turned to the lawyer, and said: "He has been quiet and industrious." An elderly businessman, a man with a long beard, begging a young girl to say a word in his favor! Let him make what private reservations he would, in the eyes of his fellow men he could find no justification. K. did not understand how the lawyer could ever have imagined that this performance would win him over. If the lawyer had not already succeeded in alienating him, this scene would have finished him once and for all. It was humiliating even to an onlooker. So the lawyer's methods, to which K. fortunately had not been long enough exposed, amounted to this: that the client finally forgot the whole world and lived only in hope of toiling along this false path until the end of his case should come in sight. The client ceased to be a client and became the lawyer's dog. If the lawyer were to order this man to crawl under the bed as if into a kennel and

bark there, he would gladly obey the order. K. listened to
everything with critical detachment, as if he had been
commissioned to observe the proceedings closely, to report
them to a higher authority, and to put down a record of
them in writing. "What has he been doing all day?" went
on the lawyer. "I locked him into the maid's room," said
Leni, "to keep him from disturbing me at my work, that's
where he usually stays, anyhow. And I could peep at him
now and then through the ventilator to see what he was
doing. He was kneeling all the time on the bed, reading the
papers you lent him, which were spread out on the window
still. That made a good impression on me, since the window
looks out on an air shaft and doesn't give much light. So
the way Block stuck to his reading showed me how faithfully he does what he is told." "I'm glad to hear that," said
the lawyer. "But did he understand what he was reading?"
All this time Block's lips were moving unceasingly; he was
obviously formulating the answers he hoped Leni would
make. "Well, of course," said Leni, "that's something I
don't know with certainty. At any rate, I could tell that he
was thorough in his reading. He never got past the same
page all day and he was following the lines with his fingers.
Whenever I looked at him he was sighing to himself as if
the reading cost him a great effort. Apparently the papers
you gave him to read are difficult to understand." "Yes,"
said the lawyer, "these scriptures are difficult enough. I
don't believe he really understands them. They're meant
only to give him an inkling how hard the struggle is that I
have to carry on in his defense. And for whom do I carry
on this hard struggle? It's almost ridiculous to put it into
words—I do it for Block. He must learn to understand
what that means. Did he read without stopping?" "Almost
without a stop," answered Leni, "he asked me only once
for a drink of water, and I handed it to him through the
ventilator. Then at about eight o'clock I let him out and

gave him something to eat." Block gave a fleeting glance at
K. as if expecting to see him impressed by this virtuous
record. His hopes seemed to be mounting, his movements
were less constrained, and he kept shifting his knees a little.
It was all the more noticeable that the lawyer's next words
struck him rigid. "You are praising him," said the lawyer.
"But that only makes it more difficult for me to tell him.
For the Judge's remarks were by no means favorable either
to Block or to his case." "Not favorable?" asked Leni. "How
can that be possible?" Block was gazing at her as intently
as if he believed her capable of giving a new and favorable
turn to the words long pronounced by the Judge. "Not
favorable," said the lawyer. "He was even annoyed when
I mentioned Block. 'Don't speak about Block,' he said. 'But
he's my client,' I said. 'You are wasting yourself on the
man,' he said. 'I don't think his case is hopeless,' said I.
'Well, you're wasting yourself on him,' he repeated. 'I don't
believe it,' said I, 'Block is sincerely concerned about his
case and devotes himself to it. He almost lives in my house
to keep in touch with the proceedings. One doesn't often
find such zeal. Of course, he's personally rather repulsive,
his manners are bad, and he is dirty, but as a client he is
beyond reproach'—I said 'beyond reproach,' and it was a
deliberate exaggeration. To that he replied: 'Block is
merely cunning. He has acquired a lot of experience and
knows how to keep on postponing the issue. But his ignorance is even greater than his cunning. What do you
think he would say if he discovered that his case had
actually not begun yet, if he were to be told that the bell
marking the start of the proceedings hadn't even been
rung?'—Quiet there, Block," said the lawyer, for Block was
just rising up on trembling legs, obviously to implore an
explanation. This was the first time the lawyer had addressed Block directly at any length. With lackluster eyes
he looked down; his glance was partly vague and partly

turned upon Block, who slowly sank back under it on his knees again. "That remark of the Judge's has no possible significance for you," said the lawyer. "Don't get into a panic at every word. If you do it again I'll never tell you anything. I can't begin a statement without your gazing at me as if your final sentence had come. You should be ashamed to behave like that before my client. And you're destroying his confidence in me. What's the matter with you? You're still alive, you're still under my protection. Your panic is senseless. You've read somewhere or other that a man's condemnation often comes unexpectedly from some chance person at some odd time. With many reservations that is certainly true, but it is equally true that your panic disgusts me and appears to betray a lack of the necessary confidence in me. All that I said was to report a remark made by a Judge. You know quite well that in these matters opinions differ so much that the confusion is impenetrable. This Judge, for instance, assumes that the proceedings begin at one point, and I assume that they begin at another point. A difference of opinion, nothing more. At a certain stage of the proceedings there is an old tradition that a bell must be rung. According to the Judge, that marks the beginning of the case, I can't tell you now all the arguments against him, you wouldn't understand them, let it be sufficient for you that there are many arguments against his view." In embarrassment Block sat plucking at the hair of the fur rug lying before the bed; his terror of the Judge's utterance was so great that it ousted for a while his subjection to the lawyer and he was thinking only of himself, turning the Judge's words round and surveying them from all sides. "Block," said Leni in a tone of warning, catching him by the collar and jerking him upward a little. "Leave the rug alone and listen to the lawyer."

[*This chapter was never completed.*]

CHAPTER NINE

In the Cathedral

AN ITALIAN colleague, who was on his first visit to the town and was one of the Bank's most influential clients, was to be taken in charge by K. and shown some of the town's art treasures and monuments. It was a commission that K. would once have felt to be an honor, but at the present juncture, now that all his energies were needed even to retain his prestige in the Bank, he accepted it reluctantly. Every hour that he spent away from the Bank was a trial to him; true, he was by no means able to make the best use of his office hours as once he had done, he wasted much time in the merest pretense of doing real work, but that only made him worry the more when he was not at his desk. In his mind he saw the Assistant Manager, who had always spied upon him, prowling every now and then into his office, sitting down at his desk, running through his papers, receiving clients who had become almost old friends of K.'s in the course of many years, and luring them away from him, perhaps even discovering mistakes that he had made, for K. now saw himself continually threatened by mistakes intruding into his work from all sides which he was no longer able to circumvent. Consequently if he were charged with a mission, however honorable, which involved his leaving the office on business or even taking a short journey—and missions of that kind by some chance had recently come his way fairly often—then he could not help suspecting that there was a plot to get him out of the way while his work was investigated, or at least that he was considered far from indispensable in the office. Most of these missions he could easily have refused. Yet he did not dare do so, since, if there were even the smallest ground for his suspicions, a refusal to go would only have been taken as an admission of fear. For that reason he accepted every one of them with apparent equanimity, and on one occasion when he was expected to take an exhausting two days' journey he even said nothing about a severe chill he had, to avoid the risk of having the prevailing wet autumnal weather advanced as an excuse for his not going. When he came back from this journey with a racking headache, he discovered that he had been selected to act as escort next day for the Italian visitor. The temptation to refuse, for this once, was very great, especially since the charge laid upon him was not strictly a matter of business; still, it was a social duty toward a colleague and doubtless important enough, only it was of no importance to himself, knowing, as he did, that nothing could save him except work well done, in default of which it would not be of the slightest use to him in the unlikely event that the Italian were to find him the most enchanting companion; he shrank from being exiled from his work even for a single day, since he had too great a fear of not being allowed to return, a fear which he well knew to be exaggerated, but which oppressed him all the same. The difficulty on this occasion was to find a plausible excuse; his knowledge of Italian was certainly not very great, but it was at least adequate, and there was a decisive argument in the fact that he had some knowledge of art, acquired in earlier days, which was absurdly overestimated in the Bank owing to his having been for some time, purely as a matter of business, a member of the Society for the Preservation of Ancient Monuments. Rumor had it that the Italian was also a connoisseur, and if so, the choice of K. to be his escort seemed the natural one.

It was a very wet and windy morning when K. arrived in his office at the early hour of seven o'clock, full of irritation at the program before him, but determined to accomplish at least some work before being distracted from it by the visitor. He was very tired, for he had spent half the night studying an Italian grammar as some slight preparation; he was more tempted by the window, where he had recently been in the habit of spending too much time, than by his desk, but he resisted the temptation and sat down to work. Unfortunately at that very moment the attendant appeared, reporting that he had been sent by the Manager to see if the Chief Clerk was in his office yet, and, if he was, to beg him to be so good as to come to the reception room; the gentleman from Italy had already arrived. "All right," said K., stuffed a small dictionary into his pocket, tucked under his arm an album for sightseers, which he had procured in readiness for the stranger, and went through the Assistant Manager's office into the Manager's room. He was glad that he had turned up early enough to be on the spot immediately when required; probably no one had really expected him to do so. The Assistant Manager's office, of course, was as empty as in the dead of night; very likely the attendant had been told to summon him too, and without result. When K. entered the reception room the two gentlemen rose from their deep armchairs. The Manager smiled kindly on K., he was obviously de-

lighted to see him, he performed the introduction at once,
the Italian shook K. heartily by the hand and said laughingly that someone was an early riser. K. did not quite
catch whom he meant, for it was an unfamiliar phrase the
sense of which did not dawn on him at once. He answered
with a few fluent sentences which the Italian received with
another laugh, meanwhile nervously stroking his bushy
iron-gray mustache. This mustache was obviously per-
fumed; one was almost tempted to go close up and have
a sniff at it. When they all sat down again and a preliminary conversation began, K. was greatly disconcerted
to find that he only partly understood what the Italian was
saying. He could understand him almost completely when
he spoke slowly and quietly, but that happened very
seldom, the words mostly came pouring out in a flood, and
he made lively gestures with his head as if enjoying the
rush of talk. Besides, when this happened, he invariably
relapsed into a dialect which K. did not recognize as
Italian but which the Manager could both speak and
understand, as indeed K. might have expected, considering
that this Italian came from the very south of Italy, where
the Manager had spent several years. At any rate, it became clear to K. that there was little chance of communica-
tion with the Italian, for the man's French was difficult to
follow and it was no use watching his lips for clues, since
their movements were covered by the bushy mustache. K.
began to foresee vexations and for the moment gave up
trying to follow the talk—while the Manager was present
to understand all that was said it was an unnecessary effort
to make—confining himself to morose observation of the
Italian lounging so comfortably and yet lightly in his armchair, tugging every now and then at the sharply peaked
corners of his short little jacket, and once raising his arms
with loosely fluttering hands to explain something * which
K. found it impossible to understand, although he was

leaning forward to watch every gesture. In the end, as K. sat there taking no part in the conversation, only mechanically following with his eyes the see-saw of the dialogue, his earlier weariness made itself felt again, and to his horror, although fortunately just in time, he caught himself absentmindedly rising to turn round and walk away. At long last the Italian looked at his watch and sprang to his feet. After taking leave of the Manager he pressed up to K. so close that K. had to push his chair back in order to have any freedom of movement. The Manager, doubtless seeing in K.'s eye that he was in desperate straits with this unintelligible Italian, intervened so cleverly and delicately that it appeared as if he were merely contributing little scraps of advice, while in reality he was briefly conveying to K. the sense of all the remarks with which the Italian kept on interrupting him. In this way K. learned that the Italian had some immediate business to attend to, that unfortunately he was pressed for time, that he had no intention of rushing round to see all the sights in a hurry, that he would much rather—of course only if K. agreed, the decision lay with K. alone—confine himself to inspecting the Cathedral, but to inspect that thoroughly. He was extremely delighted to have the chance of doing so in the company of such a learned and amiable gentleman—this was how he referred to K., who was trying hard to turn a deaf ear to his words and grasp as quickly as possible what the Manager was saying—and he begged him, if it were convenient, to meet him there in a couple of hours, say at about ten o'clock. He had hopes of being able to arrive there for certain about that time. K. made a suitable rejoinder, the Italian pressed the Manager's hand, then K.'s hand, then the Manager's hand again, and, followed by both of them, turning only half toward them by this time but still maintaining a flow of words, departed toward the door. K. stayed a moment or two with the Manager, who was looking particularly unwell that day. He felt that he owed K. an apology and said—they were standing intimately together—that he had at first intended to escort the Italian himself, but on second thought—he gave no definite reason—he had decided that K. had better go. If K. found that he could not understand the man to begin with he mustn't let that upset him, for he wouldn't take long to catch the sense of what was said, and even if he didn't understand very much it hardly mattered, since the Italian cared little whether he was understood or not. Besides, K.'s knowledge of Italian was surprisingly good and he would certainly acquit himself well. With that K. was dismissed to his room. The time still at his disposal he devoted to copying from the dictionary various unfamiliar words which he would need in his tour of the Cathedral. It was an unusually exasperating task; attendants came in with letters, clerks arrived with inquiries, standing in the doorway when they saw that K. was busy, yet not removing themselves until he answered, the Assistant Manager did not miss the chance of making a nuisance of himself and appeared several times, taking the dictionary out of K.'s hand and with obvious indifference turning the pages over; even clients were dimly visible in the antechamber whenever the door opened, making deprecating bows to call attention to themselves, but uncertain whether they had been remarked or not—all this activity rotated around K. as if he were the center of it, while he himself was occupied in collecting the words he might need, looking them up in the dictionary, copying them out, practicing their pronunciation, and finally trying to learn them by heart. His once excellent memory seemed to have deserted him, and every now and then he grew so furious with the Italian who was causing him all this trouble that he stuffed the dictionary beneath a pile of papers with the firm intention of preparing himself no further, yet he could not help seeing that it would not do to march the Italian round the art treasures of the Cathedral in dumb silence, and so with even greater rage he took the dictionary out again.

Just at half past nine, as he was rising to go, the telephone rang; Leni bade him good morning and asked how he was; K. thanked her hastily and said he had no time to talk to her, since he must go to the Cathedral. "To the Cathedral?" asked Leni. "Yes, to the Cathedral." "But why the Cathedral?" asked Leni. K. tried to explain briefly to her, but hardly had he begun when Leni suddenly said: "They're goading you." Pity which he had not asked for and did not expect was more than K. could bear, he said two words of farewell, but even as he hung up the receiver he murmured half to himself and half to the faraway girl who could no longer hear him: "Yes, they're goading me."

By now it was growing late, he was already in danger of not being in time for the appointment. He drove off in a taxicab; at the last moment he remembered the album which he had found no opportunity of handing over earlier, and so took it with him now. He laid it on his knees and drummed on it impatiently with his fingers during the whole of the journey. The rain had slackened, but it was a raw, wet, murky day, one would not be able to see much in the Cathedral, and there was no doubt that standing about on the cold flagstones would make K.'s chill considerably worse.

The Cathedral Square was quite deserted, and K. recollected how even as a child he had been struck by the fact that in the houses of this narrow square nearly all the window blinds were invariably drawn down. On a day like this, of course, it was more understandable. The Cathedral seemed deserted too, there was naturally no reason why anyone should visit it at such a time. K. went through both of the side aisles and saw no one but an old woman

muffled in a shawl who was kneeling before a Madonna
with adoring eyes. Then in the distance he caught sight of
a limping verger vanishing through a door in the wall. K.
had been punctual, ten o'clock was striking just as he
entered, but the Italian had not yet arrived. He went back
to the main entrance, stood there undecidedly for a while
and then made the circuit of the building in the rain, to
make sure that the Italian was perhaps not waiting at some
side door. He was nowhere to be seen. Could the Manager
have made some mistake about the hour? How could anyone be quite sure of understanding such a man? Whatever
the circumstances, K. would at any rate have to wait half
an hour for him. Since he was tired he felt like sitting
down, went into the Cathedral again, found on a step a
remnant of carpet-like stuff, twitched it with his toe
toward a near-by bench, wrapped himself more closely in
his greatcoat, turned up his collar, and sat down. By way
of filling in time he opened the album and ran idly through
it, but he soon had to stop, for it was growing so dark that
when he looked up he could distinguish scarcely a single
detail in the neighboring aisle.

Away in the distance a large triangle of candle flames
glittered on the high altar; K. could not have told with any
certainty whether he had noticed them before or not. Perhaps they had been newly kindled. Vergers are by profession stealthy-footed, one never notices them. K. happened
to turn round and saw not far behind him the gleam of another candle, a tall, thick candle fixed to a pillar. It was
lovely to look at, but quite inadequate for illuminating the
altarpieces, which mostly hung in the darkness of the side
chapels; it actually increased the darkness. The Italian was
as sensible as he was discourteous in not coming, for he
would have seen nothing, he would have had to content
himself with scrutinizing a few pictures piecemeal by the
light of K.'s pocket torch. Curious to see what effect it

would have, K. went up to a small side chapel near by, mounted a few steps to a low balustrade, and bending over it shone his torch on the altarpiece. The light from a permanent oil lamp hovered over it like an intruder. The first thing K. perceived, partly by guess, was a huge armored knight on the outermost verge of the picture. He was leaning on his sword, which was stuck into the bare ground, bare except for a stray blade of grass or two. He seemed to be watching attentively some event unfolding itself before his eyes. It was surprising that he should stand so still without approaching nearer to it. Perhaps he had been set there to stand guard. K., who had not seen any pictures for a long time, studied this knight for a good while, although the greenish light of the oil-lamp made his eyes blink. When he played the torch over the rest of the altarpiece he discovered that it was a portrayal of Christ being laid in the tomb, conventional in style and a fairly recent painting. He pocketed the torch and returned again to his seat.

In all likelihood it was now unnecessary to wait any longer for the Italian, but the rain was probably pouring down outside, and since it was not so cold in the Cathedral as K. had expected, he decided to stay there for the present. Quite near him rose the great pulpit, on its small vaulted canopy two plain golden crucifixes were slanted so that their shafts crossed at the top. The outer balustrade and the stonework connecting it with the supporting column were wrought all over with foliage in which little angels were entangled, now vivacious and now serene. K. went up to the pulpit and examined it from all sides; the carving of the stonework was very carefully wrought, the deep caverns of darkness among and behind the foliage looked as if caught and imprisoned there; K. put his hand into one of them and cautiously felt the contour of the stone; he had never known that this pulpit existed. By pure chance he noticed a verger standing behind the nearest row of benches, a man in a loose-hanging black garment with a snuffbox in his left hand; he was gazing at K. What's the man after? thought K. Do I look a suspicious character? Does he want a tip? But when he saw that K. had become aware of him, the verger started pointing with his right hand, still holding a pinch of snuff in his fingers, in some vaguely indicated direction. His gestures seemed to have little meaning. K. hesitated for a while, but the verger did not cease pointing at something or other and emphasizing the gesture with nods of his head. "What does the man want?" said K. in a low tone, he did not dare to raise his voice in this place; then he pulled out his purse and made his way along the benches toward him. But the verger at once made a gesture of refusal, shrugged his shoulders, and limped away. With something of the same gait, a quick, limping motion, K. had often as a child imitated a man riding on horseback. A childish old man, thought K., with only wits enough to be a verger. How he stops when I stop and peers to see if I am following him! Smiling to himself, K. went on following him through the side aisle almost as far as the high altar; the old man kept pointing at something, but K. deliberately refrained from looking round to see what he was pointing at, the gesture could have no other purpose than to shake K. off. At last he desisted from the pursuit, he did not want to alarm the old man too much; besides, in case the Italian were to turn up after all, it might be better not to scare away the verger.

As he returned to the nave to find the seat on which he had left the album, K. caught sight of a small side pulpit attached to a pillar almost immediately adjoining the choir, a simple pulpit of plain, pale stone. It was so small that from a distance it looked like an empty niche intended for a statue. There was certainly no room for the preacher to take a full step backward from the balustrade. The vaulting of the stone canopy, too, began very low down and curved forward and upward, although without ornamentation, in such a way that a medium-sized man could not stand upright beneath it, but would have to keep leaning over the balustrade. The whole structure was designed as if to torture the preacher; there seemed no comprehensible reason why it should be there at all while the other pulpit, so large and finely decorated, was available.

And K. certainly would not have noticed it had not a lighted lamp been fixed above it, the usual sign that a sermon was going to be preached. Was a sermon going to be delivered now? In the empty church? K. peered down at the small flight of steps which led upward to the pulpit, hugging the pillar as it went, so narrow that it looked like an ornamental addition to the pillar rather than a stairway for human beings. But at the foot of it, K. smiled in astonishment, there actually stood a priest ready to ascend, with his hand on the balustrade and his eyes fixed on K. The priest gave a little nod and K. crossed himself and bowed, as he ought to have done earlier. The priest swung himself lightly on to the stairway and mounted into the pulpit with short, quick steps. Was he really going to preach a sermon? Perhaps the verger was not such an imbecile after all and had been trying to urge K. toward the preacher, a highly necessary action in that deserted building. But somewhere or other there was an old woman before an image of the Madonna; she ought to be there too. And if it were going to be a sermon, why was it not introduced by the organ? But the organ remained silent, its tall pipes looming faintly in the darkness.

K. wondered whether this was not the time to remove himself quickly; if he did not go now he would have no chance of doing so during the sermon, he would have to stay as long as it lasted, he was already behindhand in the office and was no longer obliged to wait for the Italian; he looked at his watch, it was eleven o'clock. But was there really going to be a sermon? Could K. represent the congregation all by himself? What if he had been a stranger merely visiting the church? That was more or less his position. It was absurd to think that a sermon was going to be preached at eleven in the morning on a weekday, in such dreadful weather. The priest—he was beyond doubt a priest, a young man with a smooth, dark face—was obviously mounting the pulpit simply to turn out the lamp, which had been lit by mistake.

It was not so, however; the priest after examining the lamp screwed it higher instead, then turned slowly toward the balustrade and gripped the angular edge with both hands. He stood like that for a while, looking around him without moving his head. K. had retreated a good distance and was leaning his elbows on the foremost pew. Without knowing exactly where the verger was stationed, he was vaguely aware of the old man's bent back, peacefully at rest as if his task had been fulfilled. What stillness there was now in the Cathedral! Yet K. had to violate it, for he was not minded to stay; if it were this priest's duty to preach a sermon at a certain hour regardless of circumstances, let him do it, he could manage it without K.'s support, just as K.'s presence would certainly not contribute to its effectiveness. So he began slowly to move off, feeling his way along the pew on tiptoe until he was in the broad center aisle, where he advanced undisturbed except for the ringing noise that his lightest footstep made on the stone flags and the echoes that sounded from the vaulted roof faintly but continuously, in manifold and regular progression. K. felt a little forlorn as he advanced, a solitary figure between the rows of empty seats, perhaps with the priest's eyes following him; and the size of the Cathedral struck him as bordering on the limit of what human beings could bear. When he came to the seat where he had left the album he simply snatched the book up without stopping and took it with him. He had almost passed the last of the pews and was emerging into the open space between himself and the doorway when he heard the priest lifting up his voice. A resonant, well-trained voice. How it rolled through the expectant Cathedral! But it was no congregation the priest was addressing, the words were unambiguous and inescapable, he was calling out: "Joseph K.!"

K. paused and stared at the ground before him. For the moment he was still free, he could continue on his way and vanish through one of the small, dark, wooden doors that faced him at no great distance. It would simply indicate that he had not understood the call, or that he had understood it and did not care. But if he were to turn round he would be caught, for that would amount to an admission that he had understood it very well, that he was really the person addressed, and that he was ready to obey. Had the priest called his name a second time K. would certainly have gone on, but as everything remained silent, though he stood waiting a long time, he could not help turning his head a little just to see what the priest was doing. The priest was standing calmly in the pulpit as before, yet it was obvious that he had observed K.'s turn of the head. It would have been like a childish game of hide-and-seek if K. had not turned right round to face him. He did so, and the priest beckoned him to come nearer. Since there was now no need for evasion, K. hurried back—he was both curious and eager to shorten the interview—with long flying strides toward the pulpit. At the first rows of seats he halted, but the priest seemed to think the distance still too great; he stretched out an arm and pointed with sharply bent forefinger to a spot immediately before the pulpit. K. followed this direction too; when he stood on the spot indicated he had to bend his head far back to see the priest at all. "You are Joseph K.," said the priest, lifting one hand from the balustrade in a vague gesture. "Yes," said K., thinking how frankly he used to give his name and what a burden it had recently become to him; nowadays people he had never seen before seemed to know his name. How pleasant it was to have to introduce oneself before being recognized! "You are an accused man," said the priest in a very low voice. "Yes," said K., "so I have been informed." "Then you are the man I seek," said the priest. "I am the prison chaplain." "Indeed," said K. "I had you summoned here," said the priest, "to have a talk with you." "I didn't know that," said K. "I came here to show an Italian round the Cathedral." "That is beside the point," said the priest. "What is that in your hand? Is it a prayer book?" "No," replied K., "it is an album of sights worth seeing in the town." "Lay it down," said the priest. K. threw it away so violently that it flew open and slid some way along the floor with disheveled leaves. "Do you know that your case is going badly?" asked the priest. "I have that idea myself," said K. "I've done what I could, but without any success so far. Of course, my petition isn't finished yet." "How do you think it will end?" asked the priest. "At first I thought it must turn out well," said K., "but now I frequently have my doubts. I don't know how it will end. Do you?" "No," said the priest, "but I fear it will end badly. You are held to be guilty. Your case will perhaps never get beyond a lower Court. Your guilt is supposed, for the present, at least, to have been proved." "But I am not guilty," said K.; "it's a mistake. And, if it comes to that, how can any man be called guilty? We are all simply men here, one as much as the other." "That is true," said the priest, "but that's how all guilty men talk." "Are you prejudiced against me too?" asked K. "I have no prejudices against you," said the priest. "Thank you," said K.; "but all the others who are concerned

in these proceedings are prejudiced against me. They are
influencing outsiders too. My position is becoming more and
more difficult." "You are misinterpreting the facts of the
case," said the priest. "The verdict is not suddenly arrived
at, the proceedings only gradually merge into the verdict."
"So that's how it is," said K., letting his head sink. "What
is the next step you propose to take in the matter?" asked
the priest. "I'm going to get more help," said K., looking
up again to see how the priest took his statement. "There
are several possibilities I haven't explored yet." "You cast
about too much for outside help," said the priest disap-
provingly, "especially from women. Don't you see that it
isn't the right kind of help?" "In some cases, even in many,
I could agree with you," said K., "but not always. Women
have great influence. If I could move some women I know
to join forces in working for me, I couldn't help winning
through. Especially before this Court, which consists almost
entirely of petticoat-hunters. Let the Examining Magistrate
see a woman in the distance and he knocks down his desk
and the defendant in his eagerness to get at her." The priest
leaned over the balustrade, apparently feeling for the first
time the oppressiveness of the canopy above his head.
What fearful weather there must be outside! There was
no longer even a murky daylight; black night had set in.
All the stained glass in the great window could not illumine
the darkness of the wall with one solitary glimmer of light.
And at this very moment the verger began to put out the
candles on the high altar, one after another. "Are you angry
with me?" asked K. of the priest. "It may be that you don't
know the nature of the Court you are serving." He got no
answer. "These are only my personal experiences," said K.
There was still no answer from above. "I wasn't trying to
insult you," said K. And at that the priest shrieked from
the pulpit: "Can't you see one pace before you?" It was an

angry cry, but at the same time sounded like the unwary shriek of one who sees another fall and is startled out of his senses.

Both were now silent for a long time. In the prevailing darkness the priest certainly could not make out K.'s features, while K. saw him distinctly by the light of the small lamp. Why did he not come down from the pulpit? He had not preached a sermon, he had only given K. some information which would be likely to harm him rather than help him when he came to consider it. Yet the priest's good intentions seemed to K. beyond question, it was not impossible that they could come to some agreement if the man would only quit his pulpit, it was not impossible that K. could obtain decisive and acceptable counsel from him which might, for instance, point the way, not toward some influential manipulation of the case, but toward a circumvention of it, a breaking away from it altogether, a mode of living completely outside the jurisdiction of the Court. This possibility must exist, K. had of late given much thought to it. And should the priest know of such a possibility, he might perhaps impart his knowledge if he were appealed to, although he himself belonged to the Court and as soon as he heard the Court impugned had forgotten his own gentle nature so far as to shout K. down.

"Won't you come down here?" said K. "You haven't got to preach a sermon. Come down beside me." "I can come down now," said the priest, perhaps repenting of his outburst. While he detached the lamp from its hook he said: "I had to speak to you first from a distance. Otherwise I am too easily influenced and tend to forget my duty."

K. waited for him at the foot of the steps. The priest stretched out his hand to K. while he was still on the way down from a higher level. "Have you a little time for me?" asked K. "As much time as you need," said the priest, giving K. the small lamp to carry. Even close at hand he still wore a certain air of solemnity. "You are very good to me," said K. They paced side by side up and down the dusky aisle. "But you are an exception among those who belong to the Court. I have more trust in you than in any of the others, though I know many of them. With you I can speak openly." "Don't be deluded," said the priest. "How am I being deluded?" asked K. "You are deluding yourself about the Court," said the priest. "In the writings which preface the Law that particular delusion is described thus: before the Law stands a doorkeeper. To this doorkeeper there comes a man from the country who begs for admittance to the Law. But the doorkeeper says that he cannot admit the man at the moment. The man, on reflection, asks if he will be allowed, then, to enter later. 'It is possible,' answers the doorkeeper, 'but not at this moment.' Since the door leading into the Law stands open as usual and the doorkeeper steps to one side, the man bends down to peer through the entrance. When the doorkeeper sees that, he laughs and says: 'If you are so strongly tempted, try to get in without my permission. But note that I am powerful. And I am only the lowest doorkeeper. From hall to hall, keepers stand at every door, one more powerful than the other. And the sight of the third man is already more than even I can stand.' These are difficulties which the man from the country has not expected to meet, the Law, he thinks, should be accessible to every man and at all times, but when he looks more closely at the doorkeeper in his furred robe, with his huge, pointed nose and long, thin, Tartar beard, he decides that he had better wait until he gets permission to enter. The doorkeeper gives him a stool and lets him sit down at the side of the door. There he sits waiting for days and years. He makes many attempts to be allowed in and wearies the doorkeeper with his importunity. The doorkeeper often engages him in brief conversation, asking him about his home and about other matters, but the questions are put quite impersonally, as great men put questions, and always conclude with the statement that the man cannot be allowed to enter yet. The man, who has equipped himself with many things for his journey, parts with all he has, however valuable, in the hope of bribing the doorkeeper. The doorkeeper accepts it all, saying, however, as he takes each gift: 'I take this only to keep you from feeling that you have left something undone.' During all these long years the man watches the doorkeeper almost incessantly. He forgets about the other doorkeepers, and this one seems to him the only barrier between himself and the Law. In the first years he curses his evil fate aloud; later, as he grows old, he only mutters to himself. He grows childish, and since in his prolonged study of the doorkeeper he has learned to know even the fleas in his fur collar, he begs the very fleas to help him and to persuade the doorkeeper to change his mind. Finally his eyes grow dim and he does not know whether the world is really darkening around him or whether his eyes are only deceiving him. But in the darkness he can now perceive a radiance that streams inextinguishably from the door of the Law. Now his life is drawing to a close. Before he dies, all that he has experienced during the whole time of his sojourn condenses in his mind into one question, which he has never yet put to the doorkeeper. He beckons the doorkeeper, since he can no longer raise his stiffening body. The doorkeeper has to bend far down to hear him, for the difference in size between them has increased very much to the man's disadvantage. 'What do you want to know now?' asks the doorkeeper, 'you are insatiable.' 'Everyone strives to attain the Law,' answers the man, 'how does it come about, then, that in all these years no one has come seeking admittance but me?' The doorkeeper perceives that the man is nearing his end and his hearing is failing, so he bellows in his ear: 'No one but you could gain admittance through this door, since this door was intended for you. I am now going to shut it.'"

"So the doorkeeper deceived the man," said K. immediately, strongly attracted by the story. "Don't be too hasty," said the priest, "don't take over someone else's opinion without testing it. I have told you the story in the very words of the scriptures. There's no mention of deception in it." "But it's clear enough," said K., "and your first interpretation of it was quite right. The doorkeeper gave the message of salvation to the man only when it could no longer help him." "He was not asked the question any earlier," said the priest, "and you must consider, too, that he was only a doorkeeper, and as such fulfilled his duty." "What makes you think he fulfilled his duty?" asked K. "He didn't fulfill it. His duty might have been to keep all strangers away, but this man, for whom the door was intended, should have been let in." "You have not enough respect for the written word and you are altering the story," said the priest. "The story contains two important statements made by the doorkeeper about admission to the Law, one at the beginning, the other at the end. The first statement is: that he cannot admit the man at the moment, and the other is: that this door was intended only for the man. If there were a contradiction between the two, you would be right and the doorkeeper would have deceived the man. But there is no contradiction. The first statement, on the contrary, even implies the second. One could almost say that in suggesting to the man the possibility of future admittance the doorkeeper is exceeding his duty. At that time his apparent duty is only to refuse admittance and indeed many commentators are surprised that the suggestion should be made at all, since the doorkeeper appears to be a precisian with a stern regard for duty. He does not once leave his post during these many years, and he does not shut the door until the very last minute; he is conscious

of the importance of his office, for he says: 'I am powerful';
he is respectful to his superiors, for he says: 'I am only the
lowest doorkeeper'; he is not garrulous, for during all these
years he puts only what are called 'impersonal questions';
he is not to be bribed, for he says in accepting a gift: 'I
take this only to keep you from feeling that you have left
something undone'; where his duty is concerned he is to be
moved neither by pity nor rage, for we are told that the
man 'wearied the doorkeeper with his importunity'; and
finally even his external appearance hints at a pedantic
character, the large, pointed nose and the long, thin, black
Tartar beard. Could one imagine a more faithful doorkeeper? Yet the doorkeeper has other elements in his character which are likely to advantage anyone seeking admittance and which make it comprehensible enough that he
should somewhat exceed his duty in suggesting the possibility of future admittance. For it cannot be denied that
he is a little simple-minded and consequently a little con-
ceited. Take the statements he makes about his power and
the power of the other doorkeepers and their dreadful aspect
which even he cannot bear to see—I hold that these statements may be true enough, but that the way in which he
brings them out shows that his perceptions are confused
by simpleness of mind and conceit. The commentators note
in this connection: 'The right perception of any matter and
a misunderstanding of the same matter do not wholly ex-
clude each other.' One must at any rate assume that such
simpleness and conceit, however sparingly manifest, are
likely to weaken his defense of the door; they are breaches
in the character of the doorkeeper. To this must be added
the fact that the doorkeeper seems to be a friendly creature
by nature, he is by no means always on his official dignity.
In the very first moments he allows himself the jest of inviting the man to enter in spite of the strictly maintained
veto against entry; then he does not, for instance, send the

man away, but gives him, as we are told, a stool and lets him sit down beside the door. The patience with which he endures the man's appeals during so many years, the brief conversations, the acceptance of the gifts, the politeness with which he allows the man to curse loudly in his presence the fate for which he himself is responsible—all this lets us deduce certain feelings of pity. Not every doorkeeper would have acted thus. And finally, in answer to a gesture of the man's he bends down to give him the chance of putting a last question. Nothing but mild impatience—the doorkeeper knows that this is the end of it all—is discernible in the words: 'You are insatiable.' Some push this mode of interpretation even further and hold that these words express a kind of friendly admiration, though not without a hint of condescension. At any rate the figure of the doorkeeper can be said to come out very differently from what you fancied." "You have studied the story more exactly and for a longer time than I have," said K. They were both silent for a little while. Then K. said: "So you think the man was not deceived?" "Don't misunderstand me," said the priest, "I am only showing you the various opinions concerning that point. You must not pay too much attention to them. The scriptures are unalterable and the comments often enough merely express the commentators' despair. In this case there even exists an interpretation which claims that the deluded person is really the doorkeeper." "That's a far-fetched interpretation," said K. "On what is it based?" "It is based," answered the priest, "on the simple-mindedness of the doorkeeper. The argument is that he does not know the Law from inside, he knows only the way that leads to it, where he patrols up and down. His ideas of the interior are assumed to be childish, and it is supposed that he himself is afraid of the other guardians whom he holds up as bogies before the man. Indeed, he fears them more than the man does, since the man is de-

termined to enter after hearing about the dreadful guardians of the interior, while the doorkeeper has no desire to
enter, at least not so far as we are told. Others again say
that he must have been in the interior already, since he is
after all engaged in the service of the Law and can only
have been appointed from inside. This is countered by
arguing that he may have been appointed by a voice calling from the interior, and that anyhow he cannot have been
far inside, since the aspect of the third doorkeeper is more
than he can endure. Moreover, no indication is given that
during all these years he ever made any remarks showing
a knowledge of the interior, except for the one remark
about the doorkeepers. He may have been forbidden to do
so, but there is no mention of that either. On these grounds
the conclusion is reached that he knows nothing about the
aspect and significance of the interior, so that he is in a
state of delusion. But he is deceived also about his relation
to the man from the country, for he is inferior to the man
and does not know it. He treats the man instead as his own
subordinate, as can be recognized from many details that
must be still fresh in your mind. But, according to this
view of the story, it is just as clearly indicated that he is
really subordinated to the man. In the first place, a bond-
man is always subject to a free man. Now the man from
the country is really free, he can go where he likes, it is
only the Law that is closed to him, and access to the Law
is forbidden him only by one individual, the doorkeeper.
When he sits down on the stool by the side of the door and
stays there for the rest of his life, he does it of his òwn
free will; in the story there is no mention of any compul-
sion. But the doorkeeper is bound to his post by his very
office, he does not dare go out into the country, nor apparently may he go into the interior of the Law, even
should he wish to. Besides, although he is in the service of
the Law, his service is confined to this one entrance; that is

to say, he serves only this man for whom alone the entrance is intended. On that ground too he is inferior to the man. One must assume that for many years, for as long as it takes a man to grow up to the prime of life, his service was in a sense an empty formality, since he had to wait for a man to come, that is to say someone in the prime of life, and so he had to wait a long time before the purpose of his service could be fulfilled, and, moreover, had to wait on the man's pleasure, for the man came of his own free will. But the termination of his service also depends on the man's term of life, so that to the very end he is subject to the man. And it is emphasized throughout that the doorkeeper apparently realizes nothing of all this. That is not in itself remarkable, since according to this interpretation the doorkeeper is deceived in a much more important issue, affecting his very office. At the end, for example, he says regarding the entrance to the Law: 'I am now going to shut it,' but at the beginning of the story we are told that the door leading into the Law always stands open, and if it always stands open, that is to say at all times, without reference to the life or death of the man, then the doorkeeper cannot close it. There is some difference of opinion about the motive behind the doorkeeper's statement, whether he said he was going to close the door merely for the sake of giving an answer, or to emphasize his devotion to duty, or to bring the man into a state of grief and regret in his last moments. But there is no lack of agreement that the doorkeeper will not be able to shut the door. Many indeed profess to find that he is subordinate to the man even in knowledge, toward the end, at least, for the man sees the radiance that issues from the door of the Law while the doorkeeper in his official position must stand with his back to the door, nor does he say anything to show that he has perceived the change." "That is well argued," said K., after repeating to himself in a low voice several passages from the priest's exposition. "It is well argued, and I am inclined to agree that the doorkeeper is deceived. But that has not made me abandon my former opinion, since both conclusions are to some extent compatible. Whether the doorkeeper is clear-sighted or deceived does not dispose of the matter. I said the man is deceived. If the doorkeeper is clear-sighted, one might have doubts about that, but if the doorkeeper himself is deceived, then his deception must of necessity be communicated to the man. That makes the doorkeeper not, indeed, a deceiver, but a creature so simple-minded that he ought to be dismissed at once from his office. You mustn't forget that the doorkeeper's deceptions do himself no harm but do infinite harm to the man." "There are objections to that," said the priest. "Many aver that the story confers no right on anyone to pass judgment on the doorkeeper. Whatever he may seem to us, he is yet a servant of the Law; that is, he belongs to the Law and as such is beyond human judgment. In that case one must not believe that the doorkeeper is subordinate to the man. Bound as he is by his service, even only at the door of the Law, he is incomparably greater than anyone at large in the world. The man is only seeking the Law, the doorkeeper is already attached to it. It is the Law that has placed him at his post; to doubt his dignity is to doubt the Law itself." "I don't agree with that point of view," said K., shaking his head, "for if one accepts it, one must accept as true everything the doorkeeper says. But you yourself have sufficiently proved how impossible it is to do that." "No," said the priest, "it is not necessary to accept everything as true, one must only accept it as necessary." A melancholy conclusion," said K. "It turns lying into a universal principle." *

K. said that with finality, but it was not his final judgment. He was too tired to survey all the conclusions arising from the story, and the trains of thought into which it was leading him were unfamiliar, dealing with impalpabilities better suited to a theme for discussion among Court officials than for him. The simple story had lost its clear outline, he wanted to put it out of his mind, and the priest, who now showed great delicacy of feeling, suffered him to do so and accepted his comment in silence, although undoubtedly he did not agree with it.

They paced up and down for a while in silence, K. walking close beside the priest, ignorant of his whereabouts. The lamp in his hand had long since gone out. The silver image of some saint once glimmered into sight immediately before him, by the sheen of its own silver, and was instantaneously lost in the darkness again. To keep himself from being utterly dependent on the priest, K. asked: "Aren't we near the main doorway now?" "No," said the priest, "we're a long way from it. Do you want to leave already?" Although at that moment K. had not been thinking of leaving, he answered at once: "Of course, I must go. I'm the Chief Clerk of a Bank, they're waiting for me, I only came here to show a business friend from abroad round the Cathedral." "Well," said the priest, reaching out his hand to K., "then go." "But I can't find my way alone in this darkness," said K. "Turn left to the wall," said the priest, "then follow the wall without leaving it and you'll come to a door." The priest had already taken a step or two away from him, but K. cried out in a loud voice, "Please wait a moment." "I am waiting," said the priest. "Don't you want anything more from me?" asked K. "No," said the priest. "You were so friendly to me for a time," said K., "and explained so much to me, and now you let me go as if you cared nothing about me." "But you have to leave now," said the priest. "Well, yes," said K., "you must see that I can't help it." "You must first see who I am,"

said the priest. "You are the prison chaplain," said K., grop-
ing his way nearer to the priest again; his immediate return to the Bank was not so necessary as he had made out,
he could quite well stay longer. "That means I belong to
the Court," said the priest. "So why should I want anything
from you? The Court wants nothing from you. It receives
you when you come and it dismisses you when you go."

CHAPTER TEN

The End

ON THE evening before K.'s thirty-first birthday—it was about nine o'clock, the time when a hush falls on the streets —two men came to his lodging. In frock coats, pallid and plump, with top hats that were apparently irremovable. After some exchange of formalities regarding precedence at the front door, they repeated the same ceremony more elaborately before K.'s door. Without having been informed of their visit, K. was sitting also dressed in black in an arm-chair near the door, slowly pulling on a pair of new gloves that fitted tightly over the fingers, looking as if he were expecting guests. He stood up at once and scrutinized the gentlemen with curiosity. "So you are meant for me?" he asked. The gentlemen bowed, each indicating the other with the hand that held the top hat. K. admitted to himself that he had been expecting different visitors. He went to the window and took another look at the dark street. Nearly all the windows at the other side of the street were also in darkness; in many of them the curtains were drawn.

223

At one lighted tenement window some babies were playing behind bars, reaching with their little hands toward
each other although not able to move themselves from the
spot. "Tenth-rate old actors they send for me," said K. to
himself, glancing round again to confirm the impression.
"They want to finish me off cheaply." He turned abruptly
toward the men and asked: "What theater are you playing
at?" "Theater?" said one, the corners of his mouth twitching
as he looked for advice to the other, who acted as if he
were a dumb man struggling to overcome a stubborn
disability. "They're not prepared to answer questions," said
K. to himself and went to fetch his hat.

While still on the stairs the two of them tried to take K.
by the arms, and he said: "Wait till we're in the street, I'm
not an invalid." But just outside the street door they fastened on him in a fashion he had never before experienced.
They kept their shoulders close behind his and, instead of
crooking their elbows, wound their arms round his at full
length, holding his hands in a methodical, practiced, irre-
sistible grip. K. walked rigidly between them, the three of
them were interlocked in a unity which would have
brought all three down together had one of them been
knocked over. It was a unity such as can hardly be formed
except by lifeless matter.

Under the street lamps K. attempted time and time
again, difficult though it was at such very close quarters,
to see his companions more clearly than had been possible
in the dusk of his room. Perhaps they are tenors," he
thought, as he studied their fat double chins. He was repelled by the painful cleanliness of their faces. One could
literally see that the cleansing hand had been at work in
the corners of the eyes, rubbing the upper lip, scrubbing
out the furrows at the chin.*

When that occurred to K. he halted, and in consequence
the others halted too; they stood on the verge of an open,

deserted square adorned with flower beds. "Why did they send you, of all people!" he said; it was more a cry than a question. The gentlemen obviously had no answer to make, they stood waiting with their free arms hanging, like sickroom attendants waiting while their patient takes a rest. "I won't go any farther," said K. experimentally. No answer was needed to that, it was sufficient that the two men did not loosen their grip and tried to propel K. from the spot; but he resisted them. I shan't need my strength much longer, I'll expend all the strength I have, he thought. Into his mind came a recollection of flies struggling away from the flypaper till their little legs were torn off. The gentlemen won't find it easy.

And then before them Fräulein Bürstner appeared, mounting a small flight of steps leading into the square from a low-lying side-street. It was not quite certain that it was she, but the resemblance was close enough. Whether it were really Fräulein Bürstner or not, however, did not matter to K.; the important thing was that he suddenly realized the futility of resistance. There would be nothing heroic in it were he to resist, to make difficulties for his companions, to snatch at the last appearance of life by struggling. He set himself in motion, and the relief his warders felt was transmitted to some extent even to himself. They suffered him now to lead the way, and he followed the direction taken by the girl ahead of him, not that he wanted to overtake her or to keep her in sight as long as possible, but only that he might not forget the lesson she had brought into his mind. "The only thing I can do now," he told himself, and the regular correspondence between his steps and the steps of the other two confirmed his thought, "the only thing for me to go on doing is to keep my intelligence calm and analytical to the end. I always wanted to snatch at the world with twenty hands, and not for a very laudable motive, either. That was wrong, and am I to show now that not even a year's trial has taught me anything? Am I to leave this world as a man who has no common sense? Are people to say of me after I am gone that at the beginning of my case I wanted to finish it, and at the end of it I wanted to begin it again? I don't want that to be said. I am grateful for the fact that these half-dumb, senseless creatures have been sent to accompany me on this journey, and that I have been left to say to myself all that is needed."

Fräulein Bürstner meanwhile had gone round the bend into a side street, but by this time K. could do without her and submitted himself to the guidance of his escort. In complete harmony all three now made their way across a bridge in the moonlight, the two men readily yielded to K.'s slightest movement, and when he turned slightly toward the parapet they turned, too, in a solid front. The water, glittering and trembling in the moonlight, divided on either side of a small island, on which the foliage of trees and bushes rose in thick masses, as if bunched together. Beneath the trees ran gravel paths, now invisible, with convenient benches on which K. had stretched himself at ease many a summer. "I didn't mean to stop," he said to his companions, shamed by their obliging compliance. Behind K.'s back the one seemed to reproach the other gently for the mistaken stop they had made, and then all three went on again.*

They passed through several steeply rising streets, in which policemen stood or patrolled at intervals; sometimes a good way off, sometimes quite near. One with a bushy mustache, his hand on the hilt of his saber, came up as of set purpose close to the not quite harmless-looking group. The two gentlemen halted, the policeman seemed to be already opening his mouth, but K. forcibly pulled his companions forward. He kept looking round cautiously to see if the policeman were following; as soon as he had put a corner between himself and the policeman he started to run, and his two companions, scant of breath as they were, had to run beside him.

So they came quickly out of the town, which at this point merged almost without transition into the open fields. A small stone quarry, deserted and desolate, lay quite near to a still completely urban house. Here the two men came to a standstill, whether because this place had been their goal from the very beginning or because they were too exhausted to go farther. Now they loosened their hold of K., who stood waiting dumbly, took off the top hats and wiped the sweat from their brows with pocket handkerchiefs, meanwhile surveying the quarry. The moon shone down on everything with that simplicity and serenity which no other light possesses.

After an exchange of courteous formalities regarding which of them was to take precedence in the next task— these emissaries seemed to have been given no specific assignments in the charge laid jointly upon them—one of them came up to K. and removed his coat, his waistcoat, and finally his shirt. K. shivered involuntarily, whereupon the man gave him a light, reassuring pat on the back. Then he folded the clothes carefully together, as if they were likely to be used again at some time, although perhaps not immediately. Not to leave K. standing motionless, exposed to the night breeze, which was rather chilly, he took him by the arm and walked him up and down a little, while his partner investigated the quarry to find a suitable spot. When he had found it he beckoned, and K.'s companion led him over there. It was a spot near the cliffside where a loose boulder was lying. The two of them laid K. down on the ground, propped him against the boulder, and settled his head upon it. But in spite of the pains they took and all the willingness K. showed, his posture remained contorted and unnatural-looking. So one of the men begged the other to let him dispose K. all by himself, yet even that did not improve matters. Finally they left K. in a position which was not even the best of the positions they had already tried out. Then one of them opened his frock coat and out of a sheath that hung from a belt girt round his waistcoat drew a long, thin, double-edged butcher's knife, held it up, and tested the cutting edges in the moonlight. Once more the odious courtesies began, the first handed the knife across K. to the second, who handed it across K. back again to the first. K. now perceived clearly that he was supposed to seize the knife himself, as it traveled from hand to hand above him, and plunge it into his own breast. But he did not do so, he merely turned his head, which was still free to move, and gazed around him. He could not completely rise to the occasion, he could not relieve the officials of all their tasks; the responsibility for this last failure of his lay with him who had not left him the remnant of strength necessary for the deed. His glance fell on the top story of the house adjoining the quarry. With a flicker as of a light going up, the casements of a window there suddenly flew open; a human figure, faint and insubstantial at that distance and that height, leaned abruptly far forward and stretched both arms still farther. Who was it? A friend? A good man? Someone who sympathized? Someone who wanted to help? Was it one person only? Or was it mankind? Was help at hand? Were there arguments in his favor that had been overlooked? Of course there must be. Logic is doubtless unshakable, but it cannot withstand a man who wants to go on living. Where was the Judge whom he had never seen? Where was the high Court, to which he had never penetrated? He raised his hands and spread out all his fingers.*

But the hands of one of the partners were already at K.'s throat, while the other thrust the knife deep into his heart and turned it there twice. With failing eyes K. could still see the two of them immediately before him, cheek leaning against cheek, watching the final act. "Like a dog!" he said; it was as if the shame of it must outlive him.

Appendices

The Unfinished Chapters

ON THE WAY TO ELSA

ONE day, just as he was about to leave the Bank, K. was rung up on the telephone and summoned to come to the Law Court at once. He was warned against disobedience. All his unprecedented statements: that the judicial examinations were unnecessary, that they led to no result and never could, that in the future he would refuse to appear, that he would ignore all summonses, whether by telephone or in writing, and would send any messengers packing—all those statements had been duly filed and had already done him considerable harm. And why should he refuse to obey? Was it not true that, regardless of time and money, every effort was being made to clarify his complicated case? Did he really wish to obstruct this wantonly and allow those violent measures to take their course from which he had so far been spared? Today's summons was his last chance. Let him act as he pleased, but let him remember that the High Court of Justice could not permit itself to be treated with contempt.

As it happened K. had announced a visit to Elsa for that evening, reason enough for not attending at Court. He was glad to be able to justify his nonappearance in this way, though he would naturally never make use of it as an excuse and would probably not have gone even if the evening had been entirely free and completely at his own disposal. Nevertheless, conscious of his own rights, he asked through the telephone what would happen if he failed to put in an appearance. "We shall know where to find you," was the answer. "And shall I be punished for not having come of my own accord?" asked K., and smiled in anticipation of the reply. "No," was the answer. "Splendid," said K., "then what motive could I have for complying with this summons?" "It is not usual to bring the powers of the Court upon one's own head," said the voice, becoming fainter and finally dying away. It is very rash not to do so, thought K. as he hung up; for after all one should try to find out what those powers are.

Without hesitation he drove off to Elsa. Leaning back comfortably in the corner of the carriage, his hands in his coat-pockets—for it was already getting chilly—he surveyed the bustling streets. With a certain satisfaction he reflected that, if the Court were really sitting, he was causing it considerable inconvenience. He had not said outright whether he were coming or not. So the Judge would be waiting and perhaps a whole assembly as well; and only K., to the disappointment of the gallery in particular, would not be there. Unperturbed by the Court, he was going where he wanted to go. Just for a moment he was uncertain whether he had not absentmindedly given the coachman the address of the Court, so he called out Elsa's address loudly. The coachman nodded his head; that was the address he had been given. From then onward K. gradually put the Court out of his mind and thoughts of the Bank began to preoccupy him exclusively as they had been wont to do.

JOURNEY TO HIS MOTHER

Suddenly, at lunch, it occurred to him that he wanted to visit his mother. Spring was nearly over now, which made it three years since he had seen her last. On that occasion she had begged him to come to her on his birthday; in spite of a good many difficulties he had complied and had even promised to spend all his future birthdays with her, a promise which, it must be owned, he had already broken twice. To make up for this, he decided not to wait for his birthday, although it was only a fortnight off, but to go at once. Yet, as he told himself, there was no particular reason to go at the actual moment; on the contrary, the news which he received regularly every two months from a cousin, who owned a business in the little town and administered the money K. sent for his mother, was more reassuring than ever before. It is true that his mother's eyesight was failing; but then K. had expected that for many years from the doctors' reports; and her general health had improved. Several of the disabilities of old age, instead of becoming more noticeable, were less so, or at least she complained less. His cousin was of the opinion that this was possibly connected with her excessive piety during the last few years. K. had noticed slight signs of that on his last visit with something like repugnance; and in one of his letters his cousin had described very vividly how the old lady, who used to drag herself along with such difficulty, now stepped out quite vigorously when he gave her his arm on the way to church. And K.

could believe his cousin implicitly, for he was an alarmist as a rule and apt to exaggerate the bad rather than the good side in his reports.

But be that as it might, K. had now decided to go. Among other distressing manifestations he had lately noticed a certain plaintiveness in himself, a tendency to give way without a struggle to all his desires. Well, in this case that failing at least served a good purpose.

He went to the window in order to collect his thoughts. He then ordered the meal to be cleared away at once and sent the attendant off to Frau Grubach to announce his departure and to fetch his suitcase packed with whatever she thought necessary. After that he gave Kühne a few instructions to cover the time of his absence; and on this occasion it hardly even vexed him that Kühne, in an ill-mannered fashion that had now become habitual, received the directions with averted head, as if he knew perfectly well what he had to do and only put up with K.'s injunctions as a pure formality. Finally K. went to the Manager. When he asked the latter for two days' leave to go and see his mother, the Manager naturally asked if she were ill. "No," said K. without further explanation. He was standing in the middle of the room, his hands crossed behind his back and frowning as he had thought it over. Had he perhaps been too precipitate in his preparations for departure? Wouldn't it have been better to stay here? Why did he want to go? Was sentimentality the cause of the journey? And might not such sentimentality result in something important missed, an opportunity to intervene, which might after all occur any day, any hour, now that his trial had apparently been at a standstill for weeks, and hardly one definite piece of news had reached him? Besides, might he not frighten the old lady, which was naturally not his intention, but which might very easily happen against his will, since so many things were happening now against his will? And his mother was not clamoring to see him; on the contrary. In the past his cousin's letters had been full of her repeated urgent invitations; but not for a long time now. So he was not going for his mother's sake; that much was clear. But if he were going for his own sake, cherishing any kind of hopes, then he was an irreclaimable fool, and he would be repaid for his folly there by the resultant despair. But, as if all these doubts were not his own, but were being insinuated into his mind by others, he came out of his trance and adhered to his resolution. Meanwhile the Manager, either by chance or more probably out of respect for K.'s silence, had been bending over a newspaper. He now looked up and, rising, shook hands with K., wishing him a pleasant journey without further questions.

K. then waited in his office for the return of the attendant, pacing up and down and monosyllabically warding off the Assistant Manager, who came in several times to inquire the reason for his departure. When at last the suitcase arrived, he hastened down at once to the cab which had been ordered earlier. He was already halfway down when at the last moment the official Kullich appeared at the head of the stairs holding a letter he had begun to write and obviously anxious for instructions. K. waved him away; but the fair-haired, chuckleheaded young man misunderstood the gesture and waving the paper came dashing down after K. in perilous leaps and bounds. The latter was so much incensed by this that, when Kullich overtook him on the outside staircase, he snatched the letter from him and tore it up. He looked back when he had got into the cab, and there stood Kullich, who had probably not even yet realized what he had done amiss, rooted to the spot and staring after the departing cab, while the porter beside him saluted deferentially. So K. was still one of the highest officials in the Bank; if he tried to deny it, the porter would contradict him. As for his mother, whatever he could say

to the contrary, she believed him to be the Bank Manager
and had done so for years. He would not sink in her
estimation, whatever other injury his prestige had suffered.
Perhaps it was a good sign that he had convinced himself
just as he was leaving that he could snatch a letter away
from an official who actually had some connection with the
Court and tear it up without any kind of apology and without reprisals.

Deleted from here on.

. . . On the other hand he had not been able to do what
he would have liked to do most of all: administer two
ringing blows on Kullich's pale round cheeks. From another point of view this is just as well; for K. hates Kullich,
and not Kullich alone, but Rabensteiner and Kaminer too.
He believes that he has hated them from the beginning.
Their appearance in Fräulein Bürstner's room had, it is
true, first brought them to his notice; but his hatred is
older. And latterly K. has been almost sick with that hatred,
for he cannot satisfy it. It is so difficult to get at them.
They are now the lowest of all the officials; and as they are
all three completely inferior, they will never get promotion
except through the pressure of their years of seniority and
even then more slowly than anyone else. So that it is next
to impossible to hinder their careers. No hindrance engi-
neered by anyone else can ever be as great as Kullich's
stupidity, Rabensteiner's laziness, and Kaminer's cringing
and repulsive modesty. The only thing one could attempt
against them would be to have them dismissed; and as a
matter of fact that would be very easy to compass. A word
from K. to the Manager would be enough. But K. shrinks
from that. Perhaps he might do it, if the Assistant Manager,
who openly or in secret favors everything K. hates, were
to take their part. But oddly enough the Assistant Manager

makes an exception in this case and wants the same thing
as K.

PROSECUTING COUNSEL *

In spite of his knowledge of men and the experience of
the world which K. had acquired during his long service in
the Bank, the company he met at dinner in the evenings
had always impressed him as particularly calculated to inspire respect and he never denied in his inmost thoughts
that it was a great honor for him to belong to such a
society. It consisted almost exclusively of judges, prosecuting counsel, and lawyers, although a few quite young officials and lawyers' clerks were also admitted; but they sat
right at the bottom of the table and were only allowed to
take part in the debates when questions were addressed to
them directly, such questions being nearly always put in
order to divert the rest of the company. Hasterer in particular, a prosecuting counsel who generally sat next to
K., loved to embarrass the young men in this way. When
he spread out his great hairy hand in the middle of the
table and turned toward the lower end, everyone sat up
and took notice. And if one of those below the salt took
up the question and could not make head or tail of it, or
stared thoughtfully into his mug of beer, or opened and
shut his jaws instead of speaking; or even—and that was
worst of all—championed an erroneous or discredited opinion in an endless flood of words, then the older men turned
round smiling in their chairs and really began to enjoy

* This fragment would have followed immediately after the
seventh chapter of the novel. It is begun on the same sheet of paper
on which the last sentences of that chapter are transcribed. M. B.

themselves. The solidly serious professional conversations were their exclusive prerogative.

K. had been introduced into this society by a lawyer who was the legal representative of the Bank. At one time K. had been obliged to hold long conferences with this lawyer lasting late into the evening; and so it had come about quite naturally that he had taken his supper at the lawyer's table and had enjoyed the society he met there. He found himself among a whole company of learned and eminent men who wielded a certain power and whose recreation consisted in exerting themselves to find the solution of thorny problems which had only the slightest connection with everyday life. K. himself could naturally take little part in all this; but it enabled him to learn a good deal which sooner or later might profit him in the Bank; and besides, there was the possibility of establishing personal relations with the Court, which were always useful. Moreover the members of the dining club seemed to like his society. He was soon accepted as an authority on business matters, and his opinion on such questions was accepted as incontrovertible, although with some ironical reservations. It frequently happened that when two of the diners could not agree on a point of commercial law they appealed to K. for his opinion on the facts of the case, and his name was then bandied about in all the retorts and counter-retorts and even figured in the most abstruse speculations long after he had ceased to follow the trend of the argument. Gradually however many obscurities were cleared up, for he had a helpful counselor by his side in the person of Hasterer, the prosecuting counsel, who became very friendly with him. He even frequently accompanied him home at night; and it took K. a long time to get used to walking arm in arm with this giant of a man who could have completely concealed him in the folds of his cloak.

In the course of time they became so intimate that all

distinctions of education, profession, and age were obliterated; they associated with each other as if they had
always belonged together; and if sometimes one of them
seemed superficially superior to the other, then it was not
Hasterer, but K., whose practical experience generally
proved right in the end, because it had been acquired at
first hand, which is never the case at a lawyer's desk.

Of course this friendship was soon common knowledge
among the members of the dining club; they began to
forget who K.'s original sponsor had been; for in any case
it was now Hasterer who stood surety for him, and he
would have had every right, had anyone ever questioned
his title to a seat at that table, to refer the doubter to
Hasterer. This gave K. a peculiarly privileged position, for
Hasterer was respected as much as he was feared. Granted
the force and ingenuity of his legal arguments, still many
others were at least his equals in that respect; but no one
could compete with him in the ferocity with which he de-
fended his opinions. K. had the impression that when
Hasterer failed to convince an opponent, he managed at
least to intimidate him, for many recoiled as soon as he
stretched out a finger in their direction. It almost seemed
at such times as if the opponent were on the point of forgetting that he was among friends and colleagues, that after
all it was only a theoretical discussion and that in reality
nothing could possibly happen to him; for he would fall
silent and it needed courage even to shake his head. Everyone felt apprehensive when the opponent was seated at a
considerable distance and Hasterer, realizing that he was
too far off to make him see reason, pushed back his plate
and got up slowly in order to get into contact with him.
Those seated near him bent their heads back the better to
see his face. On the other hand such incidents were relatively rare, for it was only legal questions which really had
the power to rouse him, especially those about trials which

he had conducted or was conducting himself. When such questions were not involved, he was a quiet and friendly person, with an amiable way of laughing and a passion for the good things of the table. It could even happen at times that, paying no heed to the general conversation, he would turn to K., and with his arm along the back of his friend's chair, would question him in a lowered voice about the Bank and then talk about his own work or about his lady-friends, who were almost as troublesome as the Law Courts. With no one else at the table was he ever seen to speak like this; and in fact if Hasterer were to be asked for a favor—generally in order to reconcile him with a colleague—K. was often approached first to act as mediator, a task he always undertook willingly and with ease and brought to a successful conclusion. Altogether, far from exploiting his relationship with Hasterer in such matters, he was very courteous and modest with everyone; and (much more important than modesty and courtesy) he knew how to differentiate correctly between the various grades in the legal hierarchy and to treat everyone according to his rank. This admittedly was due to Hasterer, who never tired of instructing him in the art. It was the only set of rules which he himself never broke even in the stormiest debate. That was why he only addressed the young men at the bottom of the table, who had hardly as yet achieved a rank, in general terms, treating them, not as individuals, but as a conglomerate mass. Yet it was just those men who showed him the greatest respect; and when he rose up from the table at about eleven o'clock to go home, one of them was immediately by his side to help him on with his heavy coat, and another to hold the door open for him with a low bow, and to keep it open of course for K. when he left the room with Hasterer.

At the beginning of their friendship K. had accompanied Hasterer part of the way home, or else Hasterer had done

the same by K.; but as time went on the evenings generally ended by Hasterer inviting K. to come back home with
him and stay a while. They would then often sit together
for an hour over brandy and cigars. Those evenings were
so much to Hasterer's taste that he could not bring himself
to forego them even when he had a woman called Helen
living with him for a few weeks. She was a fat female of
uncertain age with yellowish skin and dark curls clustering
round her forehead. At first K. never saw her except in
bed, shamelessly sprawling, reading a serial novel and paying no heed to their conversation. Only when it was getting
late, she would stretch and yawn or even throw one of her
serial numbers at Hasterer if she could not attract his attention in any other way. The latter would then get up
smiling and K. would take his leave. But later, when
Hasterer was beginning to tire of Helen, she became a very
disturbing influence. She was now fully clad when they
arrived, generally in a dress which she doubtless thought
highly becoming and stylish, actually an old ball-dress be-
dizened with trimmings and draped with several rows of
conspicuously unsightly fringes. K. had no idea what this
dress really looked like, for he could hardly bring himself
to glance at her, and would sit for hours on end with
lowered lids while she walked up and down the room sway-
ing her hips or sat down near him. Later, as her position
became increasingly precarious, she made desperate efforts
to arouse Hasterer's jealousy by openly preferring K. It was
only misery and not malice which made her lean across the
table, exposing her bare, fat, rounded back, in order to
bring her face into close proximity with K.'s and force him
to look at her. All she gained from that was K.'s refusal to
go to Hasterer next time he was asked; and when he did
return after an interval, Helen had been sent packing for
good and all. K. took that as a matter of course. They remained together for an unusually long time that evening

and at Hasterer's instigation they drank the pledge of brotherhood. Indeed on going home he was next door to being fuddled with all the smoking and drinking.

The very next morning in the course of a business conversation the Bank Manager remarked that he believed he had seen K. the evening before. If he were not mistaken, K. had been walking arm in arm with Hasterer, the prosecuting counsel. The Manager seemed to think this so extraordinary that he named the church alongside which, close to the fountain, the encounter had taken place. Although this was typical of his usual accuracy, still, if he had been describing a *fata morgana,* he could hardly have made more of it. K. thereupon explained to him that the prosecuting counsel was a friend of his and agreed that they had in fact passed by the church the evening before. Smiling in astonishment, the Manager asked K. to sit down. This was one of the moments which so much endeared him to K.; moments in which a certain anxiety for K.'s welfare and his future made itself felt on the part of a man who was a confirmed invalid with a chronic cough and in addition overburdened with work of the utmost responsibility. It was certainly possible to label this solicitude cold and superficial (as other officials did who had experienced something similar), nothing but a stratagem by which to attach valuable assistants to his person for years at the sacrifice of a few moments of his time; but, be that as it might, K. was subjugated by the Manager in such moments. Perhaps too the Manager used a rather different tone to K. than to the others. He did not, for instance, forget his position of authority in order to be on the level with K., a regular practice of his in ordinary business intercourse; on the contrary at such times he seemed actually to have forgotten K.'s position in the Bank and spoke to him as if he were a child or an ignorant young man applying for a post who, for some obscure reason, had aroused the Manager's good will.

K. would certainly never have tolerated such a method of address from anyone else, nor from the Manager himself, if the solicitude of the latter had not seemed genuine, or rather if the mere possibility of the solicitude revealed in such moments had not completely disarmed him. He realized that this was a weakness; its cause was possibly to seek in the fact that in this respect there really was something childish about him still, because he had never known a father's care, his own having died very young. K. had left home early and had always repelled rather than invited the tenderness of his mother, who still lived, half blind, in the sleepy little town and whom he had last visited about two years ago.

"I knew nothing whatsoever about this friendship," said the Manager; and only a faint friendly smile softened the severity of the words.

THE HOUSE

Without any very definite purpose at first K. had tried on several occasions to find out where the office was situated which had sent out the first notification of his case. He discovered it without difficulty. Both Titorelli and Wolfahrt told him the exact number of the house as soon as he asked them. Later Titorelli completed the information with a smile which he always had ready for any private plans not submitted for his approval. This, he declared, was the office which, more than any other, was entirely negligible. It only executed the commissions entrusted to it, being merely the most remote agent of the great Court of Impeachment. It was true that this latter was not accessible to defendants, and that if one of them wanted something from the Court of Impeachment—there were naturally many such wishes, although it was not always wise to express them—then admittedly he would have to apply to the above-named subordinate court. Nevertheless, neither would he penetrate to the real Court of Impeachment by doing so, nor would he ever succeed in bringing his wishes to its notice.

K. already knew the painter's technique; he therefore did not contradict him, nor did he pursue his inquiries, he merely nodded his head and stored up the information. It seemed to him, and not for the first time, that as far as tormenting went, Titorelli was more than a match for the lawyer, the only difference being that K. was not so much at Titorelli's mercy, and could shake him off without more ado if and when he had a mind to. Besides Titorelli was extremely communicative, not to say garrulous, although less so of late; and finally K. had it in his power to plague Titorelli himself.

And plague him he did in connection with the matter in hand, often speaking of that house in a tone which implied that he was keeping something back from Titorelli; hinting that he was in contact with the office situated there, but that his connection with it had not yet progressed far enough to be made known with impunity. But if Titorelli thereupon pressed him for more detailed disclosures, K. would change the subject abruptly and not refer to it again for a long time. Little triumphs of this sort procured him moments of pleasure. At such times he believed that he now understood the people in the proximity of the Court much better than before and could make them dance to his piping. He felt that he had almost become one of them, or at least that he shared in flashes the clearer view which their position on the first step leading up to the Court somehow assured them. What matter then if in the end he should after all lose his position down here? Even then there was still a possibility of salvation there. He need only slip into their ranks; and, if they had been unable to help him with his case because they were too lowly placed or for any other reason, they could still shelter him and hide him. Indeed if he did it circumspectly and secretly, they were in no position to refuse him this service, especially not Titorelli, whose close acquaintance and benefactor he had after all become.

It was not every day that K. nourished such hopes as this. As a rule he was still clear-sighted enough and on his guard against overlooking or overleaping any kind of obstacle. But in moments of absolute exhaustion, generally in the evening when the day's work was done, he took comfort from the most trifling incidents, and equivocal ones into the bargain, which the day had brought forth. Lying as a rule full length on the sofa in his office—he could no longer leave his office without resting for an hour on his sofa—he would mentally piece his observations together. He did not restrict himself narrowly to those persons who were connected with the Court; in his half-sleeping state they all mingled together. He then forgot the tremendous tasks which the Court had to fulfill; he thought of himself as the only defendant and of all the others as officials and lawyers thronging the corridors of a law court; even the dullest walked with bowed heads, pursed lips, and the fixed gaze induced by weighty thoughts. In these visions Frau Grubach's lodgers always made their appearance as a closed group. They stood shoulder to shoulder with open mouths, like an accusing chorus. There were many unfamiliar faces among them, for it was long enough since K. had taken the slightest interest in the affairs of the boarding-house; and because of the many unknown faces he felt uncomfortable when scrutinizing the group. But this had to be done sometimes when he was searching for Fräulein Bürstner among them. For instance, glancing rapidly along the group he would suddenly encounter a pair of totally unfamiliar eyes shining into his own and arresting his attention. Then of course he could not see Fräulein Bürstner; but, in order to make assurance doubly sure, he looked again, and there she was, right in the middle, her arms round two men standing beside her. He could hardly have cared less, especially as there was nothing new about the scene, it being merely the indelible impression made upon him by a photograph taken at the seaside which he had once seen in Fräulein Bürstner's room. All the same it had the effect of making him avoid the group; and although he often returned to the place, he now hastened through the building, up and down, with long strides. He knew his way about all the rooms very well; remote passages he could never have seen in his life seemed as familiar to him as if he had always lived there, and details kept on impressing themselves on his mind with painful clarity. For instance there was a foreigner strolling about in the antechamber dressed like a bullfighter, with a wasp waist and an abbreviated little coat of coarse yellow lace standing out stiffly; this man, without pausing for a moment in his perambulations, allowed K.'s astonished gaze to follow him unremittingly. Stooping low, K. circled round him, gaping at him with wide-open eyes. He knew all the patterns of the lace, all the torn fringes, all the oscillations of the little coat, and still he couldn't see enough of it. Or rather, he had seen enough of it long ago; or, better still, he had never wanted to look at it at all, and yet he couldn't tear himself away. What masquerades foreign countries provide, he thought, and opened his eyes wider still. And he kept on following this man about until he flung himself round on the sofa and pressed his face into the leather upholstery.

Deleted from here on.

He lay like this for a long time and really rested now.

He still went on thinking, but it was in the dark and undisturbed. Best of all he liked to think of Titorelli. Titorelli
was sitting in an armchair and K. was kneeling beside
him, stroking his arms and cajoling him in every possible
way. The painter knew quite well what K. was aiming at,
but he pretended not to know and this tormented K. a
little. Yet K. for his part knew that he would finally succeed; for Titorelli was a frivolous person and easy to win
over, being without a strict sense of duty, so that it was a
mystery how the Court had come to have any dealings with
a man like that. Here if anywhere, he realized, it would
be possible to break through. He was not disconcerted by
Titorelli's shameless smile, directed with lifted head into
empty space; he persisted in his request and even went so
far as to stroke Titorelli's cheeks. He did this slackly, almost sluggishly, taking an inordinate pleasure in prolong-
ing the situation, for he was certain of success. How easy it
was to outwit the Court! Finally, as if he were obeying a
law of nature, Titorelli bent down toward him and took
K.'s hand in a firm clasp, while a slow and friendly lower-
ing of his eyelids showed that he was ready to grant K.'s
desire. K. rose to his feet; he naturally felt rather solemn;
but Titorelli would have nothing more to do with solemnity. He seized hold of K. and started to run, pulling K.
after him. In the twinkling of an eye they were in the Law
Courts and flying along the stairs, upward and downward
too, without the slightest effort, gliding along as easily as a
buoyant craft through water. And at the very moment when
K. looked down at his feet and came to the conclusion that
this lovely motion had no connection with the humdrum
life he had led until now—at that very moment over his
bent head the transformation occurred. The light which
until then had been behind them changed and suddenly
flowed in a blinding stream toward them. K. looked up,
Titorelli nodded assent and turned him round. He was in

the corridor of the Law Courts again, but everything was
quieter and simpler and there were no conspicuous details.
He took it all in at a glance, detached himself from
Titorelli, and went his way. He was wearing a new long
dark suit which comforted him by its warmth and weight.
He knew what had happened to him; but he was so happy
about it that he could not bring himself to acknowledge it.
In the corner of one of the passages he found his other
clothes in a heap: the black jacket, the pin-striped trousers,
and on the top the shirt stretched out with crumpled
sleeves.

CONFLICT WITH THE ASSISTANT MANAGER

One morning K. felt much fresher and more resilient than
usual. Thoughts of the Court hardly intruded at all; or
when they did, it seemed as if it would be easy enough to
get a purchase on this immeasurably vast organism by
means of some hidden lever which admittedly he would
first have to grope for in the dark; but that then it would
be child's play to grasp it, uproot the whole thing, and
shatter it. This unwonted state of mind actually induced
K. to invite the Assistant Manager to his room in order
to discuss a business matter which had been pending for
some time. On such occasions the Assistant Manager always
acted as if his relationship with K. had not altered in the
least during the last months. He came in as calmly as he
used to do in the earlier days of his incessant rivalry with
K.; he listened calmly to K.'s expositions, showed his sym-
pathetic interest by little remarks on a confidential, indeed
comradely, nature, and only put him out of countenance,
although not necessarily with intent, by refusing to be di-
verted by a hair's breadth from the matter in hand. It was

no exaggeration to say that he concentrated his whole mind on this; whereas K.'s thoughts, faced with such a model of conscientiousness, began to stray in all directions and forced him to leave the matter in question almost without a struggle to the Assistant Manager. On one occasion he had been woolgathering to such an extent that he only began to take notice when the Assistant Manager suddenly got up and went back to his office in silence. K. had no idea what had happened. It was possible that the conference had come to a normal end; but it was equally possible that the Assistant Manager had broken it off because K. had unwittingly offended him, or because he had been talking nonsense, or because the Assistant Manager had realized that he was not attending and that his thoughts were elsewhere. But worse than that, it might well be that K. had made some ludicrous proposal or that his adversary had wormed one out of him and was now hastening to put it into execution to K.'s detriment. On the other hand, no further mention was made of this particular matter. K. was unwilling to bring it up and the Assistant Manager remained uncommunicative; meanwhile there had at least so far been no visible repercussions. At all events K. had not been frightened off by this incident. Let a suitable opportunity present itself, and let him but feel at all equal to it, and there he would be at the Assistant Manager's door either to go in to him or to invite him to his office. The time had passed for lying low as he had done before. He no longer hoped for an early decisive victory which would free him at one blow from all his anxieties and restore his previous relationship with the Assistant Manager. K. realized that he must persist; for should he bow to the facts and retreat, then there was the danger that never again in all probability would he be able to advance. The Assistant Manager must not be allowed to continue in the belief that K. was dead and done for; he must not be permitted to sit quietly in his office secure in that belief; his peace of mind must be attacked. He must be made to realize as often as possible that K. was still alive, and that like all living things he might yet one day astonish the world with new potentialities, however little danger there seemed of that just now. K. sometimes told himself, it is true, that in adopting this method he was simply and solely fighting for his honor; for it could surely profit him nothing to keep on opposing the Assistant Manager in all his weakness, thus increasing the latter's sense of power and giving him the opportunity to observe the present state of affairs accurately and take his measures accordingly. But K. could not have altered his conduct had he wished to do so; he was the victim of self-delusion; at times he was absolutely convinced that the psychological moment had come to measure himself against the Assistant Manager, and the most unfortunate experiences never taught him better. What he had not achieved in ten cases, he believed that he would accomplish in the eleventh, although everything without exception had always turned out to his disadvantage. When after such encounters he was left exhausted, bathed in sweat, and drained of thought, he never knew whether it had been hope or despair which had impelled him into the presence of his enemy. Yet the next time it was hope again and nothing but hope with which he hastened to the Assistant Manager's door.

The passage in square brackets was deleted by the author.

[On that morning the hope seemed to be particularly well founded. The Assistant Manager came in slowly, his hand to his head and complaining of a headache. K.'s first reaction was to reply to this, but then he thought better of it, and embarked immediately on business without paying the slightest attention to his opponent's headache. Now,

whether the pains were not very acute, or whether his
interest in the subject under discussion allayed them for
the moment; whatever the reason, the Assistant Manager
removed his hand from his forehead during the course of
the conversation and answered in his usual style, promptly
and almost without stopping to think, like one of those
model pupils who answer before the question is well out
of the master's mouth. This time K. was able to meet him
on his own ground and refute him several times. But the
thought of the Assistant Manager's headache kept on nag-
ging at him, as if it told in his enemy's favor instead of
against him. He bore and mastered his pains so admirably!
Sometimes he would smile irrespective of what he was saying, as if he were boasting of the fact that, though he had
a headache, this did not hinder his mental processes. They
were speaking of quite other things, but at the same time
a soundless dialogue was taking place between them, in
which the Assistant Manager, without denying the violence
of his headache, kept on hinting that the pains were harm-
less and therefore quite different from those K. was accustomed to have. And however much K. contradicted him,
the way in which the Assistant Manager dealt with his
pains gave K. the lie. But at the same time it was an example to him. He too could barricade himself against all those
carking cares which had nothing to do with his profession.
He need only stick more closely to his work than ever before and introduce new methods into the Bank whose
establishment and maintenance would provide him with a
permanent occupation; he must also strengthen his slightly
slackened ties with the world of commerce by visits and
journeys, report more frequently to the Manager, and try
to obtain special commissions from him.]

It was the same again today. The Assistant Manager
came in at once, then remained standing near the door,

polished his pince-nez (a new habit of his), and looked
first at K. and then, in order not to occupy himself too
conspicuously with the Chief Clerk, he surveyed the whole
room carefully. It seemed as if he were seizing the opportunity to test his eyesight. K. withstood this byplay and
even smiled slightly as he asked the Assistant Manager to
be seated. He sat down himself in his armchair, moving
it as close to the Assistant Manager as possible, took up
the relevant papers at once, and began his report. At first
his vis-à-vis hardly seemed to be listening. Round the top
of K.'s desk ran a little carved balustrade. The desk was a
piece of excellent workmanship and the balustrade too was
firmly attached to the wood. But the Assistant Manager
made a show of discovering just at that moment that it was
loose, and he tried to repair the damage by tapping it with
his forefinger. K. thereupon offered to interrupt his report,
but the other would not consent to this, declaring that he
could hear and follow everything perfectly. In the meantime, however, K. could not elicit a single factual observation from him, whereas the balustrade seemed to demand
extraordinary measures; for the Assistant Manager now
brought out his penknife and, using K.'s ruler as a lever, he
tried to lift up the balustrade, evidently in order the better
to thrust it back. In his report K. had embodied a proposal
of an entirely new kind which, he assured himself, could
not fail to impress the Assistant Manager greatly; and as
he now came to this proposal he could hardly pause to take
breath, enthralled as he was by his own production, or
rather uplifted by the consciousness, daily becoming rarer,
that he still had a part to play in the Bank and that his
ideas had the power to vindicate him. Perhaps indeed this
was the best way to defend himself, and not only in the
Bank, but in his trial too, a far better way probably than
any other line of defense he had so far adopted or con-

templated. Reading at top speed, K. could not spare the time to ask the Assistant Manager in so many words to desist from his labors at the balustrade; all he could manage while he was reading was to run his hand reassuringly along the balustrade, almost unconsciously indicating that there was nothing wrong with it; and that even if there were, listening was more important at the moment and also more befitting than any attempt to put it right. But this manual task had roused the other's zeal, as often happens with energetic persons whose occupation is exclusively mental. One piece of the balustrade had now been successfully levered up, and the problem was how to get the little pillars back into the appropriate holes. That was the most ticklish part of the whole operation. The Assistant Manager got to his feet and tried to force the balustrade back into position with both hands; but try how he might, he did not succeed. While reading his report and elaborating it as he went on, K. had only vaguely noticed that his companion had stood up. Although he had rarely quite lost sight of the latter's amateur carpentry, still he took it for granted that this abrupt movement was somehow also connected with his report. So he got up too and, with one finger underlining a group of figures, he held out a sheet of paper to the Assistant Manager. But in the meantime the other had realized that his hands alone would never do the trick, and therefore, taking a sudden decision, he sat down with his whole weight on the balustrade. Success certainly crowned this effort. The little pillars went crashing back into their holes, but one of them broke in the process and the delicate upper strip split in two. "Rotten wood," said the Assistant Manager crossly.

A FRAGMENT

It was drizzling when they came out of the theater. K. was already tired out by the play and the poor performance; and the thought that he would have to put up his uncle for the night depressed him profoundly. For today of all days he had set his heart on a talk with F[räulein] B[ürstner], and perhaps there might have been an opportunity to get hold of her, but his uncle's presence put it entirely out of the question. Actually there was a night train which his uncle could catch; but there seemed not the slightest chance of persuading him to leave today when he was so much preoccupied with K.'s trial. However K. made the attempt, although without much hope of success. "My dear uncle," he said, "I'm afraid that I shall really need your help in the near future. I can't quite see yet in what connection; but I shall certainly need it." "You can count on me," said his uncle; "for I can think of nothing else but how to help you." "That's just like you," said K.; "only I'm afraid that my aunt will be vexed if I have to ask you to return here in a day or two." "Your trial is more important than annoyances of that sort." "I can't quite agree with you there," said K., "but whether or no, I don't want to deprive my aunt of your society more than is necessary; and as it looks as if I shall want you in the course of the next few days, what about going home in the meantime?" "Tomorrow?" "Yes, tomorrow," said K., "or perhaps even now with the night train; that might be best."

The Passages Deleted
by the Author

Page 10

The interrogation seems to be limited to looks, thought K.; well, I'll give him a few minutes' grace. I wish I knew what kind of an official body it can be which goes in for such elaborate arrangements in a case like mine which, from the official point of view, offers no prospects of any kind. For elaborate is the only word to use for this whole setup. Three people already wasted on me, two rooms not belonging to me disarranged, and over there in the corner another three young men are standing and looking at Fräulein Bürstner's photographs.

Page 11

As someone said to me—I can't remember now who it was—it is really remarkable that when you wake up in the morning you nearly always find everything in exactly the same place as the evening before. For when asleep and dreaming you are, apparently at least, in an essentially different state from that of wakefulness; and therefore, as that man truly said, it requires enormous presence of mind or rather quickness of wit, when opening your eyes to seize hold as it were of everything in the room at exactly the same place where you had let it go on the previous evening. That was why, he said, the moment of waking up was the riskiest moment of the day. Once that was well over without deflecting you from your orbit, you could take heart of grace for the rest of the day.

Page 12

As you know, employees always know more than their employers.

Page 18

The thought that by doing this he was perhaps making it easier for them to keep his own person under observation, which they had possibly been instructed to do, seemed to him such a ludicrous notion, that he buried his head in his hands and remained like that for several minutes in order to come to his senses. "A few more ideas like that," he said to himself, "and you really will go mad." Then he raised his rather grating voice all the louder.

Page 22

A soldier was doing sentry duty up and down before the house. So now they had even put a watch on the house. K. had to lean out very far to see him, for he was walking close to the wall. "Hallo!" he called out to him, but not loud enough for the man to hear. However it soon became apparent that he was only waiting for a servant girl who had gone across the road to a public house to fetch some beer, for she now appeared in the lighted doorway. K. asked himself if he had believed even for a moment that

the sentry had been meant for him. He could not answer
the question.

Page 26
"What a tiresome person you are; it's impossible to tell
whether you are serious or not." "There's something in
that," said K., delighted to be chatting with a pretty girl;
"there's something in that. I am never serious, and therefore I have to make jokes do duty both for jest and earnest.
But I was arrested in earnest."

Page 38
Instead of "local political meeting," "socialist meeting"
was originally used.

Page 46
All K. could see was that her blouse was unbuttoned
and hanging round her waist, that a man had dragged her
into a corner and was pressing her body to his, she being
bare from the waist up except for her vest.

Page 58
K. had just been going to catch hold of the woman's
hand which she was obviously if timorously stretching out
to him, when the student's words caught his attention.
He was a voluble, overbearing young man, so that perhaps it would be possible to get more precise information
from him about the charges brought against K. And if only
K. had this information then undoubtedly he could put a
stop to the whole proceedings immediately with one wave
of his hand, to everyone's dismay.

Page 88
Yes, it was even certain that he would also have rejected

this proposal even if it had been combined with bribery, which would probably have offended him still more. For, as long as his case was pending, K.'s person must surely be inviolable to all the officials connected with the case.

Page 100

Even this praise left the girl unmoved, nor did it seem to make any real impression on her when K.'s uncle replied: "Maybe. All the same I'll send a nurse round to you, if possible today. If she does not prove satisfactory, you can always dismiss her; but give her a trial to please me. These surroundings and the oppressive silence you are living in are enough to finish anyone off." "It's not always so quiet here," said the lawyer; "I'll only agree to that hospital nurse if I must." "You must," said K.'s uncle.

Page 106

The desk, which took up almost the whole length of the room, stood near the windows and was placed in such a way that the lawyer had his back to the door, so that a visitor was obliged to cross the whole width of the room like the veriest intruder before he could see the lawyer's face, unless indeed the latter were kind enough to turn round toward him.

Page 134

No, K. had nothing whatsoever to hope for if his trial became common knowledge. Anyone who did not rise up as a judge to condemn him out of hand would certainly try to humiliate him at the very least, that being now such an easy thing to do.

Page 182

It was quite dark in the room; there were probably heavy stuff curtains at the windows which allowed no shimmer of light to shine through. Slightly stimulated because he had been running, K. automatically took several long strides. Then he came to a halt and realized that he had no idea which part of the room he was in. The lawyer was obviously asleep and his breathing was inaudible because it was his habit to creep right under the feather quilt.

Page 186

. . . as if he were waiting for a sign of life from the accused. . . .

Page 188

"You are not speaking frankly to me, and you never have spoken frankly to me. So that if, at least in your own opinion, you are being misjudged, you have only yourself to blame. I am not afraid of being misjudged, because I am being frank with you. You have pounced upon my case as if I were quite free; and it almost seems to me now as if you had not only conducted it badly, but as if, omitting to take any serious steps, you had also tried to conceal the state of the case from me, thus obstructing any intervention on my part, so that one day, somewhere, in my absence, judgment will be pronounced. I do not say that you meant to do all that. . . ."

Page 192

It would have been very tempting now to laugh at Block. Leni took advantage of K.'s absentmindedness and, since he was holding her hands, she rested her elbows on the back of his armchair and began to rock it gently. At first K. paid no attention to this, but watched Block cautiously lifting up the feather quilt, obviously in order to find the lawyer's hands, which he wished to kiss.

Page 200

. . . if one did not know what he was talking about, one would have taken it, at first sight at least, to be the falling of water into the basin of a fountain.

Page 220

When he had said that, he faltered. It came home to him that he had been talking about a legend and judging it and yet that he knew nothing whatsoever about its source of origin and that he was equally in the dark about the interpretations. He had been drawn into a train of thought which was totally foreign to him. So after all this priest was like all the others? Only willing to speak about K.'s case allusively, in order to mislead him perhaps and finally fall silent? Revolving these thoughts, K. had neglected the lamp, which began to smoke, although he only noticed this when the smoke was eddying round his chin. Then he tried to turn the lamp down and it went out. He stood still. It was quite dark and he had no idea which part of the church he was in. As there was no sound anywhere near him either, he asked: "Where are you?" "Here," said the priest and took his hand. "Why did you let the lamp go out? Come with me and I'll take you to the vestry where there is a light."

K. was glad enough to be able to leave the Cathedral proper. The height and breadth of the space around him oppressed him, impenetrable as it was to his gaze except for a tiny circumference. More than once, although well aware of the futility of doing so, he had looked up, and darkness, nothing but darkness, had literally flown toward him from all sides. Led by the priest, he hastened after him.

A lamp was burning in the vestry, a still smaller lamp than the one K. was carrying; and it hung down so low that it hardly illuminated anything but the floor of the vestry which, though narrow, was probably as lofty as the

Cathedral itself. "It's so dark everywhere," said K. and put his hand over his eyes as if they were aching from the strain of finding his way about.

Page 224

Their eyebrows looked as if they had been stuck on to their foreheads, and they danced up and down, independent of the movements made in walking.

Page 226

They went along several paths mounting upward. There were policemen about here and there, either standing or strolling, sometimes in the distance, sometimes very near. One of them with a bushy mustache, his hand on the hilt of the saber entrusted to him by the state, strode up, purposefully it seemed, toward the rather suspect-looking group. "The state is offering to come to my assistance," whispered K. into the ear of one of the men. "What if I transferred the trial into the domain where the writ of the state law runs? The outcome might very well be that I would have to defend you two gentlemen against the state!"

Page 228 ORIGINAL VERSION OF THE LAST SENTENCES IN THE PENULTIMATE PARAGRAPH.

. . . were there arguments in his favor that had been overlooked? Of course there must be. Logic is doubtless unshakable, but it cannot withstand a man who wants to go on living. Where was the Judge? Where the High Court of Justice? I have something to say. I lift up my hands.

Postscript to the First Edition

(1925)

ALL Franz Kafka's utterances about life were profound and original, and so too was his attitude toward his own work and to the question of publication altogether. It would be impossible to overrate the gravity of the problems with which he wrestled in this connection, and which for that reason must serve as a guide for any publication of his posthumous works. The following indications may help to give at least an approximate idea of his attitude.

I wrested from Kafka nearly everything he published either by persuasion or by guile. This is not inconsistent with the fact that he frequently during long periods of his life experienced great happiness in writing, although he never dignified it by any other name than "scribbling." Anyone who was ever privileged to hear him read his own prose out loud to a small circle of intimates with an intoxicating fervor and a rhythmic verve beyond any actor's power was made directly aware of the genuine irrepressible joy in creation and of the passion behind his work.

If he nevertheless repudiated it, this was firstly because certain unhappy experiences had driven him in the direction of a kind of self-sabotage and therefore also toward nihilism as far as his own work was concerned; but also independently of that because, admittedly without ever saying so, he applied the highest religious standard to his art; and since this was wrung from manifold doubts and difficulties, that standard was too high. It was probably immaterial to him that his work might nevertheless greatly help many others who were striving after faith, nature, and wholeness of soul; for in his inexorable search for his own salvation, his first need was to counsel, not others, but himself.

That is how I personally interpret Kafka's negative attitude toward his own work. He often spoke of "false hands" beckoning to him while he was writing; and he also maintained that what he had already written, let alone published, interfered with his further work. There were many obstacles to be overcome before a volume of his saw the light of day. All the same, the sight of the books in print gave him real pleasure, and occasionally, too, the impression they made. In fact there were times when he surveyed both himself and his works with a more benevolent eye, never quite without irony, but with friendly irony; with an irony which concealed the infinite pathos of a man who admitted of no compromise in his striving for perfection.

No will was found among Kafka's literary remains. In his desk among a mass of papers lay a folded note written in ink and addressed to me. This is how it runs:

DEAREST MAX, my last request: Everything I leave behind me (in my bookcase, linen-cupboard, and my desk both at home and in the office, or anywhere else where anything may have got to and meets your eye), in the way of diaries, manuscripts, letters (my own and others'), sketches, and so on, to be burned unread; also all writings and sketches which you or others may possess; and ask those others for them in my name. Letters which they do not want to hand over to you, they should at least promise faithfully to burn themselves.

Yours,

FRANZ KAFKA

A closer search produced an obviously earlier note written in pencil on yellowed paper, which said:

DEAR MAX, perhaps this time I shan't recover after all. Pneumonia after a whole month's pulmonary fever is all too likely; and not even writing this down can avert it, although there is a certain power in that.

For this eventuality therefore, here is my last will concerning everything I have written:

Of all my writings the only books that can stand are these: *The Judgment, The Stoker, Metamorphosis, Penal Colony, Country Doctor* and the short story: *Hunger Artist.* (The few copies of *Meditation* can remain. I do not want to give anyone the trouble of pulping them; but nothing in that volume must be printed again.) When I say that those five books and the stort story can stand, I do not mean that I wish them to be reprinted and handed down to posterity. On the contrary, should they disappear altogether that would please me best. Only, since they do exist, I do not wish to hinder anyone who may want to, from keeping them.

But everything else of mine which is extant (whether in journals, in manuscript, or letters), everything without exception in so far as it is discoverable or obtainable from the addressees by request (you know most of them yourself; it is chiefly . . . and whatever happens don't forget the couple of notebooks in . . .'s possession)—all these things, without exception and preferably unread (I won't absolutely forbid you to look at them, though I'd far rather you didn't and in any case no one else is to do so)—all these things without exception are to be burned, and I beg you to do this as soon as possible.

FRANZ

If, in spite of these categorical instructions, I nevertheless refuse to perform the holocaust demanded of me by my friend, I have good and sufficient reasons for that.

Some of them do not admit of public discussion; but in my opinion those which I can communicate are themselves amply sufficient to explain my decision.

The chief reason is this: when in 1921 I embarked on a new profession, I told Kafka that I had made my will in which I had asked him to destroy this and that, to look through some other things, and so forth. Kafka thereupon showed me the outside of the note written in ink which was later found in his desk, and said: "My last testament will be quite simple—a request to you to burn everything." I can still remember the exact wording of the answer I gave him: "If you seriously think me capable of such a thing, let me tell you here and now that I shall not carry out your wishes." The whole conversation was conducted in the jesting tone we generally used together, but with the underlying seriousness which each of us always took for granted in the other. Convinced as he was that I meant what I said, Franz should have appointed another executor if he had been absolutely and finally determined that his instructions should stand.

I am far from grateful to him for having precipitated me into this difficult conflict of conscience, which he must have foreseen, for he knew with what fanatical veneration I listened to his every word. Among other things, this was the reason why, during the whole twenty-two years of our unclouded friendship, I never once threw away the smallest scrap of paper that came from him, no, not even a post card. Nor would I wish the words "I am far from grateful" to be misunderstood. What does a conflict of conscience, be it ever so acute, signify when weighed in the balance against the inestimable blessing I owe to his friendship which has been the mainstay of my whole existence!

Other reasons are: the instructions in the penciled note were not followed by Franz himself; for later he gave the explicit permission to reprint parts of *Meditation* in a journal; and he also agreed to the publication of three further short stories which he himself brought out, together with *Hunger Artist*, with the firm Die Schmiede. Besides, both sets of instructions to me were the product of a period when Kafka's self-critical tendency was at its height. But during the last year of his life his whole existence took an unforeseen turn for the better, a new, happy, and positive turn which did away with his self-hatred and nihilism. Then, too, my decision to publish his posthumous work is made easier by the memory of all the embittered struggles preceding every single publication of Kafka's which I extorted from him by force and often by begging. And yet afterwards he was reconciled with these publications and relatively satisfied with them. Finally in a posthumous publication a whole series of objections no longer applies; as, for instance, that present publication might hinder future work and recall the dark shadows of personal grief and pain. How closely nonpublication was bound up for Kafka with the problem of how to conduct his life (a problem which, to our immeasurable grief, no longer obtains) could be gathered from many of his conversations and can be seen in this letter to me:

. . . I am not enclosing the novels. Why rake up old efforts? Only because I have not burned them yet? . . .

Next time I come I hope to do so. Where is the sense in keeping such work which is "even" bungled from the aesthetic point of view? Surely not in the hope of piecing a whole together from all these fragments, some kind of justification for my existence, something to cling to in an hour of need? But that, I know, is impossible; there is no help for me there. So what shall I do with the things? Since they can't help me, am I to let them harm me, as must be the case, given my knowledge about them?

I am well aware that something remains which would prohibit publication to those of outstandingly delicate feelings. But I believe it to be my duty to resist the very insidious lure of such scruples. My decision does not rest on any of the reasons given above but simply and solely on the fact that Kafka's unpublished work contains the most wonderful treasures, and, measured against his own work, the best things he has written. In all honesty I must confess that this one fact of the literary and ethical value of what I am publishing would have been enough to decide me to do so, definitely, finally, and irresistibly, even if I had had no single objection to raise against the validity of Kafka's last wishes.

Unhappily Kafka performed the function of his own executor on part of his literary estate. In his lodgings I found ten large quarto notebooks—only the covers remained; their contents had been completely destroyed. In addition to this he had, according to reliable testimony, burned several writing pads. I only found one file in his lodgings (about a hundred aphorisms on religious subjects), an autobiographical sketch which must remain unpublished for the moment, and a pile of papers which I am now putting in order. I hope that among them several finished or almost finished short stories may be found. I was also entrusted with an incomplete beast-tale and a sketchbook.

The most valuable part of the legacy consists in those works which were removed before the author's grim intentions could be fulfilled and conveyed to a place of safety. These are three novels. "The Stoker," a story already published, forms the first chapter of a novel whose scene is laid in America; and, as the concluding chapter is extant, there is probably no essential gap in the story. This novel is in the keeping of a woman-friend of the author. I obtained possession of the two others, *The Trial* and *The Castle*, in 1920 and 1923; and this is a great consolation to me now. For these works will reveal the fact that Kafka's real significance, which has been thought until now with some reason to lie in his specialized mastery of the short story, is in reality that of a great epic writer.

These works will probably fill about four volumes of the posthumous edition; but they are far indeed from rendering the whole magic of Kafka's personality. The time has not yet come for the publication of his letters, each single one of which shows the same truth to nature and intensity of feeling as his literary work; but meanwhile a small circle of Kafka's friends will see to it that all the utterances of this incomparable human being which remain in their memory shall be collected forthwith. To give only one instance: how many of the works which, to my bitter disappointment, were not to be found in his lodgings, were read out to me by my friend, or read at least in part, and their plots sketched in part. And what unforgettable, entirely original, and profound thoughts he communicated to me! As far as my memory and my strength permit, nothing of all this shall be lost.

I took the manuscript of *The Trial* into my keeping in June 1920 and immediately put it in order. The manuscript has no title; but Kafka always called it *The Trial* in conversation. The division into chapters as well as the chapter headings are his work; but I had to rely on my own judgment for the order of the chapters. However, as my friend had read a great part of the novel to me, memory came to the aid of judgment. Franz regarded the novel as unfinished. Before the final chapter given here a few more stages of the mysterious trial were to have been described. But as the trial, according to the author's own statement made by word of mouth, was never to get as far as the highest Court, in a certain sense the novel could never be terminated—that is to say, it could be prolonged into infinity. At all events, the completed chapters taken in conjunction with the final chapter which rounds them off, reveal both the meaning and the form with the most convincing clarity; and anyone ignorant of the fact that the author himself intended to go on working at it (he omitted to do so because his life entered another phase) would hardly be aware of gaps. My work on the great bundle of papers which at that time represented this novel was confined to separating the finished from the unfinished chapters. I am reserving the latter for the final volume of the posthumous edition; they contain nothing essential to the development of the action. One of these fragments, under the title "A Dream," was included by the author himself in the volume called *A Country Doctor*. The completed chapters have been united here and arranged in order. Only one of the unfinished chapters, which was obviously very nearly complete, has been inserted as Chapter VIII with a slight transposition of four lines. I have of course altered nothing in the text. I have only expanded the numerous contractions (for instance, "Fräulein Bürstner" for "F. B." and "Titorelli" for "T."), and I have corrected a few little slips which had obviously only been left in the manuscript because the author had never subjected it to a final revision.

MAX BROD

Postscript to the Second Edition

(1935)

This, the second edition of Kafka's great novel-fragments, has a different aim and is guided by different laws from the first (now historical) edition. The overriding purpose then was to render accessible an autonomous poetical world, baffling in its nature and not a perfect whole. Everything which might have accentuated its fragmentary character and made it more difficult of approach was therefore avoided. Today, when Kafka's work is gaining in appeal year by year and has also arrested the attention of theologians, psychologists, and philosophers, it is now desirable to work as far as possible toward a critical edition with variant readings.

The difficulty facing Kafka philologists is unusually great. For, although his style is only comparable with J. P. Hebel's or Kleist's, still its unique charm is heightened by the presence of Prague and generally speaking Austrian elements in the run of the sentence and its cadence. In the present edition an effort has therefore been made to approximate the punctuation, style, and syntax to the accepted German usage; but only so far as seemed compatible with the distinctive melody of the author's speech. The guiding rule of this method therefore was not grammatical; it was based on a repeated recital of the sentences and paragraphs in question until evidence of correctness had been obtained. As the manuscript in its extant form was not intended for publication, and would therefore have undergone a final revision by the author, there is also some uncertainty about the passages deleted by him. Some of them would probably have been replaced after a further revision. Nevertheless, the intention of the author in the context of the novel has been rigorously respected. Those deletions which represent an enrichment of the work either in form or in content have been given in an appendix and completed by the chapters which had to be eliminated from the first edition as too fragmentary.

Contrary to the practice of the first edition, the order of the words as well as the repetition of the same word two or three times in the same sentence have been faithfully adhered to on principle throughout, except when a slip of the author's could be established with absolute certainty. Only quite obvious mistakes in the manuscript have been corrected.

In the first edition the eighth chapter was brought to a conclusion by means of a slight change of position of four lines. These have been replaced in their original context, and the chapter appears, as in the original, incomplete.

MAX BROD

Postscript to the Third Edition

(1946)

A FURTHER scrutiny of the manuscript undertaken recently makes it appear not impossible that Kafka intended the episode now designated as the fifth chapter to be in fact the second. Although Kafka gave titles to the chapters, he did not number them. I put them in order on internal evidence; and I was also guided by special indications, as for instance the repetition of the last words of one chapter on the first page of the next. This must have been the original form. Later Kafka separated the single chapters from each other, and each time he added the above-mentioned final words at the end of each chapter in a very abbreviated copy, often written in his personal shorthand. Such duplicate passages at least prove that chapters marked in this way originally belonged together. Whether it was the author's intention to retain this order or to relinquish it must forever remain doubtful.

MAX BROD

274

Excerpts from Kafka's Diaries

THE FOLLOWING passages are taken from Kafka's diaries between August, 1914, and April, 1915. They refer to *The Trial* and to Kafka's writing in general during this period.

AUGUST 6 [1914]. What will be my fate as a writer is very simple. My talent for portraying my dreamlike inner life has thrust all other matters into the background; my life has dwindled dreadfully, nor will it cease to dwindle. Nothing else will ever satisfy me. But the strength I can muster for that portrayal is not to be counted upon: perhaps it has already vanished forever, perhaps it will come back to me again, although the circumstances of my life don't favor its return. Thus I waver, continually fly to the summit of the mountain, but then fall back in a moment. Others waver too, but in lower regions, with greater strength; if they are in danger of falling, they are caught

The Diaries of Franz Kafka, Vol. II, 1914-1923
Copyright © 1949 by Schocken Books Inc.

up by the kinsman who walks beside them for that very purpose. But I waver on the heights; it is not death, alas, but the eternal torments of dying.

AUGUST 15. I have been writing these past few days, may it continue. Today I am not so completely protected by and enclosed in my work as I was two years ago, nevertheless I have the feeling that my monotonous, empty, mad bachelor's life has some justification. I can once more carry on a conversation with myself, and don't stare so into complete emptiness. Only in this way is there any possibility of improvement for me.

AUGUST 21. Began with such hope and was then repulsed by all three stories; today more so than ever. It may be true that the Russian story ought to be worked on only after *The Trial*. In this ridiculous hope, which apparently has only some mechanical notion behind it of how things work, I start *The Trial* again. — The effort wasn't entirely without result.

AUGUST 29. The end of one chapter a failure; another chapter, which began beautifully, I shall hardly—or rather certainly not—be able to continue as beautifully, while at the time, during the night, I should certainly have succeeded with it. But I must not forsake myself, I am entirely alone.

AUGUST 30. Cold and empty. I feel only too strongly the limits of my abilities, narrow limits, doubtless, unless I am completely inspired. And I believe that even in the grip of inspiration I am swept along only within these narrow limits, which, however, I then no longer feel because I am being swept along. Nevertheless, within these limits there is room to live, and for this reason I shall probably exploit them to a despicable degree.

SEPTEMBER 1. In complete helplessness barely wrote two pages. I fell back a great deal today, though I slept well. Yet if I wish to transcend the initial pangs of writing (as well as the inhibiting effect of my way of life) and rise up into the freedom that perhaps awaits me, I know that I must not yield. My old apathy hasn't completely deserted me yet, as I can see, and my coldness of heart perhaps never. That I recoil from no ignominy can as well indicate hopelessness as give hope.

SEPTEMBER 13. Again barely two pages. At first I thought my sorrow over the Austrian defeats and my anxiety for the future (anxiety that appears ridiculous to me at bottom, and base too) would prevent me from doing any writing. But that wasn't it, it was only an apathy that forever comes back and forever has to be put down again. There is time enough for sorrow when I am not writing. The thoughts provoked in me by the war resemble my old worries over F[elice] in the tormenting way in which they devour me from every direction. I can't endure worry, and perhaps have been created expressly in order to die of it. When I shall have grown weak enough—it won't take very long—the most trifling worry will perhaps suffice to rout me. In this prospect I can also see a possibility of postponing the disaster as long as possible. It is true that, with the greatest effort on the part of a nature then comparatively unweakened, there was little I was able to do against my worries over F[elice]; but I had had the great support of my writing only in the first days of that period; henceforth I will never allow it to be taken from me.

OCTOBER 7. I have taken a week's vacation to push the novel on. Until today—it is Wednesday night, my vacation ends Monday—it has been a failure. I have written little and feebly. Even last week I was on the decline, but could not foresee that it would prove so bad. Are these three days enough to warrant the conclusion that I am unworthy of living without the office?

OCTOBER 15. Two weeks of good work; full insight into my situation occasionally.

OCTOBER 25. My work almost completely at a standstill. What I write seems to lack independence, seems only the pale reflection of earlier work.

NOVEMBER 1. Yesterday, after a long time, made a great deal of progress; today again virtually nothing; the two weeks since my vacation have been almost a complete loss. — Part of the day—it's Sunday—has been beautiful. In Chotek Park read Dostoevsky's pamphlet in his own defense. The guard at the castle and the corps headquarters. The fountain in the Thun Palace. — Much self-satisfaction all day. And now I completely balk at any work. Yet it isn't balking; I see the task and the way to it, I simply have to push past small obstacles but cannot do it.

NOVEMBER 30. I can't write any more. I've come up against the last boundary, before which I shall in all likelihood again sit down for years, and then in all likelihood begin another story all over again that will again remain unfinished. This fate pursues me. And I have become cold again, and insensible; nothing is left but a senile love for unbroken calm.

DECEMBER 8. Yesterday for the first time in ever so long an indisputable ability to do good work. And yet wrote only the first page of the "mother" chapter,* for I had barely slept at all two nights, in the morning already had had indications of a headache, and had been too anxious

* Published as a fragment in Appendix I of this book, under the title "Journey to His Mother."

about the next day. Again I realized that everything written down bit by bit rather than all at once in the course of the larger part (or even the whole) of one night is inferior, and that the circumstances of my life condemn me to this inferiority.

DECEMBER 13. Instead of working—I have written only one page (exegesis of the "Legend" **)—looked through the finished chapters and found parts of them good. Always conscious that every feeling of satisfaction and happiness that I have, such as, for example, the "Legend" in particular inspires in me, must be paid for, and must be paid for moreover at some future time, in order to deny me all possibility of recovery in the present.

DECEMBER 14. My work goes forward at a miserable crawl, in what is perhaps its most important part, where a good night would stand me in such stead.

DECEMBER 19. Yesterday wrote "The Village School-master" ["The Giant Mole"] almost without knowing it, but was afraid to go on writing later than a quarter to two; the fear was well founded, I slept hardly at all, merely suffered through perhaps three short dreams and was then in the office in the condition one would expect. Yesterday Father's reproaches on account of the factory: "You talked me into it." Then went home and calmly wrote for three hours in the consciousness that my guilt is beyond question, though not so great as Father pictures it. Today, Saturday, did not come to dinner, partly in fear of Father, partly in order to use the whole night for working; yet I wrote only one page that wasn't very good.

The beginning of every story is ridiculous at first. There

** Exegesis of "Before the Law"; "Before the Law" was originally published in the collection *A Country Doctor,* and then incorporated into Chapter IX of *The Trial.*

seems no hope that this newborn thing, still incomplete and tender in every joint, will be able to keep alive in the completed organization of the world, which, like every completed organization, strives to close itself off. However, one should not forget that the story, if it has any justification to exist, bears its complete organization within itself even before it has been fully formed; for this reason despair over the beginning of a story is unwarranted; in a like case parents should have to despair of their suckling infant, for they had no intention of bringing this pathetic and ridiculous being into the world. Of course, one never knows whether the despair one feels is warranted or unwarranted. But reflecting on it can give one a certain support; in the past I have suffered from the lack of this knowledge.

DECEMBER 31. Have been working since August, in general not little and not badly, yet neither in the first nor in the second respect to the limit of my ability, as I should have done, especially as there is every indication (insomnia, headaches, weak heart) that my ability won't last much longer. Worked on, but did not finish: *The Trial,* "Memoirs of the Kalda Railroad," "The Village School-master," "The Assistant Attorney," * and the beginnings of various little things. Finished only: "In the Penal Colony" and a chapter of "Der Verschollene," ** both during the two-week vacation. I don't know why I am drawing up this summary, it's not at all like me!

JANUARY 6 [1915]. For the time being abandoned "Village Schoolmaster" and "The Assistant Attorney." But almost incapable too of going on with *The Trial.*

---

* This story has not been preserved.
** "The Man Who Disappeared," the title Kafka first gave to *Amerika.*

JANUARY 20. The end of writing. When will it take me up again?

JANUARY 29. Again tried to write, virtually useless.

JANUARY 30. The old incapacity. Interrupted my writing for barely ten days and already cast out. Once again prodigious efforts stand before me. You have to dive down, as it were, and sink more rapidly than that which sinks in advance of you.

FEBRUARY 7. Complete standstill. Unending torments.

MARCH 11. How time flies; another ten days and I have achieved nothing. It doesn't come off. A page now and then is successful, but I can't keep it up, the next day I am powerless.

MARCH 13. [. . .] Lack of appetite, fear of getting back late in the evening; but above all the thought that I wrote nothing yesterday, that I keep getting further and further from it, and am in danger of losing everything I have laboriously achieved these past six months. Provided proof of this by writing one and a half wretched pages of a new story that I have already decided to discard and then in despair, part of the blame for which my listless stomach certainly shares, read Herzen in the hope that he might somehow carry me on.

MARCH 23. Incapable of writing a line.

APRIL 27. [. . .] Incapable of living with people, of speaking. Complete immersion in myself, thinking of myself. Apathetic, witless, fearful. I have nothing to say to anyone —never.